THE DIMENSION RIDERS

CW00434637

DOCTOR WHO – THE NEW ADVENTURES

Also available:

THE NEW

DOCTOR WHO

ADVENTURES

THE DIMENSION RIDERS

Daniel Blythe

First published in Great Britain in 1993 by
Doctor Who Books
an imprint of Virgin Publishing Ltd
332 Ladbroke Grove
London W10 5AH

ISBN 0 426 20397 6

Cover illustration by Jeff Cummins

Phototypeset by Intype, London

Printed and bound in Great Britain by
Cox & Wyman Ltd, Reading, Berks

With thanks

Mum (for time, space and continual encouragement)
& Dad (for food and technology)
And all those who read and commented

And stealing from between the doors of vision
With breath of space beyond they came, fragmenting
Time, and borne on winds that charred
The earth itself

Jazlon Krill, The Darkside Epics

CONTENTS

THE DIMENSION RIDERS:
DRAMATIS PERSONAE

THE DOCTOR, a wandering Time Lord
ACE, his companion
BERNICE SUMMERFIELD, his companion

TERRAN SURVEY CORPS

Captain ROMULUS TERRIN, Commander of the
  Starship Icarus
Lieutenant-Commander LISTRELLE QUALLEM, First
  Officer
Lieutenant-Commander DARIUS CHEYNOR, Second
  Officer
Dr FERRIS MOSTRELL, Medical Officer
Lieutenant ALBION STRAKK
TechnOp ROSABETH McCARRAN
Surveyor MATTHIAS HENSON
Surveyor TANJA RUBCJEK
Troopers
TechnOps

STATION Q4

Supervisor SEPTIMUS BALLANTYNE
Co-ordinator HELINA VAIQ
Crew Members and TechnOps

OXFORD

JAMES RAFFERTY, Professor of Extra-Terrestrial
  Studies
THE PRESIDENT of St Matthew's College
AMANDA, a Time Lord android
TOM CHEYNOR, postgraduate student
HARRY, a porter

THE GARVOND, a creature from the Time Vortex
TIME SOLDIERS

Prologue

Input

For a full day and night, the Cardinal's mind wrestled with the creatures in the Matrix.

The observers monitored his breathing and the beating of his hearts, and occasionally they would hear words half-forming on his parched lips. No one knew what demons had assailed him, but when he finally emerged from his ordeal, he was drained and grey. He was helped to the recuperation chamber by two Capitol guards, and accompanied by his fellow statesmen, but it soon became clear that the mind games had caused more damage than had been at first apparent.

The systems indicated that regeneration was imminent, and the watchers relaxed, confident that the Cardinal, refreshed in his new body, would be able to tell them what he had found at the heart of the Panotropic Net.

The regeneration never came. The incredulous medics checked the systems, and checked again. There could be no doubt. The Cardinal was dead. Subsequent analysis was to reveal that he had come to the end of the twelve regenerations of a Time Lord body. And yet his last incarnation had been only his second.

Somehow, the Cardinal's life had been eaten away from within. Some force with its roots deep in the Matrix had stolen his remaining regenerations, and he had aged to death.

Fearful members of the High Council suspected what had caused the Cardinal's accident. As some pointed out, his hearts had been healthy, his constitution strong. And if

1

the suspicions were correct, then a long-buried menace had once again been released upon the universe.

(from 'The Worshipful And Ancient Law Of Gallifrey')

The captive within the silver sphere shivered with fear and anger. The probes which injected the information sent twinges into it, new data, new food. And as it had done now for some time, the sphere swung in its perpetual motion through the freezing room, a motion unending and rhythmic.

Surely there had to be an end for the prisoner. But for now, it was bent to the will of another. Through the probes, in impulses half-heard and half-felt, came the voice of its torturer.

'You can see the Time Lords' history is rich, my friend.' There was a brief pause, which could have been a clearing of the throat, or a giggle. 'Like anything rich, it goes rotten rather quickly. You know some secrets now . . .'

The prisoner was not interested in this creature's machinations. All it could articulate was a silent scream of *Freedom*, a jet of icy breath within the sphere.

'Oh later, later,' said the captor, who now sounded rather irritable. 'We have a history lesson to do first. With your power, I can summon a legend. A creature of dark history, banished long ago. Someone we both know did something very important to keep that creature trapped in the Matrix. Now supposing . . . just supposing that never happened?'

The captive bristled with fear now. It could feel information prodding and poking it, tingling like a million needles.

Two essential pivots. Earth, 1993, and deep space, in the late twenty-fourth century. Those were the breakthrough points. Two holes, between which the line was to be gashed.

'The Doctor,' said the captor's gleeful voice, 'has just returned from one of those interesting alternative universes. Now he's back in the real cosmos. Almost the

2

same time, almost the same place. I've selected our most appropriate meddler . . .'

An image of a human face was implanted on the creature's mind. On the walls, the clusters of time-lines flickered with energy. It could taste the force it was calling on, now, and the captive sensed what was, for it, akin to horror.

It knew what it was being asked to do.

The previous test of the Doctor had been a challenge, almost a diversion for it. This, though, was something new, dangerous. It was something untried.

There had to be an end.

It saw the images in its mind. The process was beginning, and nothing could be done.

Chapter 1

Time Ghosts

Half the galaxy had been abandoned, Henson knew that. But he thought the salvage squads had moved in after the first cease-fires, picked everything clean, then vanished. He had certainly not expected to see Station Q4 still intact. It was just coming into view against the blackness on his monitor.

He took the survey module in low. His instruments recorded Rubcjek's craft, the twin sister of his own, keeping a constant linear distance from him and descending at the same velocity. Henson heard her voice in his helmet. It sounded as clear as if she were whispering close in his ear. As clear as the time when she had, in fact.

'Keep this gentle. We don't know who might have got there before us.'

They could already see that something was very wrong with the space station. It ought to have been alive with the glitter of shuttles and lights, blazing with beacons, but the central globe was dark, like a forgotten asteroid. Henson's infra-red detectors should have been dancing madly. They were still. The sub-space interceptors, which should have been picking up a chattering crowd of communications before they were three hemi-traks from Lightbase, were emitting nothing but a quiet clicking. A death rattle.

Henson guided his module around the towering pillar, the central body of the station, which skewered the globe like a stick through a cherry. Rubcjek, meanwhile, was skimming at right angles along the secondary arm.

'Are you getting all this?' he murmured.

'All what, Matt? It's dead. The whole place.'

'I wish you wouldn't use emotive vocabulary.'

'Are we going in?'

'I don't think we have a choice. Scan the docking bays.'

'Have done. All reflex systems inoperative. No, wait – '

Henson held his breath as he nudged the craft back round the edge of the station's hull. He was responding to an urge to get Rubcjek's module in sight. The detectors picked her up as a glittery dart aiming for the primary arm.

'What is it, Tanja?' he snapped.

'Bays 24 and 25 are open.'

'What do you mean, open?'

Her voice, louder, nearly deafened him. 'As in not closed, all right? Head round thirty degrees, you'll get a full-face scan and see what I mean.'

'So that's the way we go in,' Henson said.

They met in the vast, cathedral-high darkness of the docking bay, two silver-suited figures picked out on each other's infra-red scanners. Henson didn't like the way he could hear the blood rushing in his head. Normally he would have looked into his partner's eyes for comfort, but the anti-glare film of gold on her helmet rendered her anonymous. Another astronaut. The second half of a two-module unit and no more.

The detectors were registering minimal air in the station itself, but strangely the level was constant. If there had been a leak, it had somehow been stabilized.

Henson did not like the idea of what they might find on the other side of the airlock. He paused with his hand a few centimetres from the release button.

Rubcjek, impatient, slammed the control.

Above their heads, the airlock door rumbled into unseen heights. They stepped into the main body of the station.

Henson swept the scanner in a forty-five degree arc, saw the readings and turned a full circle, waiting for the information. He didn't need to relay it.

5

'Massive structural instability,' Rubcjek had reached the same conclusion, her voice barely audible in his ear. 'Internal molecular disruption of all surfaces.'

'You mean the whole damn place is falling apart,' Henson responded flatly. His glove pushed an internal bulkhead, and came away with a handful of dust. He was sure that the aural sensors were picking up creaks and groans, like the sounds of metal and joints under massive pressure. He stepped further into the corridor, the detector pad a guiding hand in the unknown.

And then he found the first crew member.

It was not the ragged uniform, hanging in threads, that made him stop in horror, nor the way the snapped body was rammed up against the bulkhead at an obscenely unnatural angle, the spine evidently broken. Henson's fear and disgust, making his call to his partner stick in his throat, was caused by his sight of the crewman's face. The skin was a yellowish-grey, blotched with brown, and it had shrunk so that it barely covered the skull. All that remained of the jawbone was a rivulet of dust around the neck. The eye-sockets were empty, and the hands were claws with only shredded remnants of parchment-like skin hanging from the bone.

Rubcjek joined him. She shuddered once, briefly, almost as if to get the standard reaction out of the way. Then she swept the scanner across the man's shrivelled body, reading the input relayed by the Röntgen ray.

Henson kept his voice level. 'So how did it happen?'

The answer, when it came, was equally calm, as if Rubcjek were hoping to forestall the hatred, the incredulity.

'This man is three hundred years old, Henson. He died of natural causes.'

In the control centre, still and dusty, they found more. Some still bore the remains of flesh. Others had decayed to no more than bones, shreds of ancient uniforms hanging on the rib-cages, grinning skulls meeting the two surveyors' gazes as if in mockery of their horror. One of the tallest skeletons was sitting upright in the Supervisor's chair. His hand, or what remained of it, was gripped firmly around the disc of the distress button.

Henson was at the control panels, sweeping dust and debris aside. He flicked a couple of switches experimentally, and to his surprise the relevant panels were illuminated. 'There's power left in these circuits,' he said.

Rubcjek did not answer. Henson looked up, and saw that her attention was fixed on something else. He joined her on what had been the mezzanine gallery of the control centre.

Two more crew members were fixed rigidly in their seats, facing each other. One of them had his hand stretched out as if to clutch something. And then Henson looked down, following Rubcjek's gesture. On the table between the two men he saw the dusty remains of a chess-set. From the positions of the few pieces that had not crumbled beyond recognition, it was evident that a game had been in progress. The absurdity of the tableau clicked in his mind like a confusion of coloured dots resolving themselves into a picture.

'What now?' Rubcjek asked.

Henson hurried back into the centre of the room. 'Power,' he said. 'I'll see what I can do.' He set his earpiece to detect the widest range possible, and as the hissing he had expected echoed in his head, he tried the best combination of controls he could think of.

'I've re-pressurized the lower levels,' he called, 'and the others should stabilize soon.'

He swung around, and his scanner failed to pick up an image of his partner. The grinning skulls met his gaze impassively.

'Tanja?'

The dusty stillness did not allow an answer to be heard.

Henson moved to the bulkhead as fast as his spacesuit would allow. He shut off the wide-range relay, but the hissing sound in his ears did not abate.

'Rubcjek! Report, please!' He drew his side-arm, swinging in a wide arc with the detector in his left hand and the weapon in the other. The sound grew in intensity. It

7

was alien, but strangely lulling, like the sea, and it was filling Henson's mind.

The detector readings were going wild. Nothing clear was readable on its tiny screen. The sound was now unbearably loud, and he was seized with a sudden insane urge to tear the helmet from his head. The sound was almost visible, tumbling towards him like an avalanche, chunks of noise smashing the landscape of his mind. And borne upon it came –

The impact was incredible. The room rushed towards Henson, *through* him, until he was enveloped by a blackness beyond.

Tanja, was the word he tried to scream into the void.

And then the dust settled in the control centre, leaving no trace of the survey team.

Her mirror-lenses reflected the bustling crowds of Terminal Two. She strode onwards with a regular, almost automated pace, trim brown legs encased in white boots, her perfect figure outlined in black and silver. The briefcase at her side, black and oblong, was glossy enough to send light bouncing back towards the fittings high above her.

She was aware of the exact position of the four blue-uniformed guards in the departure hall. It was going to be difficult with all these people.

The earphone crackled. 'Target fifty metres and closing.' She strode onwards.

The departure board was flashing Last Call for the 1200 flight to Paris Charles De Gaulle. She registered it out of the corner of her eye. A couple with a laden trolley cut straight across her path, but she did not slacken her pace. It was almost as though they were not there.

'Target thirty metres and closing.'

The security gate came into view. She tightened her grip on the reflective briefcase. Still advancing. Heels clicking like a clock's breath. Ironic, as Time was her reason for being there.

'Target twenty metres and closing.'

The important thing was the swiftness of the immediate moves. Her reflexes were going to be quicker than those of anyone else in the hall, and it was just a question of making it to the exit. After that, they would not know where she had gone.

Timing had to be accurate. But then timing was not a problem for her.

'Target ten metres.'

The data rush identified the target. Visual confirmed it. The face under the thinning grey hair was the right one. He was reaching for his boarding pass.

She swung the case up and threw it vertically into the air. The target rotated ninety degrees as he became aware of the movement. When the case came back down into her hands, its halves had split open and it came to rest on her palms like a giant bird. The material of the case was curving, fluttering, and around her the people and their reaction seemed to have been slowed as if they were battling against driving winds.

She saw the terror in the grey eyes of the target. Then the laser-tube snicked up from the centre of the case and sent three pulses. He was slammed into the barrier, three red stars torn into his suit.

She snapped the case shut and headed for the exit. If at all possible, she did not want to have to eliminate any other life-forms.

Someone screamed. As Time gathered its natural momentum again, about five hundred people hit the floor of Terminal Two in panic. An alarm began to howl dementedly.

As the glass doors swished open, she was aware of the four primitive projectiles that thudded into her back. They tore the fabric of her dress. Her index finger pressed a button on the handle of the briefcase, and a black sports car sprang into view, directly in front of the terminal.

She slipped into the driver's seat just as three of the blue-uniformed guards emerged from the building. Their bullets spattered the tinted windscreen like rain. And then, above the noise of the alarm, came a new sound. It

9

was like the trumpeting of a thousand elephants, mixed with the screams of tearing metal, and it emanated from the car.

The black car's headlights sprang from their concealed sockets, glowing red as the cacophony intensified. The car began to fade. It paled to a smudge of grey, and then to nothingness. Where it had stood, there was a swirl of dust.

Inside the departure hall, panicking travellers were picking themselves up.

Three seconds later, the target achieved critical blood loss and died.

Chapter 2

Perception and Inception

The seventh incarnation of the Doctor pondered his reflection in an immobile pool of H_2O. His eyesight was sharper than that of any human, so he could see the lines and weariness, even in this makeshift mirror. He had always thought, until now, that this seventh face of his was pleasantly ageless beneath its new fedora hat, but he had to admit that recent events were beginning to take their toll. This part of his life seemed to have become the longest, the most painful. And the loneliest. Time was etching itself on his face, drying like lichen, ageing him towards ... what? The battles, the tortuous paradoxes, had left him drained, but still he carried on. And now, despite his brand new cream-coloured waistcoat and the latest in a collection of paisley cravats – bought for him by Bernice in a January sale in London – not to mention a newly dry-cleaned suit, he still felt the element of disguise, the knowledge that the body beneath was punished, deteriorating.

Even by Time Lord standards, he was an old man.

He straightened up, breathing the air. A little more carbon monoxide than he would have liked, but on the whole very reasonable. Straining his eyes against the sun, he looked at the beauty of the honey-brown tower beyond the Botanical Gardens and smiled. It was not the first time he had been to this city, and he found it a relaxing place.

Lunch had been provided by his old friend Professor Rafferty, and although both of his current travelling companions had been invited, only one had accepted. Bernice had been fascinated by the Professor of Extra-Terrestrial Studies, a newly created and controversial post. She was, though, under strict instructions from the Doctor to 'avoid saying anything anachronistic. Don't forget, there may have been a few hushed-up incidents with invaders, but these humans have only just taken the first step into space.' He knew Bernice was keen to spend some time in the seat of learning and he did not see why it should not be now – earlier, he had given her a homing device to locate the TARDIS, as he could not guarantee to park it in the same place when he returned.

The Doctor had taken his leave at four o'clock, saying he had a few things to attend to. He had left Bernice interrogating the Professor. (What exactly was High Table, then? How high was it? What was the difference between sending down and rustication? Why was there a pair of oars painted on the wall of one of the quads, with an inscription proclaiming a successful 'bumping'?)

The Doctor was not alone by the pond now. Above the cawing of the rooks, he had heard a soft footfall.

He did not look at her. 'Hello, Ace. What have you found out?'

He sensed the girl give an impatient shrug. 'It's Oxford. I recognize it from the pictures. So?'

'Place . . . and time.' He held out his hand for the TARDIS key, which she gave him.

'How should I know? You set the co-ordinates. Doctor, I thought we agreed a long time ago to cut all this crap.'

'Time.' He saw her now – she had sensed that her combat suit would not be right for the environment, and had adopted a black motorcycle jacket with a pair of bright red leggings, and tied her hair back with a multi-coloured band.

'The shops are selling 1994 calendars. Must be late '93. October, probably, looking at the trees. Might be November.' She breathed deeply and closed her eyes. 'It's been raining.' Her eyes snapped open again. 'That's all.'

'November the eighteenth, 1993,' said the Doctor casually. He swung his umbrella over his shoulder and began to walk, Ace following him with a knowing look. 'And it's a Thursday.'

'Easy enough to work out.'

'Obviously,' snapped the Doctor, and he fixed her with the old gaze, the firm, impenetrable look where his eyes seemed to change colour. A look from long ago. 'So if it's a Thursday in 1993, why is everywhere shut?'

She felt the all-too-familiar chill spreading through her, not from the November air. 'Bank holiday?'

'Not as far as I know. Oh, one or two places were open, of course. Newsagents, in particular. Rather like a Sunday... and an old-fashioned Sunday at that.' He pulled something out of his pocket and threw it to her. She caught it instinctively.

A newspaper, dated November 18th, 1993. No weekday was given.

'That's not fair.'

He shrugged as they passed through the turnstile. 'A perfectly logical way of discovering the date. You must have been away for too long.' He paused, tapping the handle of his umbrella under his chin as he watched the traffic in Oxford High Street. The Thursday traffic?

Ace threw the newspaper into a rubbish-bin. She didn't care about the Doctor's games any more. They had just seen a world die, a world full of people she had known and cared for, and the Doctor had left her to work out the explanation. This was 1993. The same time-zone, a different world. It had just come home to her that she was back in the real universe – if she went back to Perivale now, she would find Manisha's grave. Manisha was dead. Everyone was dead.

'Back to the TARDIS,' the Doctor murmured, and strode off, his scarf blowing in the wind. 'I somehow feel that's where I'll be able to think best.'

Ace stared after him for a moment.

There was a choice between going with the Doctor, who hardly even seemed to speak to her these days, and staying in Oxford. It was a no-win thing. This world was already becoming hateful, oppressive. Twentieth-century Earth, in the real Universe, held little attraction now. At least if she went with him there might be an escape from the horror of it all.

She passed the rubbish-bin without looking at the newspaper she had discarded. The fluttering headline read MINISTER MURDERED AT HEATHROW.

About twenty seconds later, the rubbish in the bin began to twinkle with a gentle red and green light. The light seemed to centre on the newspaper, and anyone watching would have seen the black headline, and the text beneath it, fade to an almost imperceptible grey. It took the words another minute to fade from the newspaper completely, leaving a blank wad of paper in the rubbish-bin.

Professor Rafferty had taken to the unusual lady whom the Doctor had brought to his office, and had answered her questions as best he could. He was quite used to the Doctor being accompanied by personable young women, but this one seemed somehow different – sophisticated yet practical, and with an expression of vague amusement which he rather liked. Her burgundy trouser-suit and black boots were of the highest quality, he noticed.

Bernice Summerfield, for her part, was living out history. And she found Rafferty, with his slightly shabby suit and rather worn academic attractiveness, to be a pleasant companion. When the Professor, suddenly realizing the time, had leapt to his feet, saying, 'I have to go and give the finalists their cosmology revision seminar,' she had felt her heart sink, but she had been gratified when he added, 'Feel free to have a look around until the Doctor gets back.' And he treated her to a rather nervous smile before dashing from his study with a bundle of charts and three-inch diskettes under his arm.

So she had taken him at his word, burrowing in his oak bookshelves and breathing the rich mustiness of each book. Although she had not said as much to Rafferty, the Doctor had booked her a room at the Randolph Hotel, so she had at least two days in Oxford, longer if she wanted. That was sufficient, she had thought with amusement, for the Doctor to pop out and save the galaxy a couple of times before tea. Some of the books, she noticed, were in near-lost languages like German and Italian. The book she was dipping into now appeared to have little to do with cosmology, but Rafferty's collection was refreshingly eclectic – Bernice liked that.

She sipped her tea – it tasted real, full of hidden strength – and read, trying to recall her knowledge of the old languages. *Die Kunst ist lang, und kurz ist unser Leben . . .* Art is long, and our life is short. She smiled ruefully, thinking how much Johann Wolfgang von Goethe would have appreciated a Faustian voyage in the Doctor's TARDIS.

The knock at the door disturbed her thoughts.

'Come in,' she called. This might be quite entertaining, she said to herself.

The young man in a denim jacket who put his head round the door blinked a couple of times. 'Oh. I wanted to see the Professor.'

'Amazingly enough, I'd deduced that much,' said Bernice with a smile. 'Tea?'

'Well, I – wasn't planning to stay long, actually. I wanted to borrow a couple of books.' He came in, extended his hand. 'I'm Tom.'

'Bernice Summerfield. Call me Benny.'

He took a biscuit from the tray. 'Must I?'

She raised her eyebrows. 'I'd never really thought. I suppose you can call me what you like. The Professor's gone to give a lecture.' She sprawled in the chair from which Rafferty had deconstructed hundreds of student projects. 'Do have a biscuit,' she added, as Tom, munching happily, scanned the bookshelf.

'Mm. Cheers. So, um, you a visitor here?' Tom, who knew an interesting woman when he saw one, glanced at her.

'For the moment. I haven't seen much of the town yet, though. Can you manage?'

Tom shrugged helplessly. 'He must have taken it with

him. Never mind.' He was about to leave, but the sight of Bernice listlessly gazing at the *Daily Telegraph* stopped him in his tracks. 'Are you doing anything?'

Bernice spread her hands. 'Sitting. Reading. Getting rather bored, actually – oh, yes, I'd forgotten. Quaint. Use of the gerund to express the future.'

Tom looked a little blank. 'I mean, if you want me to show you round . . .'

'How charming. A real student.' Bernice, the social chameleon, remembered some fragments of dialogue from old 2D broadcasts. 'So, we're going to, ah, check out a couple of happening bands? Shoot some pool?'

Tom blinked slowly. 'I was thinking of taking you to the Queen's Lane Coffee House, actually.' He felt the need to defend himself. 'It is only half past three,' he pointed out lamely.

'Then the day is young,' said Bernice with a smile, as Tom opened the door for her.

The head porter of St Matthew's College knew that they had really gone too far this time. He blamed the medical students – they had had their rowdy drinks and dinner the previous night, and this surely had to be something to do with them. Where the hell had they got an old police box from, anyhow? He didn't think they made those things any more. It must have taken about ten of them to lift it – the things were damned heavy, from what he remembered. Anyhow, whoever had put it there, it had to be taken away. The lawn might be ruined if they left it any longer. He had lifted the receiver ready to call a couple of the handymen when he saw two people, a man and a girl, brazenly striding across the lawn. Would you believe it? Ignoring all the signs. And they were heading for that blasted police box.

The man appeared to have a key for it, too. What the blazes were they playing at? The porter, resolute now, slammed the receiver down and hurried out of the lodge to deal with this himself. If, as it appeared, this had something to do with tourists, he was going to relish clearing it up even more than he would have done had it been a student prank.

He was sure that he heard a faint creaking sound as he opened the lodge door. He made a mental note to have the hinges oiled. A moment later he forgot it entirely as he stood blinking in the pale November sun, looking at the empty lawn where the police box had stood.

He was even more astonished when, less than a minute later, the creaking sound that he had heard began to echo through the quadrangle once more, and a light started to flash in the air about ten feet above the ground. Approximately fifty feet from its original position, the blue police box shimmered back into view on the lawn of St Matthew's College.

The porter gathered his resolve and strode towards it. When he reached the edge of the lawn, he blinked. He wondered if it was maybe the unexpected sunlight, playing tricks with his eyes. There was no police box.

Baffled, he looked all around the quad, seeing only students strolling in twos and threes.

If he had looked at the lawn more closely, he might have seen the square depression in the centre of the grass.

The TARDIS, though, was in the Vortex. The breathing of the time rotor showed they were in flight. Ace, who had flopped into a basket-chair near the hatstand, thought it best not to ask why the console room was suffused with a dim red glow, which appeared to be emanating from the time rotor itself.

'Exactly how many rooms have we lost, then?' Ace asked.

'Lost?' The Doctor was engrossed in the console. 'Nothing's been lost. Just changed.'

'So where's the chemistry lab? You can't fool me. You're not the only one who takes a stroll round the corridors. Have you told Benny her collection's gone?'

'I don't think she needs telling.' The Doctor's hands were flickering over the controls with their usual pianist-like dexterity. 'No, no,' he said agitatedly, and started to gnaw at his fingers like a worried child. 'That's not right at all.'

'Don't tell me. It's having another sulk, and you don't know your way around this one properly.' Ace sat back with her hands behind her head, rather enjoying the Doctor's discomfiture. After recent events, she rather felt he needed telling that he could not always do things his way. 'I mean,' she said, 'it's his, isn't it? Well, yours, I mean, but the other one.'

'The TARDIS is the TARDIS. The architectural configuration has been in progress for some time, but then I wouldn't expect you to know that.' He looked up, glaring at her as if an earlier comment had registered. 'And it never sulks!'

'So what's up?'

'The path tracer claims we have just left the fifty-fourth sector of charted space. These co-ordinates.' He jabbed at the monitor on the console. 'they bear absolutely no relation to the space-time co-ordinates for Oxford in 1993. Which *should* be our last trace.'

'And the TARDIS thinks we've come from somewhere else?' Ace was intrigued despite herself.

'From the other side of the galaxy.'

In the dark silence of the space-station, the dust began to dance on the fallen skull of a crew member.

The breeze intensified, became a wind whipping up the dust and debris into a whirlpool. A swirl of twinkling lights, no more than a few centimetres across, came into being in the centre of the corridor. It sparkled and fizzed like the bubbles in a glass of champagne, and glowed blood-red.

The intrusion grew to the size of a football, bathing the cracked steel walls and the tattered skeleton in its crimson glow. And it grew bigger still.

At the heart of the storm of lights, an oblong prism came into view. It was naturally blue, and seemed purple in the light of the whirlpool. The light on its top side was slowly pulsing.

* * *

Nothing had seriously stirred the vaults of the TARDIS library for centuries. Even the Doctor or one of his companions, searching for information or a first-edition Dickens, had trodden with awe, breathed with care, lifted the books from their shelves with reverence.

If the Doctor had been in charge of the library's organization himself, then the books would have been in no order whatsoever. The yellowing First Folio of *King Lear* would have jostled for space with the Penguin paperbacks. The diskettes containing the complete works of the 21st-century environmentalists would have been shoved in next to the tablets engraved with Linear B. The TARDIS knew better than that. The architectural configuration circuits had reorganized the library long ago.

Under the second tower of mini-diskettes, one of the gravity pads, used for access to the top shelves, began to glow, indicating that someone had stepped on to it to use it. But there was no one to be seen.

Or was there?

Just for a second, like a picture in a burning flame of red and green, a figure appeared. There was a brief impression of a close-fitting uniform and a visored helmet. And then it faded and the gravity pad thumped back to the floor.

In the highest reaches of the library, where forgotten tomes in thick hide rested under films of dust, crackles of reddish light threaded like snakes. A wind blew, ruffling pages in sequence, like a Mexican wave at a football ground. And from somewhere amidst the echoing vaults came a chilling, inhuman howl of despair.

'It might just be a fault in the communications circuits between the memory bank . . .' The Doctor ducked under the console, 'and the output.' He flipped open a panel and, fishing a laseron probe from his pockets, began to make a few experimental prods and pokes.

The time rotor was still rising and falling regularly, and Ace wondered whether she ought to keep an eye on it. It was just then that the ship seemed to shudder imperceptibly, and Ace felt ripples beneath her feet as she heard something just beyond sound. As if someone had struck a gong deep within her subconscious . . .

'Doctor – '

'Not now, Ace!' A shower of sparks erupted from under the console, followed by a Gallifreyan curse which Ace recognized. Her instant translation, though, was blotted from her mind by a second reverberation of the gong. And it was then that she realized what the doom-laden tolling was.

Something fizzed and crackled on the wall nearest the double doors. Ace's eyes widened as she saw a swirl of red and green lights gathering in one of the roundels. Just as she opened her mouth to call the Doctor, her mind was shaken by the third resonant clang of the cloister bell.

It lasted just a second, but she saw the creature jump.

It was a humanoid, outlined in flickering red and green and leaving a trail behind it like after-images. It carried some kind of chunky weapon while the face was visored and wore something that looked like a futuristic filter-mask. It leapt in slow motion from the roundel to the door, as if passing through on its way to somewhere else. And then it was gone.

The Doctor's head popped back up. 'Ace, get me the artron meter and the vector gauge.' He did a double take when she failed to respond. 'Ace?' The Doctor followed her horrified gaze, but saw nothing in the corner of the console room. 'What is it?'

'Something was here, Doctor. Something was inside the TARDIS.'

In his fourth incarnation, or even his fifth, the Doctor would have scoffed at such an idea, saying that nothing could have entered the TARDIS while it was in the Vortex. The Doctor, however, had learnt a great deal from experience, although he knew there had always been something up with the temporal grace circuits.

'And I heard the cloister bell! Only it wasn't sounding in the console room. It was sounding inside my head.'

'Fascinating.' The Doctor's face was shadowed with

troubles, dark with foreboding in the dim chamber. 'The TARDIS chooses to give a telepathic warning and sends it exclusively to you . . . and the intruder is seen only by *you*. As if it knew . . .' The Doctor approached her, eyes burning with the reflection of the time rotor. 'Tell me exactly what you saw, Ace.'

At 3.23 p.m. on November 18th, 1993 – a Thursday – a black Porsche, like a wedge cut from the night, sidled in to park outside the Randolph Hotel in Oxford.

The girl who checked in was tall and attractive, with short black hair and mirrored sunglasses. She carried a briefcase at her side, as dark and glossy as the car she drove.

The receptionist did not report the arrival. Had the day been the following Sunday, she would have recognized, with a jolt, the face that was all over the newspapers and TV as the wanted assassin of the Home Office minister. But as the murder had yet to take place, she did not bat an eyelid.

Chapter 3

Atmosphere Normal

'No,' said Bernice. 'I think we'll give it a miss.'

She tucked the leaflet back into its holder. The 'living museum' seemed rather too stilted for her. The idea of trundling around a plastic Oxford in a motorized desk, looking at waxworks while a commentary crackled through a walkman, seemed too much like those which she could visit on colonies in her own 25th century. She was here to see the real Oxford, and said as much to her new friend Tom.

He found this funny. 'The problem is,' he explained, as they strolled through the covered market, 'that it's different things to different people. Like the American couple who collared me once and said, sure, fifteenth-century buildings are beautiful, but where can we find a really *old* college? So I directed them to St Catz. They deserved it.' Bernice was not to know that St Catherine's College had been founded in the 1960s, and was a glorious example of what should not be done with glass and concrete.

Bernice stood at one of the junctions, taking in the bewildering array of shops – overflowing florists, tiny sandwich bars exuding the aroma of real coffee, bookshops. Her eyes alighted on one of the latter. The Doctor had told her – possibly in jest – that some second-hand bookshops in 20th-century Oxford were dimensionally transcendental, and she was keen to test the theory. She browsed for a while, happy to let Tom chatter, and purchased a Julian Barnes paperback and a battered copy of A. L. Rowse's *Oxford in the History of the Nation*.

'Of course,' Tom said, 'you have to be here in Trinity

term really. That's from April to June. The best thing is to stay up all night and hear the choir sing from Magdalen Tower at dawn. You know Magdalen Tower? Then if you can go to a ball, that's great. Would you like to go to a ball? We had the Episodic Dreamers at ours last year. You could –'

'How long have you known the Professor?' Bernice inquired, cutting him off in full flow. She fumbled with unfamiliar money at the till.

'Rafferty?' Tom frowned. 'He's my supervisor. I've been a student of his for five years. Since I was an undergrad. Why do you ask?'

Bernice grinned, without looking at Tom. 'Just curious.'

When they left the shop, neither of them noticed the slim, dark-haired girl in mirrorshades detach herself from behind Marxist Literature and follow them.

Intangible.
Always just beyond perception, a mind even more devious than I had suspected.

Fragments of memory flotsam, falling like blossom on the wine-red ocean. Now, then, and to be, all coalescing. How am I to know? So many thoughts, from one mind. One mind in all those on whom I have fed.

I wait. I grow stronger.

The time rotor had stopped. Moreover, the red glow in the console room was distinctly vermilion now.

Ace strode back into the room. She had changed back into her one-piece combat suit, emblazoned with her personal logo, but she had thrown the leather biker jacket over the top.

'What are you *doing* with the corridors?' she snapped moodily. 'It took me an hour to find my way back. Like playing Tetris in black and white.'

The Doctor was in the middle of putting his own jacket on. 'You got here,' he said absently, as if it were of little importance, and started to hunt round the console room for his hat.

Ace held up a small gold cylinder. It held a stump of lipstick. 'I got lucky. Sorry about the mess.'

The Doctor glanced up to see what she meant, and Ace thought she detected the ghost of a smile. 'Ah,' he said.

'So where have we ended up?' she asked angrily. 'And why didn't you tell me we were going anywhere? What about Benny?'

He was checking the contents of his pockets. 'To take your questions in reverse order – she wants to spend some time in Oxford; you'd find out sooner or later; and where the TARDIS seems to think we have already been.' He began to check the readings on the console. It occurred to Ace that he did not seem to care whether she was there. A problem had seized him, and he was obviously searching for the answer to the exclusion of almost everything else.

'So you mean the fifty-fourth sector and all that? The co-ordinates from the tracer log?'

'Precisely! If you want to find out where you're going, you find out where you're supposed to come from, and if you haven't been there, you go there and work back. Or forward. It's perfectly simple, Romana.'

'You *what*? And who's Romana?'

The Doctor paused, looking at Ace – no, she realized, looking *through* her. 'Did I really say that? Hmm. Atmosphere normal, pressure normal. I think a little exploration is called for.'

'Why?' Ace was not entirely sure if her question was merely that of a devil's advocate.

The Doctor pulled the door-control. 'We're supposed to have been here. The least I can do is find out what it looks like. You can come if you want.'

She paused only to grab her backpack and to check that her wrist-computer was in place. She smiled at that old friend. It felt like part of her arm, these days.

She found him in semi-darkness, sniffing the air. She did so herself, and found it decidedly musty, but breathable.

'Are you going to tell me exactly what this place is?' she asked in a loud whisper.

A globe the size of a tennis-ball seemed to appear in his hand, bathing them both in scarlet radiance and giving a visibility of about three metres.

'Space Station Q4,' he murmured, 'an Earth survey outpost at the fringes of explored space for the time. The twenty-fourth century,' he added as an afterthought. 'Just before Benny's time, and after the Cyberwars.'

Ace shivered. 'Not much action,' she said. 'Must be Sunday.'

'Or a very quiet Thursday,' answered the Doctor, and began to move forward with the glo-ball. Ace followed. The Doctor had the light, after all.

At the base of the TARDIS, red and green lights crackled in a moving mesh, growing into a swirl of globules.

The light soundlessly resolved itself into a figure, which stood watching the retreating figures of the Doctor and Ace at the end of the corridor.

It was the creature Ace had seen in the TARDIS, only clearer now. About two metres tall, bipedal, suffused with light and flickering as if not quite there, phasing in and out of the present. Armed with a wide-barrelled blaster. Clad in a shining uniform like living metal. Its body seemed to blend seamlessly into its wedge-shaped helmet, which tapered to a futuristic gas-mask. Behind the helmet, two red eyes glowed fiercely with the light of battle.

Watching.

Waiting.

And slowly, rhythmically, breathing.

The sleek oblong of a spacecraft was gradually moving in on the giant X of the abandoned space-station. It moved as silently as a ghost. And emblazoned on its side was the insignia of the Terran Survey Corps.

Four micro-traks and closing.

Ace had seen too much death in the last five years. She liked to think she had come to accept it. There were moments, like now, when she realized that she had not, and that she never would. The thing about the blank eyes of a skeleton, she thought, was that you could not even give them that false peace by closing them.

The Doctor took something from the ragged uniform of the sixth skeleton they had found, the one seated in the command chair. He handed the glo-ball to Ace as he inspected the plastic and metal ID plaque.

'Still legible,' he said quietly. 'Not biodegradable, I'd imagine. Station Supervisor Septimus Ballantyne. Then his service number, and date of birth.'

'Doctor, this is well spooky. They're all dead. Everyone on this station is dead.'

'Of course they are,' he answered angrily. 'I'd estimate those remains to be approximately three hundred years old. Which makes me wonder about *this.*' With a startling suddenness, the Doctor's umbrella swung round and tapped the column of the distress console. The hand of the dead Supervisor Ballantyne was firmly clamped over the end of the column.

'He died sending a distress call,' Ace said. She swallowed hard. Somehow, a space-station full of ghosts was among the worst things she could imagine, but there was to be no showing that in front of the Doctor. Not now.

'So they left him there to rot?' The Doctor's tone was sarcastic.

'Bloody hell.' The realization had struck her.

'And take a look at this.' She saw the dim outline of the Doctor's umbrella pointing, and swung the glo-ball round. The light fell upon the two skeletal chess-players. Frozen in time. One moment, forever their deaths. While she was looking away, the Doctor slipped Ballantyne's ID plaque into his pocket.

'It's severely gross, Doctor. Do you think they could have done anything about it?'

The Doctor was surveying the chessboard. 'I fear not. They'd both lost their queens. It would have been stalemate in three moves.' He tapped both kings with the end of his umbrella. They fell, and crumbled into dust.

'Doctor – '

'Decay,' he whispered. 'Decay and death. We're dealing with three hundred years that must have passed through this station in a matter of seconds. Or less.'

'So what's it got to do with what happened in the TARDIS?'

'Nothing has happened in the TARDIS. Yet.' He frowned. 'Except those telepathic circuits. The cloister bell, and only in your mind, not mine. Most odd . . . Someone here has been playing with Time, Ace. Like playing with fire, only worse . . . you're doing it blind, and you get burnt before you've lit the match. Before you even knew you were going to. It's not just dangerous, Ace. It's madness.'

Ace was involved now, her mind working fast. She wondered, sometimes, if the Doctor knew how much she had learnt from him. She swung the globe back round to illuminate the skeleton of Ballantyne. 'Do you suppose his distress call got through?'

'That depends. One would imagine that if the station aged along with the crew, there'd have been a massive power drain. Perhaps there simply wouldn't have been enough power left to drive a distress beacon.'

The docking tube extended like a feeler from the body of the ship. It touched the fragile skin of the space-station. Contact was made.

In the station control centre, the Doctor and Ace felt the reverberation. Ace looked round in alarm, but the Doctor's eye had been caught by a flashing light on one of the seemingly dead consoles.

'So there is still power,' he said, almost to himself. 'Visitors, Ace. This is not a good place to be. Come on.'

'Where to? Back to the TARDIS?'

'Not until I've found out what's going on here. No, I want to be somewhere where we can see them, and they can't see us. Come *on*.'

The ancient doors leading from the control centre creaked open. The gap was too narrow to pass through, and they had to grab one door each and force them by hand for the last metre.

The rusted mechanism screeched in agony, but gave beneath their combined strength. The Doctor mopped his face with his paisley handkerchief. 'Machines,' he said. 'Always back to humans in the end.' He gestured to Ace, and with a resigned smile she lifted the glo-ball to light their way.

As the echo of their hurried footsteps died away, a breeze began to blow through the darkened, high room. It blew the dusty remains of the two kings from the chess-board, and as the dust fell it was caught in an aura of sparkling light. The tatters of the crew's uniforms fluttered like flags before being torn from the bones and thrown across the room. Dust, infused with radiance, swirled like smoke in the darkness.

A figure in a spacesuit, with Terran Survey Corps flashes on the shoulders, extended a hand from the dust. A ghost, reaching for help. Help that was not there.

The hatchway to the airlock thundered upwards until it was flush with the ceiling, and the beams of four infra-red scanners cut invisibly into the darkness.

The leading figure checked the readings on its detector, then inclined its head slightly before reaching up to the tinted, globe-shaped helmet it wore. There were two small hisses as the pressure-seals were broken. The leader lifted its helmet off. Cascades of reddish-gold hair fell over the shoulders of her spacesuit. She was no more than twenty-five years old.

'Atmosphere normal,' she said into the com-link at her neck.

Listrelle Quallem, first officer of the Survey Ship *Icarus*, directed her boarding party to draw their sidearms and to keep detectors on full power. Two life-forms had already been registered, and finding them was only a matter of time.

'Trooper Symdon and I will begin on level thirty and work down. Lieutenant Strakk – '

The fair-haired officer at her side nodded and awaited his instructions.

' – you and Carden start at level zero and work up. Maintain full radio contact at all times. Understood?'

'Understood, ma'am.'

'Proceed.'

They moved off in separate directions.

After about ten seconds, a grating lifted in the floor and the Doctor and Ace peered cautiously out. Their eyes were beginning to grow accustomed to the gloom.

'You know, I sometimes wonder,' mused the Doctor, 'whether service tunnels were built for the sole purpose of hiding intruders from people.'

'They were speaking English. I mean, real English. Not translated like normal.'

'I'd imagine that must be the investigation team from Earth,' the Doctor confirmed. 'That's all we need now.' He heaved himself back into the corridor, and pulled Ace up after him. 'It's just a question of time before their detectors locate us,' he added.

Ace paused in the act of replacing the hatchway cover. 'So why haven't they already?'

'Pah! Their instruments are primitive devices, primed to home in on cardiological activity.' The Doctor fumbled in his pockets and brought out a small disc of metal with flickering lights inlaid into it. 'Fortunately, they won't be equipped to deal with this. It's programmed to emit random information on the same frequency. Jams their sensors.'

Ace was impressed. 'Can I have one?'

'Possibly,' mumbled the Doctor, and slipped the device back into his pocket.

'So why are they going to find us?'

'It's not an infinitely large station, Ace,' said the Doctor apologetically. 'And besides, we're going to introduce ourselves to them. When I'm ready.'

'There has to be an explanation for this, Symdon.'

The skeleton which Quallem and the trooper had found

was in the first recreation area, slumped in the tattered frame of a deep chair. Symdon was studying the detector readouts with mounting concern.

Listrelle Quallem's eyes, behind her infra-scan goggles, were bright with anger. Life, survival, that had always been her aim, her motive at almost any cost. It made her burn with long-suppressed hatred to be so near a force that could control destruction so easily.

She activated the com-link with her voice-pattern. 'Boarding party to *Icarus*.'

High above them, a sound like the fluttering of wings echoed through the corridors.

In the near-silent and still TARDIS console room, the lights flickered once and dimmed again to a yellowish fog.

Had the Doctor been there, he would undoubtedly have known what to do about the small intrusion alert signal flashing on one of the panels of the hexagonal console. The time rotor was pulsing with a deep red that seemed to be draining the light from the rest of the room. A sound was gathering – like a wind blowing scraps of paper across a deserted courtyard, or maybe the fluttering of a flock of migrating birds. An avalanche of noise, it tumbled through the corridors of time. The ship howled. Like vicious winds, agonies of torment.

In the space between the console and the interior door, the dark red seemed to gather into a billowing shadow. The shadow acquired depth, sleekness, reflection.

When the rushing wind died away, the console room contained the low, glossy shape of a black two-seater Porsche Turbo.

Chapter 4

Vertices and Vortices

On the podium on the bridge of the starship *Icarus*, the tall and long-limbed frame of Captain Romulus Terrin leant on the command rail and surveyed the bank of monitors that relayed images of Station Q4. He had already received Quallem's report and he was wondering, as he always did, about factors beyond the immediately obvious. There had been an attack, and so it had to be investigated and the perpetrators brought to justice – that would be the same no matter what the nature of the murders. He had naturally experienced vicarious horror at Quallem's descriptions, but for him they now had more of a task than a mystery.

What he still did not understand was how the atmosphere regulators were still working properly.

At the Academy, Romulus Terrin had found that most of his trainers were living embodiments of the Peter Principle. Continually promoted for excellent achievement in their posts, they had risen in rank, were promoted again for outstanding achievement, until finally they reached a position where they moved neither up nor down. Everyone rising to the level of his or her own incompetence.

Once, during a lecture on tachyon control physics, he had risen boldly to his feet in a packed hall and, with his remote indicator, pointed out the crucial instability point in the lecturer's equation. Two years later, when giving his own lecture to a new year of cadets, he had snapped the screen dark and had gone into an elaborate conjuring routine, producing silver spheres apparently from nowhere and making gold fire leap from the desk. This

31

had met with rapturous applause from the students, but the loudest ovation of all came after the last five minutes of the lecture, during which Terrin explained the scientific principles behind each and every one of the illusions. His students had left the hall dazzled not by sleight of hand but by his perceptions.

He was profoundly aware of his own lack of knowledge, of how small the accumulated wisdom of man could be in comparison with the vastness of the universe. One of his favourite writers, André Gide, had been interested in the idea of the man perceptive enough to know the limits of his intelligence, and Terrin subscribed keenly to this idea. With it in mind, he had refused an academic chair and had instead risen to the rank of starship captain, a role for which he considered himself eminently suitable. He had already once turned down the rank of admiral in order to avoid becoming a victim of the same principle that had trapped his tutors. And now, he was continually finding his knowledge and experience challenged on every single mission. That was how he wanted it to be. For Terrin knew that those who think they have understood the universe have the most closed minds of all.

He descended the white podium to stand beside his second officer. Darius Cheynor was in his thirties, somewhat younger than Terrin, and had a long, tanned face with a slender nose and deeply etched lines of worry. His night-black hair, years ago, had been shoulder-length and full of life, like that of a rock star or an actor, but now he had the regulation short-back-and-sides required to join the Terran Survey Corps.

'Why is it taking Quallem so long to locate two traces?'

Cheynor knew his commander well enough to appreciate that the question was rhetorical, and his large brown eyes did not leave the screen. 'She will, Captain. I've never known the Lieutenant-Commander to lose a trace.'

The communications TechnOp called to the Captain. 'Sir, Lightbase is requesting an update on our position.'

'Tell them we have no further information.'

'Sir?'

'*Do it!*'

'Yes, sir.'

The move had not surprised Cheynor. 'You want the ball all to yourself, Captain,' he murmured, but not disrespectfully.

Terrin voiced both their thoughts. 'This is right out of our league, Darius. If Lightbase know what we're dealing with, they'll pull us out straight away. Send us straight back for that de-commission. They might get round to sending a survey craft full of specialists in a month or so – and then no one will ever find out what happened here.'

Cheynor knew that his Captain's unorthodox approach had paid off before. And so he wondered why he felt so uneasy.

In Oxford, there was sun and rain. The sun caught the silver threads of rainwater and made them glitter like a magical web across the town. Puddles shimmered with light and then were sliced into tatters of water by the wheels of buses. A rainbow arched from the dome of the Radcliffe Camera to somewhere far beyond the suburb of Cowley in the east, while the golden stone of the colleges, rain-darkened, was clear and sharp beneath a blue sky stained with the white and grey of clouds.

The new licensing hours were a blessing, thought Tom, even if the prices weren't. He carried the two brimming glasses of beer back to the table and smiled at Bernice, who looked at them somewhat disdainfully.

'So that's real ale,' she said.

Tom nodded. 'Cheers.'

'Oh. Cheers, then.' She took a sip. It was bitter and verging on the strength of sherry. She tried not to let her expression give too much away. 'Lovely,' she croaked. 'Very nice.'

'Here,' said Tom, casting a hand around the pub, 'is where C. S. Lewis and J. R. R. Tolkien used to get together with their mates. Like it?'

Bernice had already decided the place was full of smoke, populated with loudmouths and sportsmen, and really not her type of haunt at all. She was diplomatic. 'This, I take it,' she said, 'is the subversive tour of the town.'

'Quite right,' said Tom, and took another sip of his pint.

So this is what it's like, reflected Bernice. She hadn't seen a single gown or mortar-board yet, and had noticed only an average number of bicycles. The town seemed to bubble with life, but it was very different from the tangible academia she had expected to be able to sniff in the wind. Inhale in this Oxford, she decided, and you'd get a lungful of traffic fumes, whisky, dope and rain. She liked it, though. It had a kind of magic.

'If he's on form,' Tom said, 'then Professor Rafferty ought to be here before long.'

'Oh, yes?' Bernice answered. She smiled to herself. She half-hoped that Tom found the smile enigmatic. It was a way of distracting him from her true opinion of this beer stuff, she supposed, and she looked around the bar for another. 'Popular in this place, are you?'

'Hey. I'm everybody's favourite guy. Why do you ask?'

'Well, that girl at the bar's been giving you the eye ever since we came in. Or at least,' she added, as Tom swivelled to look with lightning reactions, 'I hope it's you, and not me. It's rather difficult to tell when she's wearing those things.'

The girl's mirrorshades reflected the vanishing daylight, which flickered briefly across them as she swivelled on her stool. She crossed her legs, affecting a nonchalant pose, as she sipped a mineral water.

'Never seen her before. More's the pity,' said Tom. He swung back round to Benny. 'You sure she was looking at me?'

'She's going,' said Bernice. 'Look.'

It was true. The girl had finished her drink, had picked up her reflective silver handbag and was heading for the door.

'Thomas, I think we've rumbled her,' Bernice murmured. She was welcoming the break from the TARDIS at the moment, but now she rather wished that the Doctor was there. Something about that girl spelt trouble.

The girl had to pass them at a distance of less than two metres to get to the pub exit. Something made Tom turn pale and take a deep gulp of his beer, not looking up until the coast was clear. Something had set him shivering, as if a blast of cold air had hit him.

'So,' said Bernice, ever observant, 'you do know her.'

He shook his head. 'I just had the strangest feeling. Like someone walking over my grave, you know . .? Only more than that. Worse.'

'Worse?' Bernice's heart had started to beat a little faster.

'Yeah.' He took another deep and desperate gulp of beer, almost too quickly. 'I don't know. Something about her gave me the creeps. And there was that sound . . .'

Bernice had heard nothing. 'What sound?'

'Didn't you hear it? Like . . . like waves. No, it was more sort of – fluttery, really . . . bats, maybe. Yeah.' He sat back in his chair, rubbed his eyes. 'It was bats. Definitely. Least, I hope *it* was, and not me.'

Bernice had already decided what to do. 'Drink up,' she said, and steeled her stomach for the onslaught ahead. 'Then we'll find Professor Rafferty.'

The manager of the Randolph Hotel in Beaumont Street was glad to see that the black car which had been obstructing the entrance had been removed. He had not seen it go, but then that was not his problem.

Meanwhile, in St Matthew's College, anyone entering the basement of its most modern block (considered an eyesore by Fellows and students alike) would have noticed that the college had acquired a new drinks machine in one shadowy corner. The girl who was walking up to it, though, knew it was there. She took a cursory look around – her dark glasses flickering redly as if absorbing data – before stepping into the back of the machine and disappearing.

After five minutes, she re-emerged and secured the unit

with her remote locking device. She did not have the long-range laser in its briefcase this time, for she was hoping not to need it. Never one to come out unarmed, though, she hoped to rely, should the need arise, on the blaster disguised as an attack alarm in her clutch-bag.

Making her way to the surface via a spiral staircase, she emerged into the drizzle and began to stride across the quadrangle with an imperious step. The rainwater seemed to bounce off her hair and body as if repelled by some interior force.

The Professor of Extra-Terrestrial studies, ironically enough, was not that far away. He was deep in conversation with the Senior Dean beside the front lawn of the college. The Dean, who was doing most of the talking and was partially sighted, was not aware of the girl striding across the lawn behind them, and thus did not realize that he had lost the professor's already wandering attention.

The girl, who was breaking college rules by walking on the lawn, was crouching and, with her head bent towards the grass, sweeping one hand, palm downwards, over an area of the lawn about a metre and a half in diameter. Professor Rafferty squinted, while nodding in pretended agreement at the Dean's suggestion for the next Joint Council meeting. He saw now that the girl was brushing the air over a flattened area of grass. The area was perfectly square, and looked like the imprint of some heavy object. She seemed to be measuring the angles and lengths of the sides with her hands.

The Professor apologized for interrupting the Dean and strode forward to the edge of the lawn.

She looked up. The scan registered a humanoid. Height, one metre sixty. Physical age in Earth cycles, 57. Intelligence rating, high. Unarmed. She relaxed, allowed her long legs to unfold, taking her to her full height.

'Can I help you at all?' the Professor asked politely. He was aware that dealing with tourists was more the province of the Head Porter, but this one looked more like a student. Rafferty, despite the thought of his pint of bitter waiting in the Eagle and Child, was keen to fulfil his function as a moral tutor.

The girl smiled. It was like the snapping of an icicle. She came towards him, her high heels making sharp imprints in the lawn which would have endangered the head gardener's blood-pressure.

'I'm not sure.' Her voice was like unpolished silver. 'May I know whom I have the pleasure of addressing?'

He extended a hand, a little warily. 'Professor James Rafferty. Astronomy, astrophysics and, ah, other responsibilities.' The Professor still, through force of habit, tended to keep his exact title to himself unless pressed.

'You can call me Amanda,' she said.

She smiled.

But not with her shaded eyes.

The glo-ball bobbed in the darkness, casting a ghostly light on the Doctor. Ace followed, just as she had always done in the time before she had become more than just another piece of cargo for him. She wondered, still, what he knew about Space Station Q4, because he always knew more than he would tell. These days, he just expected her to guess.

Ace was beginning to recognize the creaking walkways and scarred bulkheads. They passed a prone skeleton which she definitely remembered seeing, and so it was no great surprise to her when they ended up back in the control centre.

The Doctor placed the ball on one of the inert consoles and his hands brushed the debris from the panels. 'I want to find out what happened here, Ace,' he murmured. Lit from below, his face looked menacing, troubled, like a man who had borrowed the powers of evil to make them fight each other for eventual good. 'These consoles could tell me ... if only ...'

It was Ace who saw stirrings in the shadows. 'Doctor – '

The Doctor was juggling with wires behind a ripped-out monitor screen. 'It's just a matter of reanimating the passive inflectors – but then what do I do next?'

'I'll tell you,' said the fair-haired officer, whom Ace had not quite spotted in time. His Derenna–24 handgun had been trained on the Doctor's left temple ever since the Time Lord had entered the room. 'You stand perfectly still and raise your hands.'

'That sounds like an excellent suggestion,' said the Doctor, who complied without turning his head. 'Terran Survey Corps, I assume.'

'You assume correctly.'

'A little late, if you ask me. A deaf Maston could have found us more quickly than you, in fact, more quickly than I could say, *Ace, back to the TARDIS, now!*'

'I wouldn't,' said the man calmly, as Ace spun around to find another armed man in the doorway. 'Allow me to introduce myself. Lieutenant Albion Strakk, serving under Captain Terrin on the Starship *Icarus*. The gentleman in the doorway is Trooper Carden, who's been itching to shoot at something ever since we saw what happened to our colleagues. So I wouldn't even hiccup if I were you.' He spoke briefly into the microphone at his neck. 'This is Strakk. We've got them. In the control centre.' The response crackled in his ear. 'Now,' he said, 'why don't you just tell us what you're doing here?'

'You're *very* nervous,' remarked the Doctor, risking a glance at Strakk. 'And you haven't shaved this morning. I don't like being threatened by frightened men, Lieutenant. The last one was a drunk in Victoria Bus Station – before your time, of course, dreadful place anyway – '

'Carden.'

The trooper seemed to move with startling agility at Strakk's command, and grabbed Ace's hair, jamming his gun under her neck.

She struggled like an angry cat. 'We're on your side, you morons – '

'Then prove it.' Strakk, the Doctor realized, was a tense young man doing a passable impression of a calm authoritarian. Beneath his eyes, the skin was grey and creased, while his blond hair bore an incongruous quiff of grey and white.

'It's very dangerous here,' the Doctor retorted. 'There are forces on this station that might surpass my own understanding, never mind yours.'

'I – want – identification.'

'I'm the Doctor, and this is my friend Ace.'

'Not good enough.'

'Well, that satisfies most people. Try under my hat.'

Strakk, suspicious, nodded to Carden, who tapped the hat off with his gun. Ace, rubbing her neck, muttered 'Bootbrain,' under her breath.

The lieutenant looked down the plastic strip of credit cards. 'United Nations Intelligence Taskforce? Rather behind the times, aren't we, "Doctor"? Interplanetary Visa ... Prydonian Chapter Debating Forum ... *Oxford Union Society*?'

'Life member,' offered the Doctor hopefully.

'Frankly, Doctor, I'm not impressed.'

'I might have known. Cambridge man, are you?'

'Moonbase Academy, actually. They teach you to shoot rather well in all gravity conditions. So please don't waste my time.'

Closeness, now.

The perceptions and the long-embedded fears. Fire lapping at my ankles ... no, there must be more than that. I probe more deeply. Yes ... the incomplete game. Not the fear of losing, but the terror of the unknown ... of the Universe remaining unfathomable. What arrogance I have found.

I feel, through the shell of the station and other minds, through the dull intellects that surround this one; and I catch impressions ...

I gain strength.

Soon!

The doors swished open, and Quallem marched in, followed by Symdon. She gave the Doctor and Ace the kind of look that a cat bestows upon its latest bowl of meaty chunks.

'I found them tampering with the controls, ma'am,' Strakk said. 'They seem to know what's going on here.'

Ace met the stare of the new arrival. She didn't like the look of her, even though she could barely believe the girl had any authority. *This was their first officer? A bimbo barely older than her* . . . Quallem's eyes, round and green, seemed to look through Ace with distaste and the slightest hint of irrationality. In the centre of the room, the Doctor stood silently.

'Excellent,' said Quallem at last. 'Lieutenant, make the arrangements. They will be transported back to the ship immediately.'

Strakk nodded, and began a low and earnest conversation with his com-link.

Quallem, with an imperious toss of her fiery hair, turned away from her prisoners and began to slink out of the room, her reflective suit catching the glitters from the globall. She paused at the door, and glanced over her shoulder for a moment.

'Oh, by the way,' she said, 'you are under arrest.'

To Ace's fury, the Doctor's face broke into a broad smile.

'Splendid,' he said, 'not before time. I wonder if I might have a glass of water?'

Chapter 5

Temporal Distraction

Dr Ferris Mostrell never stroked his white goatee beard, but he did have an irksome habit of tapping it with his forefinger while resting his thumbs under his chin. The lights of the *Icarus'* laboratory filled the circular lenses of his glasses as he lifted his head to look at Captain Terrin.

'Bone samples,' said the medical officer, clearly and distinctly.

Terrin folded his arms. 'Bringing material back on board could be dangerous.'

'Nevertheless, we need to find out what happened down there. And do you imagine that my equipment is portable?' Terrin was almost dazzled by the reflection from Dr Mostrell's glasses. 'I need bone samples, Captain. As soon as possible.'

Terrin winced slightly. 'Very well. I'll tell Quallem.' He went to the communications panel and punched in the code with unnecessary violence.

It sparkled like a million mirror-balls in a ballroom of insanity. Tumbling lights like shattered crystals falling through moonbeams into water. It shifted, billowed, re-formed itself constantly against the blackness of space.

Slowly, the pulses of light became more regular. The cloud throbbed with new energy as if it had located its prey, and reached out into the blackness.

It sensed life.

It closed in.

Cheynor could hear his own breathing as he leaned over

the tracking TechnOp's shoulder. The TechnOp's hands caressed the opaque dome on his console, making minute alterations. Data flowed across its surface, and then Cheynor saw the red blip, like a drop of blood on the tracer.

'It seems to have variable mass and volume, sir.'

'Speed?'

'Five traks per second.'

Cheynor felt his heart thumping as if it wanted release. He straightened up and strode towards the podium, in one movement. 'Get the captain,' he said before he reached the chair. 'And go to Initial Alert.'

The lights dimmed on the bridge.

Shadows like stalagmites fell across Darius Cheynor, and for the first time ever they frightened him.

Symdon and Carden had left the control centre of Station Q4, having been dispatched to collect the samples requested by Dr Mostrell. Strakk was lounging in the corner, against the main doors, but Ace had seen hunters and fighters enough times to know the pose of relaxation for what it was. She fixed her gaze on his gun-hand, which was tight and steady on the grip of the Derenna–24. The distance between her and Strakk was about eight metres, she calculated roughly. It would not be enough. The result of a break would be likely to be messy.

Beside her the Doctor, as usual, was giving nothing away. She often used to wonder if he really formulated plans or if he just made it up as he went along, but she had stopped wondering long ago, even before first parting with him. Both interpretations were far too reductive, neither allowing for the true complexities in the way that the Doctor worked. So if he was playing along, she would too. She knew the score well enough by now.

There were three sharp clicks as Quallem re-fixed the seals on her pressure-suit. 'Move,' she said. 'We're going.' She levelled her blaster at the Doctor.

' "Please" is such a little word,' said the Doctor ruefully.

'And it doesn't cost anything,' Ace added, in Strakk's general direction.

42

The doors slid open, with loud and painful shrieks from their machinery. Quallem's pistol was right against the back of the Doctor's neck as they moved out from the centre of the room, and Strakk's was level with Ace's kidneys. Four sets of footsteps resounded like drums from hell. Before they even reached the exit, Quallem's communicator buzzed. She pressed the receive switch. 'Quallem?'

The voice of Terrin crackled through the speaker. *'Lieutenant-Commander, proceed to the airlock, now!'*

'Great minds?' said the Doctor quietly.

Quallem ignored him. 'We're just on our way, sir.'

'Then make it faster! Cheynor's tracking an unidentified trace in this vector. It'll be right on your heads in two minutes –'

Metal screamed, almost drowning out Terrin's words. Ace first thought the ceiling was collapsing on them, then she became aware of the sparkling lights beneath the thick dust on every console.

Quallem spun in a half-circle, but Strakk's gun did not waver, even when the tortured doors crashed shut with a shower of dust, sealing the four of them in the control centre.

'Someone sounds pretty miffed,' Ace muttered, looking up towards the unseen upper levels of the station. 'Lucky we didn't ring for room service.'

'Human arrogance never changes,' said the Doctor, his eyes fixed unblinkingly on the horrified face of Listrelle Quallem. 'You realize that you may not be allowed to leave this place?'

Ace looked properly at the doors for the first time. They were two triangular slabs of metal that came together in a diamond shape, outlined in a rusty brown that might once have been red, and they looked decidedly unmoveable.

The communicator was spitting static, staccato bursts growing louder like some demonic snare-drum.

'Door controls,' said Strakk, and swept the debris off the nearest console with one angry movement. He surveyed the keyboard for a second or two, wondering what to do, then he looked up at the Doctor, who widened his eyes slowly in expectation or mockery.

'I think you'll find,' the Doctor told him, 'that whatever has jammed the doors would probably expect you to try and open them.'

'*Whatever?*' This was from Quallem.

'Yes! Why do you humans always expect that everything has to be within your comprehension? It's your most irksome trait. And one I've never come to live with.'

'Doctor,' Ace interrupted, 'at the risk of being an irksome human, how the hell are we going to get out of here?'

The Doctor was, temporarily, saved from having to answer, as the static from Quallem's communicator resolved itself into the fractured voice of Terrin.

'*Lieutenant-Commander, why haven't you moved? That trace is right on top of you!*'

Quallem, almost gabbling with urgency, responded. 'Captain, we're trapped in the control centre. Can you contact Symdon or Carden? They're on one of the lower levels.'

'Then they're probably dead,' said the Doctor.

Quallem's accusing stare was more than matched by Ace's.

In the dimness of the hold where it had materialized, the TARDIS stood as an oblong block of deeper blackness.

A breath or a whisper began, like waves against a long-forgotten shore. Twisting with it into a corkscrew of sound came a deep and almost human sigh of pain. It seemed to come from the depths of the time machine itself.

When the lamp on top of the police box began to pulsate, it was not with its usual soft, blue light. Jade-green and jagged, it dashed splinters of radiance around the dusty hold. And the glow, swirling in fractal patterns, spilled over the Doctor's TARDIS and engulfed it.

When the lights dwindled like dying glow-worms, the TARDIS had disappeared.

And from the level below came a scream of terror.

They heard the scream in the control centre. It was not alien. It could be nothing other than the sound of a human being dying in the utmost agony. And it stopped after five seconds, like a tape-recording snapping to the end of its spool. When it ended, the only sound was the dead hissing from both the Survey Corps officers' radios.

Strakk looked desperately at Quallem.

The first officer, her face betraying anger and hatred, moved towards the Doctor, and before Ace could stop her she grabbed him by the collar with surprising strength and forced him up against the bulkhead.

'All right, Mr Superior, I've had enough of you! I don't know what the hell is happening here, but you do. So tell me before I kill you.'

She was at least a foot taller than the Time Lord's current body, and the discovery pleased her, enhanced her sense of power. The Doctor, meanwhile, could smell the warm metal in the barrel that was being pressed between his eyes, mingled with a sweet aroma which, had he known it, came from the freshener implant in Quallem's wisdom-tooth.

'If you really think I can tell you anything,' he said, 'then killing me is going to make you none the wiser.'

'Maybe not. But it might just make me a little happier.'

The Doctor had seen calculating humans tip over into madness before. He looked into Listrelle Quallem's face and met her eyes with an intense expression of sadness. It had been a long time since he had found a mind which he was tempted to reach out to, although he knew he really ought not to do that kind of thing any more. This one, he felt, if only he pushed further, would contain so much abandonment, bleakness . . .

'What's that noise?' Strakk asked.

Quallem let the Doctor go. He straightened his tie, smoothed his crumpled waistcoat. They were all listening now, as the fluttering, like the wings of a thousand bats, seemed to pass over their heads. It seemed then to return in a rustling wave, settling over the ceiling of the control centre with a babble like the twittering of ghostly birds.

'Creatures . . .' Quallem murmured, her gun pointing into the dark upper reaches. 'Thousands of creatures . . .'

The Doctor's face seemed to have gained more lines and shadows, and when he spoke, Ace shivered.

'No,' he said. 'It's far worse.'

He is so close now that I can touch him. Like one icicle among many on the branch of a tree, but I know which one it is that I must reach out for. I can see the light of Time reflecting on his mind.

He is here!

Ace saw it first.

'Don't suppose you're expecting visitors, Boadicea?' she asked nervously.

Quallem did not need to ask what she meant. The officer was already mesmerized by the flickering lights which had begun to form around the skull of Supervisor Ballantyne like a devilish halo, and which were now filling the eye-sockets with radiance. Slowly, the lights formed a sparkling corona of red and green, and lifted silently, like a balloon, from the skeleton.

Only the Doctor knew that it was hunting.

'What the hell is it?' Strakk breathed.

'Party pooper,' said Ace. 'Time to go home, Doctor, say something. Be nice to it!'

The Doctor, his umbrella clutched close to his chest, was the only one who seemed not to be reacting. 'It doesn't use speech, Ace. It's progressed beyond that need.'

Quallem had been breathing hoarsely for the past few seconds, and her gun-arm, slender and straight, was lifting at an inexorable angle.

The Doctor's cry of 'No, *don't*!' coincided with the first three energy bolts. They fizzed into the globe of light and were absorbed. It fed on them. Swelling like a purulent sore, it throbbed and advanced towards Quallem, becoming formless now, filling the room. Quallem's reflexes, activating a jittering finger, pumped bolt after bolt into the cloud of lights. Strakk, uncertain, aimed but did not fire.

It was then that Ace decided she had better do something.

'Doctor, let's go!' she yelled, and circled around the hovering lights. The entity was now, effectively, between them and their captors.

Quallem was screaming incoherently. The air fizzed with charged particles from her gun, slamming uselessly into the entity.

Ace felt herself shoved roughly to one side. She hit the floor, with the sounds of Quallem's panic echoing in her ears.

When she rolled over, she saw the Doctor, his arms spread wide, advancing on the growing cloud of lights as if welcoming them.

It took less than a second. The cloud swooped, and swallowed the Doctor up.

In the fading glare, Ace saw the doors juddering open once more. And then she found herself being hauled to her feet, with Quallem's gun tight against her jawbone.

Chapter 6

Communication Breakdown

'It is a capital mistake to theorize before one has data. Insensibly one begins to twist facts to suit theories, rather than theories to suit facts.'

Sir Arthur Conan Doyle, *A Scandal in Bohemia*

Tom skidded to a halt in the Porter's Lodge, and slammed his hands down on the reception desk to stop himself from falling over.

'Harry, I need to find Professor Rafferty,' he said breathlessly, as Bernice followed him into the Lodge at a rather more sedate pace.

Harry liked the leisurely life. A job as an Oxford porter suited him these days – it was nice and sedate after his time in the police force, and you got a bit of respect, too. He liked the way the gates were shut at midnight on the dot, because it appealed to his sense of order, and he liked being able to tell people not to walk on the grass. The hours were good, and everybody knew your name. He often thought that if it wasn't for the students, the job would be pretty much all he wanted. Harry sighed, put his newspaper down and looked up at Tom. 'Raining out, is it?' he asked, looking pointedly at the drips that were falling on his key-allocation list.

'If you could be so kind,' said Bernice with a flattering smile, and trod on Tom's foot, 'we would be so very grateful.'

Harry cleared his throat and perked up a little. He was never one to offend a true lady. 'Professor Rafferty should be in his rooms, miss,' he said. 'He headed there about fifteen minutes ago. Oh, he's got a visitor, though.'

'Visitor?' Bernice wondered to herself if the Doctor and Ace had come back already, and did not chide herself for the disappointment she felt.

'A young lady. Pretty thing, she was. In a black dress. Didn't say a word, though – Hey, not so fast! You'll slip over!'

Harry shrugged, and reached for his newspaper again. He perched his glasses on his nose and settled back to continue the article he had been reading.

The page was blank.

He stared uncomprehendingly at the whiteness for a few seconds, then flicked through the rest of the newspaper with mounting astonishment. There was nothing in it. The words he had been reading not two minutes ago seemed to have vanished. What he was holding looked like no more than a wad of chip-paper.

'Well, I'll be – '

He put the paper down and hurriedly tapped out a number on the internal phone.

'Bill? Yeah, listen, it's Harry here. St Matthew's. You got a moment to come round here? I've got something to show you . . .'

There was no answer from Rafferty's office, so Bernice tried the door. The oak-panelled study was just as they had left it, and there was no sign of Rafferty.

'I don't believe this,' said Bernice. She looked at Tom, who now appeared even more worried than before.

'This isn't like the Professor,' he said. 'I don't like it one bit.'

'You think he's in trouble,' Bernice murmured. 'No such thing as a quiet life, is there? I thought Oxford was supposed to be a sedate place. Next year I'll try the Lebanon for my holidays.' She was aware that her flippancy was not getting them anywhere, and Tom was hopping from one foot to another like an agitated schoolboy.

'All right,' she said. 'Calm down. We'll find him. Does he have other rooms anywhere in the university?'

'Of course – his Faculty office. But that's out east, at Cowley – '

'Come on, then. Let's get cracking.'

They turned together, and saw it at the same time.

In the doorway, a hovering whirlpool of green and red globules of light was slowly coming into being. There was a noise, a scurrying, twittering noise like hundreds of creatures.

They backed away in horror.

'That's it!' Tom hissed, his eyes open wide in horror. 'That's the sound I heard earlier!'

Bernice touched his elbow gently. 'The Doctor always says,' she whispered, keeping her eyes on the entity, 'that if you show that you mean no harm yourself, then you won't come to any.'

The whirlpool pulsed with brighter light. Like whispers on a vast auditorium, the sound grew, and the spiralling lights began to advance on them.

'On the other hand,' Bernice added, 'even the Doctor talks rubbish sometimes . . .'

'What are we going to do?'

Not for the first time, Bernice Summerfield realized that she was in a position where her combat skills were not going to be much use. For one thing, she was not armed, and for another, the nebulous invader did not look as if it could be overpowered by the martial arts. They were up against the bookshelves.

'Which floor are we on?' she asked.

'Second.'

'Oh, well. There goes another great idea.' She was scrabbling behind her, and pulled something out. The book was bound in maroon cloth and had the author's name embossed in gold.

Crackling, the energy bore down on them. It filled the room with unnatural light and squealed and chattered like a cloud of birds. A wind blew papers from the desk, scattering them like leaves.

'Do you like Henry James?' asked Bernice.

'No.'

'Good.' She flung the book. 'Fetch, boy. *Fetch*!'

The entity fell upon the pages with a roar of triumph. *The Portrait of a Lady* flared red as it was consumed, and then there was emptiness and silence.

Bernice and Tom, scarcely able to believe they were alive, lifted their eyes. The Professor's papers were scattered across the carpet, and the entity had gone. 'It worked,' breathed Bernice. 'And who said all art was useless?'

Tom, who was still shaking, lowered himself into Rafferty's chair. 'It was a trap. That thing wanted to kill us.' He wiped his forehead with his handkerchief. 'I don't feel at all well.'

'Don't be so feeble. The galaxy has far worse things in it. No, I think,' Bernice said, tapping her chin with one finger, 'that it was some sort of warning.' She knelt down and examined the carpet, picking at threads as if looking for something. 'If you want to make yourself useful,' she added, 'you could try getting the Professor on the phone.'

Tom seemed to jerk back to reality, and tottered rather uncertainly over to the telephone. 'Do you do this sort of thing every day?' he asked.

Carden had been with Terrin's crew for two years. He had been in the team that had rescued three trapped palaeontologists on the colony of Ephros, and he remembered the mission now as he picked his way through the ravaged lower decks. The men had been on a month-long mission, but a rockfall had extended it to six weeks before anyone thought to send in a rescue squad. The Icarus team had had seven days with oxygen-masks and no natural light until they had finally homed in on the life-traces in the Belvedere Cavern, the deepest and most enormous of the halls. Its huge, motionless lake reflected phosphorescence and glittering rock formations, watchful like sentries. The team, led by Cheynor, had only found one of the scientists, and he was incoherent, unable to

51

provide any details of how he had survived, let alone any clue to the whereabouts of his colleagues.

Captain Terrin, Carden remembered, had sent the amphiboid to scour the caves and drag the lake, and he and Symdon had been on the team. The old first officer, Kenley, had been in charge. It had taken another twenty-four hours of mindless tedium, of waiting for the radar to detect something in the apparently bottomless water. Then, finally, they found what they were looking for, what they had been dreading. As the infra-red camera homed in on the two floating bodies it became apparent that they had been lashed together with the palaeontologists' standard-issue cable. They also saw what Carden would never forget, the tattered flesh hanging like shreds of chicken-meat on a bone, the stubby limbs and the savage rips in the men's chests.

Afterwards they had been ordered to keep their silence about the exact condition of the bodies. Carden did not know what had gone into Kenley's report, but it did not take long to prove the case beyond doubt. They needed a spectrographic DNA analysis of the third palaeontologist's knife, of the skin under his fingernails, and of the enamel on his teeth.

The condemned man was transported to Station B5 to await trial. Carden had heard – and he was willing to believe it was not an apocryphal story – that for his last meal before the passing of his sentence (life on a penal colony) the man had requested two rare steaks. He wondered, now, whether this assignment would replace that of the murdered palaeontologists as the spectre that haunted his nightmares.

His infra-scanner picked out a grin. His heart skipped a beat as he passed the immobile skeleton, slumped like so many against the corridor wall. Only the upper half of the body could be seen, the lower ribs and pelvis resting on a fine dust which had presumably been the legs.

He moved on, hearing the floor creak beneath his boots, feeling the straining girders. He wondered how old they were now, and if they would hold.

The loudest sound in the corridor was his own breathing. So when the scream came he was in no doubt about it.

For several seconds he could not move his legs. The visible darkness seemed to crawl from corners towards him and he felt a trickle of sweat escape past his deodorizer implant.

His heart pounding, he flipped open his communicator. 'Symdon, location please?'

The static and feedback were louder than he had ever heard them before.

'Symdon, respond!'

There was something slithering up the corridor behind him.

He knew that without turning round.

Now he moved. Something propelled him, a primal urge, a human instinct for survival. He hit the next section at a run, and his infra-scanner picked out a black metal door ahead of him, patches of rust splashed like blood on its surface. Behind him, there was a sound like the rustle of bats' wings. He thumped the door-control without even thinking where it might lead. And there, in the gloom, he caught the flash of a silver star on a white-pressure suit. The protective uniform of a Survey Corps trooper. Relief washed through Carden like alcohol, but still the adrenalin was kicking him into action.

His call to Symdon stuck in his throat as he saw exactly what he was facing.

Carden had a brief, blurred image of a creature so twisted and shrivelled, so near death that it hardly looked human. The eyes were those of his friend Jed Symdon, but the skin, brittle as dried leaves, was tearing on the skull as the figure toppled forward. The hands, claws like knives protruding from mushy flesh, clutched at Carden's uniform.

In a haze of green, it was the last sight that Trooper Carden ever saw.

Headphones clattered on to the console and the TechnOp leapt to his feet.

53

Thirty faces turned in the orange light of the Icarus' bridge to look at the man, including those of Captain Terrin and Second Officer Cheynor.

'Massive feedback, sir,' mumbled the man, somewhat sheepishly.

'Captain,' called the tracker TechnOp from his glass-domed console. 'I've lost the traces.'

'*What*?' Terrin hurried over.

'All the links are down, sir. I can't get anything.'

'And nothing on audio,' said Cheynor bitterly. He met his captain's hunted expression, saw the strain even in the orange-edged shadows.

Terrin carefully put the headphones to one ear. He nodded, and looked at Cheynor. 'Some sort of massive disturbance from Q4,' he hazarded.

'That was our last contact. Sir, that means we've lost all communication with the group.'

The captain was already heading for the exit. 'Get me two guards,' he said, 'I'm going in there.'

James Rafferty had had many unusual visitors to tea in his oak-panelled study in the Faculty, indeed he had tutored several of them. He found this girl Amanda more polite than most, and if she was a little unsettling, he decided, it was only because of the aura of cool, deadly beauty which she exuded. That, and her unwillingness to remove her sunglasses. He found that looking at his own reflection every time he spoke to her put him at quite a disadvantage. His hands were steady when he poured her tea, though, and he gave her a winsome smile as he passed a plate of scones.

Amanda, comfortable in the armchair, crossed her black-stockinged legs with a quiet swish that did nothing for Professor Rafferty's blood-pressure. She held up one white palm to refuse the scones, but took the cup of tea.

'Thank you very much, Professor. It's kind of you to entertain me.'

'I gathered it was for my own benefit, young lady. We don't often find visitors examining our lawn, and it's been a long time since anyone told me they had interesting information for me.' Rafferty sighed, pressed his fingertips together and fixed his gaze on one corner of his Renoir print. 'I'm usually the one giving the information, you see. Giving it and not being believed, in the normal run of things.'

Amanda's reaction was to sip her tea, almost mechanically. There might have been a hint of a smile on her blue-painted lips, but it was difficult to tell.

Rafferty lowered his glasses on his nose and leaned forward, intertwining his fingers. It was a stance that he had used many times to warn undergraduates of the imminent approach of a Very Serious Question, but it seemed to have little effect on the girl.

'Tell me, Miss, ah – '

'Amanda.'

'Ah, yes. You said. Amanda. Are you a student here?'

'Just passing through.'

There was something about the girl's voice, Rafferty thought. Some of the young women who came to him to read chapters of their astrophysics dissertations had voices that were strained, blackened by coffee and smoke, voices with a tainted purity like crumpled sheets. But Amanda's gained its lived-in resonance from something more intangible. It sounded . . . *tensile*.

'And what was it you wanted to talk to me about?' asked the Professor, taking a gulp of tea to lubricate his dry throat.

Amanda placed her teacup on the table beside her. 'Professor, an area of one hundred and fifty-four square centimetres on the lawn of your college is currently being subjected to a controlled temporal implosion. The forces involved must be utilizing loop systems of dimensional engineering that do not exist on this planet at this time.'

Rafferty was silent. He blinked once.

'I thought,' Amanda continued, 'that you found such anomalies a challenge.'

The Professor smiled and reached for his telephone.

'I'll call the head gardener, if you're concerned,' he said airily. 'Have him roll it out.'

'*Professor Rafferty!*'

The effect of her voice was astonishing. It was like a physical force slamming the receiver back down and twisting his head to look at her blank eyes. When she continued, her tones were softer.

'Don't play the foolish Earthling with me, Rafferty. You can't pretend not to understand. Not the Professor of Extra-Terrestrial Studies at Oxford University.'

'And what do you know of extra-terrestrial life?' Rafferty realized his hands were shaking. He got up and went to the drinks cabinet.

'Suppose I were to mention Brigadier Lethbridge-Stewart of UNIT? A friend and colleague of yours, I believe.' Rafferty did not respond as he poured himself a brandy. 'He has dined at High Table in this college no less than three times in the past eighteen months. What do you discuss, I wonder?' Her voice was like a razor through satin.

'You could easily know of the Brigadier. He was the main opposition speaker at a Union debate last Michaelmas term. "This house believes that Britain needs no military defence", I think.' Rafferty took a deep gulp of brandy. 'Went down remarkably well. Won over a few of those peace-and-love students, as I recall.'

'But would I know of the Zygon Gambit?' Amanda purred, and slipped from her seat with silent grace. 'Or the Shoreditch incident?' she added, her mouth unnecessarily close to Rafferty's ear. 'Or how about your paper on the dust samples taken from the Auderly House explosion?'

'You're a remarkably well-informed young lady,' said Rafferty steadily, and finished his brandy.

'I want to call the college President.'

'Impossible. Dr Styles is in his lodgings, he's never disturbed during the day.'

'Ah, but he'll make an exception,' said Amanda, 'for me,' and she slipped the telephone receiver around Rafferty's neck to his left ear.

* * *

Captain Terrin's group had run into Quallem's near the airlock sector. Despite Ace's protestations, no one was prepared to go back to the control centre to find out what had happened to the Doctor. Quallem, in particular, seemed relieved to have one less prisoner to contend with.

Now Ace's arm was aching. Quallem had turned out to be quite unexpectedly strong, and was making a good job of marching her along the corridors with a powerful grip. The added problem was that Ace, although her eyes had become accustomed to the darkness, could not see as well as the officers with their infra-scan goggles, and every step felt like a venture into the unknown.

Strakk kept behind. Ahead of them somewhere, Ace knew, were Captain Terrin and his two guards leading the way, but she could only hear and not see them. She supposed that the darkness was useful in that it hid some of the space-station's horrors, but she was consolidating the opinion that she often found stiffs a lot less creepy than some people she could mention.

She was jolted to a halt. There was a sound of a door hissing open, which she knew had to be the airlock.

They all heard the rustle of sound further down the corridor, and saw the bluish light permeate the gloom. Ace could make out the two guards now, their guns instantly raised, but she also saw Terrin's hand raised to stop them.

'No!' snapped the captain. 'Look!'

Forming in a whirlpool of light was a space-suited figure. What they had all noticed, and what was now stopping each of them from instantly opening fire, was the Survey Corps insignia on the ghostly figure's uniform.

Transfixed, they watched the ghost reach out to them. A hand, for help. Help not offered, but needed. And faintly, in the distance, as if borne on the wind across a desolate moorland, a cry of pain. A woman's voice.

'Tanja,' murmured Strakk.

Ace and Quallem looked at him.

The image flickered now as if slipping out of phase. Blue light was strobing across the small group of humans.

Ace saw Strakk, as if in slow motion, pushing his way forward, towards the figure. Only Terrin held him back.

'Don't go! Tell us what's happening!' Strakk yelled.

The ghost of Surveyor Tanja Rubcjek glowed one last time and vanished like a guttering flame.

Terrin's reaction was instant. 'Right, everyone into the airlock. That means you, too,' he added for Ace's benefit.

Strakk's eyes were still fixed on the end of the corridor where the spectral figure had appeared. Ace, ignoring Terrin, was studying the Lieutenant, not without sympathy.

'You knew her?' she asked.

'Come on,' Quallem snarled, and Ace was shoved into the airlock before Strakk could answer. The security guards followed.

'Captain – ' Strakk began.

'Back to the ship, Lieutenant,' Terrin ordered. 'I'm going to find out what's happened to Symdon and Carden, and this strange fellow you mentioned.'

'They're all dead, sir. There's no point.'

'Strakk – '

'This place is death! It breathes it. The bloody metal stinks of it.'

Terrin laid a hand on the young lieutenant's shoulder. 'We are still the Survey Corps, Lieutenant, not the military. We have certain responsibilities. It is our business not to run away from danger, nor to tackle it head-on, but to find out. That's why we're here, that's why we collected those samples. To *know* why something happened. Otherwise there is no point to it all.'

'Point? Tanja, Matt and the others have died for that *point*, sir. And one day, Captain, your hunger for knowledge is going to get you killed as well.'

With that, Strakk, somewhat astonished at his own impertinence, strode into the airlock without looking back.

Chapter 7

On the Bridge

The starship *Icarus* was hardly what Ace had been expecting. She would have placed these people in a gleaming, slick environment, humming with human and mechanical activity. Disillusionment came fairly swiftly. First there was the elevator, which was slow and creaking. Then, as they reached their destination, she became aware that Quallem's gun was actually ushering her onto the bridge itself. It occurred to her, as it had not done before, that a survey ship would be purely functional and would not be likely to have any facilities for prisoners.

She saw a low, circular room bathed in orange light and dominated by a screen, with the captain's podium in the centre. About a dozen TechnOps were at consoles around the walls, and all of them wore headphones with radio-link mouthpieces like trackers at Mission Control. None of them looked up as the party entered, but Ace supposed they were paid not to notice things that didn't interfere with the job. The atmosphere of tension was tangible, but that was not the first thing Ace remarked upon. The Doctor had told her this was the twenty-fourth century, and although she did not count herself an expert, she did not think the equipment looked sufficiently high-tech. Some of the instrumentation had purposes that could only be guessed at, such as the opaque dome on one of the far consoles, but banks of switches, keyboards and monitors were not what the now broad-minded girl had come to expect. There was even a stand-alone PC with a printer in one corner. The rail that surrounded the central podium could have done with a lick of paint, as could some parts of the wall.

'Restrain her,' Quallem ordered, as she strode imperiously on to the bridge.

Cheynor pivoted on one heel and raised an eyebrow. 'Here?'

'I want the little bitch where I can see her.'

'Stick it, Boadicea!' Ace yelled as the two guards manhandled her into a swivel-chair.

Cheynor strode over to the chair and stood looking down at Ace with his hands clasped behind his back. 'So, you're our intruder,' he said, more surprised than anything. 'Doubtless we shall come to you in due course.'

Ace looked him up and down, seeing a man of medium height, late thirties, in a black uniform with the silver star she had come to associate with the Survey Corps. All the uniforms, Ace had noticed, looked as if they had seen better days, and the Corps insignia had evidently been added as an afterthought. Cheynor himself, despite a deep tan acquired somewhere on his travels recently, looked worn out too – deep crow's feet were etched into the skin around his eyes. Another tired one, she thought. Everything and everyone's on its last legs round here. Still, at least he seemed reasonably civil.

'Yeah, well,' she said, 'don't force yourselves. If you've more important things to do.'

Cheynor smiled. 'For the moment, it looks as if that's the case,' he said, and nodded to the guards. One of them pressed a control on the back of the chair, and three tight bands of metal sprang from the upholstery, one around Ace's neck and the others pinning down her arms. 'Sorry,' Cheynor added, sounding as if he meant it.

In the next few minutes, most of them seemed to forget she was there, so she sat and watched them all instead. She had trouble recalling all the names, but she saw the suntanned guy deep in conversation with the cold bitch Boadicea on the podium. Over the chatter of instruments, though, she could not hear what they were saying. Only at one point did she make something out, when the man said, 'not expendable' and, raising his voice apparently in anger, something about 'should have sent someone else.'

She became aware of a shadow falling over her, and looked up into a familiar pair of hunted eyes behind a grey-blond quiff.

'Comfy?' asked Strakk as he unclipped his gloves and threw them onto a chair.

'Don't you have a post to go to, or something?'

'Probably. But no one's insisted yet. It's a bit like that around here – haven't you noticed?' Strakk folded his arms and leaned against the wall.

'Tell me about it. You seemed such an efficient bunch back on the station.'

Strakk shrugged. 'It's the impression the captain quite likes to give. He knows as much as any of us that it's one long tea-break sometimes.'

'Are they all as keen as you?' Ace asked with a grin.

'Look, this ship is a hundred and fifty years old. We don't boast about it. You don't imagine they actually fund the Survey Corps properly, do you? We get the crap that the military and the medics don't need. Our last mission's lasted two years and we've all had it. So's the ship. It's being de-commissioned when we get back to Earth.'

Ace nodded, her suspicions confirmed. 'So what now?'

He looked away into the distance for a moment, his eyes seeing something that Ace could only guess at. Then he said, 'Whatever we're dealing with – you're as frightened of it as we are, aren't you?'

'Uh-huh.' Ace realized it was hurting her jaw to speak.

'Well. Sorry about the spartan accommodation. If you really have just been caught up in this, then believe me it's the safest place for you to be right now.'

'Why are you such a bastard when *she's* around?' Ace tried to jerk her head in the relevant direction, but Strakk understood and gave a bleak, fractured smile.

'Helps to get the job done,' he said.

'You sure? If you ask me, your first officer's a few bytes short of her full ROM.'

He obviously did not want to say any more about Quallem, at least not on the bridge. 'Your friend the Doctor. That creature – whatever it was – attacked him too. Why didn't he run? He just stood there.'

'The Doctor knows what he's doing.' *And maybe that's what's always worried me*, she added to herself.

'He seemed to have some idea what happened back there. If he can really help us, then . . . I want to be part of it.' Strakk met Ace's gaze. 'But for now . . .' And his eyes, almost imperceptibly, flicked back towards Quallem.

Ace got the message. *We have to follow orders.*

'You knew that girl, didn't you? You called out her name.'

'She was another surveyor,' he said dismissively. 'One of those sent here when communication gave out. She's dead. They're all dead. And Terrin still won't let it lie.'

'And if he finds something?'

Strakk laughed hollowly. 'You saw those poor sods back there. They found something too. And they can't tell us much about it.'

'The Doctor could,' said Ace.

'If we knew where he was – yeah?'

And as she looked into his mocking, half-shadowed face, she had to admit that she shared his sense of helplessness.

Chapter 8

Conversations with the Dead

The Doctor, in his long experience, had become used to recovering from shocks. He seemed to spend a disproportionate amount of his life waking up on cold floors in a prone position, with a nasty ache at the back of his head, and indeed towards the end of his fourth incarnation he had even contemplated giving up the whole intergalactic trouble-shooter life for good and retiring for an extended fishing holiday on Florana. Only recently had he actually begun to enjoy the wretched business again. There was still the unfortunate occupational hazard of the knocks and bumps, though.

He sat up, rubbing the back of his head, and replaced his hat. Rather to his surprise, he appeared undamaged. Having reassured himself of this, he looked up, for the first time, into his surroundings – and was dazzled.

The light was white, clear as mountain snow, and washed over smooth walls without emanating from any visible source. The surfaces looked to be made of the kind of material that could atomize dust at a distance of several centimetres. Such things were not unknown in the Doctor's experience. As he climbed cautiously to his feet, he was unsurprised to find that the walls formed a curving corridor, inlaid at one point with a red, diamond-shaped logo. And it was with a weary sense of time-honoured resignation that he felt the cold steel of a blaster against the back of his neck.

'Whatever you're planning to do next,' said a tobacco-choked voice, 'run it past me first, OK?'

'You know, when you get to my age,' said the Doctor

ruefully, without turning round, 'you tend to imagine that people will be pleased to see you. Just shows how wrong you can be, really.'

He heard the click of a communicator being activated. 'The intruder has been apprehended,' said the phlegm-soaked voice, and its owner paused to relish a hawk and a spit before continuing. 'Shall I bring him to the centre?' The answer was inaudible to the Doctor, but a second later the blaster jabbed him in the neck again, accompanied by the instruction, 'Move.'

'I see your manners are no improvement on your sense of hygiene,' remarked the Doctor. He glanced over his shoulder. His captor was a black-uniformed guard, built like an American footballer, and he stank of tobacco.

'Move!' The guard gave him a shove and the Doctor decided it was best to obey as he was propelled along a series of almost identical corridors. He kept asking himself where he had seen the red diamond logo, and before he had time to think about it, he and his captor were facing a heavy pair of sliding doors outlined with the same pattern. Lights flickered briefly in a side panel, presumably for identification, and then the Doctor entered a world of holograms.

There were columns of planets, whirls of galaxies, giant pools of star-charts, all beneath a vaulted roof that curved up towards a circle of blackness. He had not expected to see them, and yet they all were floating over the consoles. And all were manned by alert, young TechnOps, their hands like those of musicians over the touch-sensitive keys.

It was then that the Doctor realized where he had seen the room before.

In the centre, near the eye of a hologrammatic ion-storm that was obviously being closely monitored, there stood a padded swivel-chair. It contained a tall man with high cheekbones and close-cropped grey hair. As the Doctor was pushed roughly into the chattering, swirling world of the centre, the man straightened up from his ion

64

storm and met the Time Lord's gaze with a pair of bright blue eyes.

'We do not take kindly to stowaways.' His voice was like a spring, compressed and suggesting greater power than it actually revealed. 'I suppose you came on with the last shipment?'

The Doctor looked a little edgy. This was the part he had always found embarrassing. On this occasion, though, the difficulties were compounded by a feeling that he should not really be alive at all. 'Ah, well,' he said. 'Not exactly.'

The tall man strode over to the Doctor and looked down at him with very little effort to disguise his contempt. 'I am Station Supervisor Septimus Ballantyne,' he said. 'And I should like to know, sir, how you come to be on board Space Station Q4.'

He had wondered how long it would be before he got that familiar, queasy feeling that things were going to be complicated. And this time, they seemed to be even worse than usual.

'I see,' said the Doctor. 'I must say, Supervisor –'

'Yes?'

'You're looking very well.'

The President of St Matthew's College, Oxford was a contented man. The fortunes of the college were very healthy indeed thanks to a number of donations from benefactors. In general they tended to be anonymous, but the President had a fair idea who most of them were.

The college's reputation was similarly flourishing, now that the First Eight had bumped the much-vaunted boats of Oriel and, furthermore, now that it had cemented its position in the top five of the recently resurrected academic league, the Norrington Table. An excellent production of *A Midsummer Night's Dream* was currently drawing the crowds to the gardens every evening, and the chaplain, after a protracted theological debate with the President which had become a personal argument, had announced his intention to retire.

The President had been reading over the bursar's notes on undergraduate rent agreements when Amanda had called. She had managed, it transpired, to persuade Rafferty that his presence was not required by the President just now, and that she had to see him on private business of some urgency. Rafferty, being the perfect gentleman, had obviously understood and allowed the girl to make her own way. Amanda was quite aware that it had been all too easy, and knew Rafferty could hardly be expected not to have suspicions.

The President poured wine, and his glass was more than half-full before he looked up and, with a broad smile on his bewhiskered face, said:

'Ah, but you won't have one, will you, my dear?'

Amanda leaned back in the green leather chair. 'Alcohol,' she admitted languidly, 'has a corrosive effect on the interstitial nuclei of my anterior hypothalamus.'

'Indeed,' said the President, 'and we can't have that.'

'Absolutely not,' said Amanda.

The President cast a reflective look at the blood-red depths of the wine before taking an appreciative sip. 'Now, I want you to tell me, my dear – '

'Yes?'

'Where have you left my TARDIS?'

Terrin had seen enough.

The captain took one last look around the centre, shaking his head ruefully at the hollow skeletons. *If I could understand only a part of this*, he thought sadly.

He was not really clear why he had come back, except that he often needed time alone to think without his officers around him. They were a good crew, he knew that, but the responsibility sometimes weighed on him to the extent that he felt he was only using his brain and not his intellect. Terrin needed clarity and silence. And he was finding it here, in this deep-space graveyard.

Quallem would take care of things, he was confident of that. She was inclined to be a little over-enthusiastic at times, he thought, but she was basically a reliable officer.

It sometimes occurred to him, usually in the greyness between waking and sleeping, that the ship might be more tightly run under Quallem – that her bursts of anger and vitriol were a reaction against the laxity of the regime and the creaking, barely spaceworthy ship. A substitute for real authority. Terrin did not like to dwell on the idea.

He had known the young Listrelle in his second phase at the Academy, when she was a cadet and he was a lieutenant on a user-awareness course, studying the long-term effects of linkage with neural networks. Her hair had been a glossy bob then, and she had been thinner, almost skin and bone, but her crispness, her almost brutish dedication, had been the same. He wondered how she relaxed, until one day he had seen her in the Intuitive Fencing hall. The mask, designed to render each player totally blind, hid her face, but there was no mistaking the bright red mushroom of hair and the lithe body. Lieutenant Terrin had leaned on the gantry and watched the seventeen-year-old Listrelle whirling and parrying in the perfect union of mind and body, second-guessing her opponent, a young man, on every move. Terrin had tried the game a couple of times but he found the mask claustrophobic, and he had not been especially good at monitoring the dizzying display of heat-readouts and sound-graphs which rushed in front of his eyes at each moment of play. It had seemed to him the sort of game that Quallem would excel at.

Now, a decade later, she had been with him for almost two years – the youngest first officer ever assigned to a starship by Lightbase – and he still hardly knew her. Joshua Kenley, her predecessor, had been a very different case, a true humanitarian and the captain's personal friend. He could not imagine Quallem having close friends. There was a rumour among the junior officers that she had never had a lover, but Terrin knew this to be untrue. One did not spend a year at the Academy with someone without finding out these things.

The sound, when it came, snapped him back into the present. He whirled around from the skeleton. It was a crackling, like feet on autumn leaves ... or was it more the rush of air through the trees themselves? His panic growing, he scanned the room. Nothing came up on the infra-red readout, and yet the sound was building up.

It was behind him now. He primed his grin. It was a Derenna–36, with symbiotic sighting, and missing did not come into its vocabulary. The problem was that, right now, there was nothing to aim at.

He retreated against the wall and flipped open his communicator.

'Terrin to *Icarus*. Come in, please.'

The sound seemed to be channelled through his communicator, intensified. There was *something* in the room, he could feel it. Beginning to wish he had not backed into a corner, Terrin tried the ship again. The static crackled back at him, still intensifying.

He was still frantically trying to call when the air in front of him concealed into a bubble of twinkling red lights. The sound was like a sigh of release from a grave, borne on the wings of a thousand phantom birds. He heard it rushing in his ears as the lights blotted out the room.

The shadows lengthened on the bridge of the *Icarus*.

The tension was tangible. The only person to appear relaxed was Strakk, sprawled in a chair next to Ace with his feet up on the spare flight-monitor. Against every rule in the book, he had popped a tranquillizer about half an hour ago. He'd offered one to Ace, but she had learnt very early to say no to such things.

'So are you married, then?' she asked, trying and failing to turn her constrained neck.

He seemed to find this funny. 'No. Where are you from?'

'Perivale. West London.'

Strakk's inane grin widened. 'What, the forest?'

'No. It's ... hard to explain.'

The angry bleeping cut into the tension on the bridge. Cheynor was at the TechnOp's side in an instant.

'The captain's life-trace, sir.' The man's face was white as he looked up at the Second Officer. 'It's gone.'

'Energy turbulence increasing,' reported another crew member. 'Location ... one-two-seven, four-eight-four from current.'

'Distance, Mr Rost?' Quallem asked.

'One micro-trak.'

Cheynor's eyes met Quallem's across the bridge. 'The captain – '

Quallem was in the command chair. 'Mr Larsen, disengage boarding-link and seal all hatchways.'

The TechnOp's fingers stabbed at the relevant controls. 'Disengaging, ma'am.'

Cheynor, fury in his face, swept across the bridge. 'Lieutenant-Commander, that last order is – '

'Is precisely that.' Quallem seemed supremely indifferent to anything Cheynor had to say. 'All units, prepare for undocking. Standard escape velocity, Mr Larsen.'

'Engaged, ma'am.'

'Set course for Station P4. Mr Strakk, please take your position.'

Strakk swung his legs down and winked at Ace. 'Playtime,' he whispered. 'See you later.'

Cheynor was visibly shaking with rage. He leant on the arm of the command-chair and kept his voice discreetly low.

'May I remind you, Lieutenant-Commander, that three men are unaccounted for, including the captain – '

'They're dead, Mr Cheynor.' Quallem's green eyes were on the monitor screen. 'Their life-traces have gone. What do you want me to do? Risk more lives?'

The whine of the engines, even more tortured than usual, was growing, and the ship juddered as it disengaged from Space Station Q4.

'We have a responsibility to those men.'

'We have a duty to Lightbase.' Quallem's answer came instantly. 'As the acting captain my first priority is to report the situation so that it can be dealt with. You know as well as I do, Mr Cheynor, that we're not in range here.'

'Then send a beacon. Within the hour – '

'Within the hour we could all be dead.'

For a few moments, Cheynor remained with his gaze fixed on Quallem's white cheekbones, a mixture of emotions churning inside him. Then he turned and walked slowly from the captain's podium without looking back.

'Got problems, Boadicea?' Ace could not resist it.

Quallem turned, her hair and eyes blazing in the orange light, and strode down from the podium to Ace's chair. She took the girl's chin in a leather-gloved hand and pushed it up so that her head was hard against the back of the chair.

'You are the most impertinent little madam I have ever met,' said Acting Captain Quallem coldly, and let her go.

'Then you should get out more,' Ace called after her.

If anyone had been passing by the Hinchcliffe Building of St Matthew's College, Oxford, and had looked in at the bullet-proof window of the President's study, they would have seen an unusual sight.

The President himself had flipped open his drinks cabinet and was observing a number of small white lights on what looked like some immensely complex video-game. Meanwhile, a slim, dark-haired and frighteningly attractive girl in mirror shades was sprawled in the President's own oak chair, watching him.

Amanda should, of course, have been as incapable of feeling indifference, or other emotions, as any android. She merely awaited orders, and if she had fulfilled her last instructions without receiving any new ones, then the usual practice was to wait patiently, although androids do not feel patience or impatience, until those expected orders arrived.

Amanda, unfortunately, had been working on her personality, and the President rather liked the idea. He was especially keen on the quirk of cybergenetics that had resulted in the girl abandoning the android's apparent air of cool detachment and indifference in favour of a simulated personality whose prime trait was an air of cool detachment and indifference. It was enough to make an android engineer's heart glow with pride.

'According to the interstitial relay,' said the President, a smile on his florid countenance, 'the starship has undocked from the space-station.'

'Now,' said Amanda, 'might be a good time.' There was a click, and the President turned to see her slipping a new cartridge into her pistol.

'Heavens, no, my dear,' said the President hurriedly. 'Put the thing away. You go to Heathrow now and you're likely to blow the whole thing sky-high. Excuse the metaphor.' He shut the drinks cabinet and hurried over to his bookshelf, looking for something among the nineteenth-century novels. 'Tell me,' he said, running his finger along the tomes, 'do you find it odd, having performed an action as the dress-rehearsal for the action itself?'

'The question is irrelevant,' said Amanda. She sounded almost bored.

'Quite so. Quite so. Ah.' The President found the copy of *The Picture of Dorian Gray* that he had been looking for, and removed a slim cylinder from its spine. He smiled at Amanda. 'Here we go, then,' he said jovially, as if opening the batting for the Senior Common Room First XI, and slipped around behind her. He peeled back her skin to reveal the aperture in her neck, and inserted her new orders.

Tom and Bernice had had no success in finding Rafferty, an idea which had acquired even more urgency since the encounter with the apparition in the Professor's college study.

Now, Bernice was beginning to wonder if she truly was in the twentieth century. When she asked Tom for transport, she thought grimly, this was not what she had expected. The driving rain needled her skin and blew her hair in front of her eyes as she pedalled furiously. The lactic acid was aching in her calves, and Tom, some way ahead on his own bicycle, kept beckoning to her to hurry up. She gritted her teeth and pushed harder on the pedals.

They rode past Wadham and the King's Arms, before emerging from South Parks Road and swinging left. Tom was pedalling hard under the Bridge of Sighs. Bernice spared it an admiring glance but no more, for she was a little unnerved by the screech of brakes and the insults from behind her. I will never complain about shuttle travel again, she thought.

Halfway along New College Lane, they almost ran the Professor down.

He caught Bernice as she toppled from the unwieldy machine.

'Dear me, Miss Summerfield,' he said, 'I shouldn't have left you alone at the mercy of this young reprobate.'

'Professor,' Tom said eagerly, 'we were attacked!' The memory of his earlier fear had dissipated, and he was keen to boast about the experience now.

'It's true,' Bernice added, a little dizzily. 'This dreadful *thing* – ' She shook her head, regained her composure. 'Let's start at the beginning.'

'Yes,' said Rafferty, bewildered. 'Let's.'

Something had already told him it was going to be one of those days.

Chapter 9

Far Out and Gone

Ace was bored. One of the crewmen had clipped a pair of wafer-thin headphones over her ears, which she assumed was meant kindly. Ace, though, had heard enough of mid-millennium music to know she didn't like it. Some of it was all right. The closest parallel between twentieth-century music and what was washing through her head now was some of the ambient-dub she had heard on Earth in the late nineties; the Orb or Brian Eno. It was relaxing, in a way, and the sound quality was perfect, but she had still been relieved when the loop ended. She didn't have the heart to ask if they had any Carter USM.

It hadn't surprised Ace that Strakk doubled up on communications. Despite his keenness to point guns at people – or maybe because of it – she had gleaned the impression that security was not his first love, and that Albion Strakk would prefer something where he was less likely to end up getting greased. He was the one who, after five minutes' cruising in deep space, picked up the message.

'Communication coming through from – ' His face was a mask of disbelief as he turned to Quallem. 'From the space-station, Commander.'

'We're not in range, Mr Strakk.'

'No, ma'am. From Q4.'

Listrelle Quallem's expression said, *But they're all dead down there*. She did not look at the second officer.

'Visual.' The order came from Cheynor. Ace wondered why. The monitor picture broke up into blue and silver shards. Strakk made some calibrations, and appeared worried. 'We're losing it. Can we isolate?'

The picture began to take shape, and the crackling that went with it took on the vestiges of speech.

Ace was looking at the screen like the rest of them. It pleased her to think that, over the last few years, she had not lost her capacity for astonishment.

'It's him . . .' she murmured.

The face on the monitor was that of the Doctor.

Cheynor heard Quallem draw breath. 'You know him?'

'That's the fool who was on the station with *her*.' The first officer didn't even look at Ace, but a crimson finger-nail pointed in the direction of the restrainer chair. 'Is this some kind of joke?'

'Uh, negative, ma'am,' Strakk said, his fingers flickering over the console. 'The computer reports a high-frequency beacon, transmitting on pre-programmed schedule – ' He grinned, possibly at Ace. 'It's a recording,' he said. Ace thought she heard him add 'Cool,' under his breath.

'Then get it, someone!' Quallem yelled. 'Get the blasted sound!'

They all heard it now, strained through the interference.

'. . . grave threat. I repeat, avert your current path and advise Earth of your situation. You must believe me . . .' A huge wash of static drowned the Doctor for several seconds. ' – the most serious time-break. We have very little time ourselves . . .'

Now both the sound and picture were breaking up. The Doctor's image crackled through a snowstorm.

'Why can't we get a clear signal?' Ace asked. As usual, everyone ignored the prisoner.

'Get him back,' Cheynor said. 'We need that message!'

Strakk cupped his hand to his earphone, but was not looking hopeful. 'It's going, sir. I think it was only pro-grammed to beam once. And judging by the state of the equipment back there . . .'

Darius Cheynor's tanned face was lined with worry as he paced the shadows of the bridge. 'A pre-recorded message, programmed to beam into space at a set time . . .' He strode to Ace's chair and spun her around to face

74

him, meeting her implacable gaze. 'What does your friend know about all this, I wonder?'

'Don't raise your hopes,' she said. 'He doesn't even tell me, most of the time.'

We have made contact. We are ready for union.

In the void beyond Time, they stood ready. An army of ghosts, shimmering grey and white, crimson eyes glowing behind their masks. They were never still. Ripples, susurrations ran through them, and in the darkness there echoed a muttering like the incantations of prophets. At the flanks and the rear, new spectres were joining the hideous crew at each moment. Although moments meant nothing here. They came with a fluttering, leathery sound like the flapping of bats' wings, and stood, jittery and expectant, with their comrades. Each soldier was armed with a wide-barrelled blaster that somehow seemed part of the arm.

Prepare for transfer.

The voice, in each of their minds, was like the crashing of granite into oceans, like lightning splitting trees, like other terrors of beauty that some of the Time Soldiers half remembered.

From long ago.

Soon, said the voice, *we shall be in the Time Vortex. Prepare to ride into it, my friends. Time is almost ours.*

'Rumpelstiltskin?' said Terrin.

'No,' said the little man opposite him.

'Tiberius?'

'No.'

Terrin had been astonished to discover that he was not dead. He had woken up in a featureless room to find himself being watched by a pixie-like man with a wise, friendly face and twentieth-century clothes, who was sitting cross-legged on the floor. When he had sat up, rubbing his cramped limbs, the little man had explained to the captain that they were both, for the moment, prisoners, and that this was presumably the detention centre. The man had added that he was pleased to have some company, and he supposed the newcomer was from the Survey Corps?

Terrin had first looked in vain for a door to the cell, so that he could hammer on it and demand his release. That sort of thing never did any good, but he had an idea that etiquette somehow demanded it. Only then had he grudgingly admitted where he was from. As his mistrust of the little man mellowed, he agreed – for want of any better suggestion – that they should pass the time by guessing one another's names.

'Then I give up. Mine's Romulus. Romulus Terrin.'

'Ah. Do you have a brother?'

Terrin frowned. 'No.'

'Never mind. Well, I'm usually known as the Doctor.'

'I see. You don't have another name?'

'Only on special occasions. You can call me John Smith if you like, but it would just be for convenience.'

Terrin had met many reasonable people who, for one reason or another, preferred pseudonyms, so he didn't press the point. He sighed and continued pacing. 'So, Doctor whoever, are you going to give me your theory of where we are and how we got here?'

'You were on Q4. Like me. Somehow we were brought here, presumably by whatever attacked the crew, and your men.'

Light dawned on Terrin. 'You're the intruder. The one Quallem was talking about. I should arrest you,' he added, half-heartedly.

'There's little point,' said the Doctor, 'and besides, they've taken away your gun. Pontoon?' he added, shuffling a pack of cards that he had produced.

'What?'

'Time is my business, Captain Terrin. The date on the guard's wristwatch said March 22nd. Now, what do you make of that?' The Doctor dealt the cards solemnly.

'One week ago,' said the Captain, puzzled. 'His watch was wrong? Probably picked it up from a tax-free on one of the outposts.'

The Doctor gave the captain one of his rare smiles. 'How very quaint. You see, my interpretation is that we've travelled in Time, but not in space. This is still Station Q4, Captain – as it was, one week ago.'

'I find that very hard to believe, Doctor, and I'm a broad-minded man. When we left Earth, Professor Xoster's tachyon experiments were at a very primitive – '

'Ha! Call yourself broad-minded?' The Doctor was derisive. 'Twist,' he added and took another card.

Terrin looked suitably chastened. 'I think I might have a headache coming on,' he confessed. 'I feel like one of Robert Silverberg's characters. Or maybe Isaac Asimov. I've studied the literature and culture of the twentieth century, you see, Doctor. And I can't help noticing your own attire . . .' He shrugged. 'Are you sticking?'

'Yes.'

'Me too. I declare eighteen.' Terrin put down the ten of diamonds and the eight of clubs. 'Doctor – if I were to talk to the supervisor of the station – let him know who I am – '

'You can try,' said the Doctor, putting down his seven of hearts and eight and six of diamonds. 'But you won't get very far.'

'What do you mean?'

'Where was your ship last week?'

'Colony Franost. We were collecting samples to check for contamination and . . .' Terrin stopped. 'Oh,' he said, feeling rather stupid for the second time in five minutes.

'I'm afraid,' said the Doctor, 'you would be denounced as a pure and simple imposter. Another game?'

Terrin was doing his best to adjust to the new concept. 'Good lord. If I went there I might meet myself.'

'Take it from me,' said the Doctor as he dealt again, 'that can be profoundly embarrassing.'

The *Icarus* had now been cruising for thirty minutes, judging by Ace's watch, which automatically adjusted to the time-zone of her location. Strakk had told her that the *Icarus* ran on Central European Time, because that suited the majority of the crew, and its days and nights would ebb and flow in accordance with a link transmitter in Hamburg.

The stern face of Dr Mostrell appeared on the first officer's monitor. Cheynor had never had a field promotion, and it took him a few seconds before he realized that he was supposed to answer.

'Cheynor here.'

'Darius, those bone samples. I'm having some interesting results. I don't suppose you could come and have a look?'

Cheynor was unsure. He was not needed, but one look at the brightness of the new captain's eyes and the way she was clutching the arms of her chair, knuckles white, made it clear to him that someone was going to have to keep an eye on things up on the bridge.

'I'm indisposed, Doctor. I can send . . .' His eye roved round the bridge, till he found the ideal all-purpose candidate. The ship's professional mug, in fact, was how the choice had once described himself to a tall Draconian girl he was trying to impress. 'I can send Strakk.' Cheynor called him over. 'You're wanted, Lieutenant.'

Strakk ambled over, rubbing his eyes as if he'd just got out of bed. 'On six planets, sir,' he said, 'but don't tell the captain.' He did not expect much more than the stony expression he got from Cheynor as the reassignment card was pressed into his hand. Strakk often bemoaned the fact – mostly to women, after several glasses of Voxnic – that he was the only officer on board with a sense of humour.

A thought occurred to him at the elevator door. 'Shall I take her?' he asked, indicating the sullen Ace.

'She's a prisoner, Lieutenant.' Quallem's reproach was razor-edged.

'Yeah, I know. I just thought she could make herself useful.' He shrugged. 'I'll be responsible. We can tag her.'

Quallem was strolling among the TechnOps, checking readouts. She waved a hand, absently.

Cheynor looked from Strakk to Quallem and back

again, then gave the three-fingered authorization signal. 'Limit her to the first ten sectors,' he said.

Strakk pressed a catch on the back of the chair and the metal bonds sprang open. 'You have to wear this,' he said, clipping a metallic bracelet to her. It felt tighter than any watch she had ever worn. 'If you go off-limits,' he said, 'the shuttle bay for example, the laser will slice your hand off at the wrist. It's nasty, but it works. So behave.'

'And if I try and take it off?'

'Something in the same vein,' Strakk quipped, as he called the elevator. He saluted to Quallem as they entered. 'Leaving the bridge, Captain.'

Dear Diary, wrote Bernice.

Professor Rafferty has wired his study with microphones, hidden a video-camera in his desk and meshed the room in beams of light, any one of which, when broken, sets off his pager. He wants to be seen to act on our story, I suppose. But at the same time, he wants to get to know me a little better, which is fine by me. And James Rafferty seems to be a man who takes his pleasure as seriously as his work. So Tom has been dispatched to the Bodleian, to look up everything he can find about reports of temporal disturbances – while I have been invited to dinner at High Table.

In the Senior Common Room, Benny slipped the book into her breast pocket as the Professor handed her a second glass of sherry.

'Thank you. Should I have dressed up?'

'Oh, no ... what you're wearing will be fine. I, on the other hand, have to parade in this.' He smiled, and tugged at his academic gown.

'It's very distinguished,' Bernice reassured him, as they strolled over to the window. She looked out at the floodlit domes and spires in the rain. Their natural honey-brown was enhanced by the yellowish light, making them look wise and watchful. Silent now, but awaiting the buzzing activity of the next day.

Rafferty had waited until Tom had gone before telling Bernice about his visit from Amanda. He did not know why. Maybe, he thought, it was inculcated into him not to discuss strange occurrences in front of students until it became necessary. Otherwise – as he had found in the past, especially with his hot-headed young postgrads – they tended to dash off and do a bit of detective work on their own that was often a hindrance. He knew Bernice would be a little more composed than that.

'I'd have said she was a reporter,' Rafferty mused, 'if it weren't for the fact that she knew . . . things several levels above top secret.'

'I won't ask,' said Benny, and she smiled up at him before straightening his bow-tie. She sighed. 'You know, I seem to attract trouble, even when the Doctor's not around.'

'Yes,' Rafferty said, as if it had suddenly struck him. 'Where *is* the Doctor, anyhow?'

'No idea. I imagine that without me around, he's having the time of his life.'

The Doctor's face contorted as the muscle-bound guard pulled his hair back until the light was dazzling him.

'The name,' said Ballantyne threateningly, as he leaned over the Doctor. 'The name of your organization.'

The Doctor had been disappointed. He had built up quite a resistance to lie-detectors and instruments of mental torture over the years, and he had been preparing himself in the cell. When the interrogation had finally come, though, it had turned out to be simply the traditional cold steel room with a light shining in his face and a continual barrage of identical questions. He found it rather sad that the human race had need of this sort of thing at all, but not to have progressed in a third of a millennium was surely indicative of a lack of imagination. He had tried to point this out at the start, and had been rewarded with a cuff from the guard.

'I don't have an organization. I was in one once, it made me disorganized. Supervisor, if you don't listen to me, you and all your personnel will be dead within one week! I don't know how long we have. It may only be a matter of hours.'

'So you keep saying,' said Ballantyne, crossing his long legs as he sat down opposite the Doctor. 'Quite a prophet of doom, aren't you, Doctor?'

'They warned me at the Academy about talking to the dead. It seems they may have been right.'

The slim, dark-skinned woman at Ballantyne's side had been quiet up until now, but at the Doctor's last comment she moved into the blue light. She had enormous brown eyes and a high-boned face beneath cropped hair, and she wore a uniform similar in style to the supervisor's. Helina Vaiq, the station co-ordinator, was unsettled by the little man, and she knew Ballantyne was too.

'Supervisor,' she said. 'A word?'

In the corner, where the Doctor could not hear them, the supervisor and the co-ordinator conferred.

'I hate to tell you this, Septimus, but I don't think he's totally crazy.'

'You don't,' said Ballantyne evenly.

'His colleague might have been suffering from parapsy-chotic dementia. I thought I detected a neo-primal guilt urge too ... But this one ... unless what we've got here is a severe case of *pseudologica fantastica* ... I think he must be the genuine article.'

Ballantyne looked affronted, then horrified. 'You mean all the time he's been telling the truth?'

Septumus Ballantyne, before his elevation to station supervisor, had been a major-general in the Terran Defence Corps, and he had interrogated many life-forms on suspicion of being alien spies. There had even been a joke doing the rounds of the Institute of Interplanetary Linguists and Non-Verbal Communicators that Major-General Ballantyne kept their interpreters in business. There had been one unfortunate incident where the sub-ject of interrogation was a member of the Institute himself, a ferret-faced alien called a Bojihan who was accused of taking illicit holograms of station security zones. The accused was conversant in three of the Morestran dialects, but unfortunately knew no English. No one from Earth had ever mastered any of the fourteen main Bojihan languages, as they depended not only on pronunciation, stress and inflexion, but also on several thousand different types of squeals and grunts, a few hundred of which lay beyond the range of human hearing. Therefore the only reputable interpreters the Institute could offer in this case were other Bojihans from the same continent of the prisoner's planet. Ballantyne would have none of it, arguing that the possibilities for being conned were endless, and the Bojihan was eventually let off the hook as the charge could not be brought.

Helina Vaiq was aware of the supervisor's zeal, and this was partly why she was keen to continue the Doctor's interview (she disliked the word 'interrogation') on her own. 'Give me some time with him,' Vaiq offered. 'I need to do a proper analysis of his blink and pulse rate, but I should be able to give you a definite answer within the hour.'

Ballantyne nodded. 'And the other one?'

'I'll put someone on to him. Find out where he got the Survey Corps I.D., that sort of thing. You never know, he might be genuine too.'

'Did you ask him who he was?'

'Yes. He said I'd never believe him.'

Ballantyne heaved a sigh. 'There seems to be a lot of it about at this time of year. All right, Helina, carry on.'

Rain danced in the headlights on Broad Street. At this time of the evening, Oxford's streets were quiet, but flanked with pockets of noise. A Mazda, cobalt blue, turned the corner from South Parks Road into the Broad, past the stone heads of the Philosophers and the colourful window of the Paperback Shop. The car slowed, tyres swishing on the wet road, its engine lower than a purr. It cast in front of it a cone of light that was definitely reddish in colour. The driver was looking for something.

A figure in a denim jacket hurried along the Broad, cursing the weather and pushing his soaking hair out of his eyes. Even before today, Tom had not had a good couple of weeks. The computer system containing all the results of his tachyonics experiments had crashed, taking everything with it, and a virus had corrupted most of his floppies. The only hope now was that a lot of it was still stored on the Winchester drive that Rafferty owned. He had forgotten to ask the Professor earlier. Then he had had an argument with one of the girls he was currently interested in, about her intention to go to the Hertford College ball with another man, and this had prompted her to slam out of his life. On top of that, his motorbike had been stolen. The police at St Aldate's had been helpful, but they had found nothing matching the description of his machine. All he wanted now was to get back to the college bar and have a game of table football. The Bodleian, the Professor and Bernice could all wait.

He was wondering why the car with the funny headlights seemed to be tailing him.

He paused. Through the haze of the rain, he saw the car stop too, waiting like a predatory red-eyed beast.

Tom stepped out to cross the street, just opposite Trinity gates, and in a sudden, sickening moment he heard the rush of water and the roar of the engine. He jumped aside in panic, but the car had already screeched to a halt.

The window began to wind down. A choice profanity was just forming on Tom's lips when he saw the driver. She was young, about twenty, he supposed, with dark hair that curled at the shoulder. His own bedraggled face was reflected twice in her mirror-lenses.

'You look very wet. Can I give you a lift?'

The voice reminded him of the way his late Siamese, Audrina, used to rub herself around his calves before settling down and going to sleep. And the face was –

'It is Tom, isn't it?' she added sweetly.

He nodded, trying to convince himself that Bernice had been right and he really did know her. After all, there had been that Archery Club party at St Anne's . . . and the mid-term bop at the NukeSoc where he . . . hmm. He realized he could have given quite a few attractive girls his name and number in the past week without remembering it, and this one was decidedly interesting.

'Thanks,' he said. 'That's kind.'

His heart was beating fast. He had not forgotten that strange, unearthly feeling from the pub. The inside of the Mazda smelt of warm leather and Dior, and he smiled at her gratefully, only realizing now how cold and wet he had been.

'Are you . . . Did I see you at NukeSoc?'

'Where?'

'Nuclear Research Society. The dinner.'

'No,' she said, as the car moved off.

'Ah.' He tried again. 'English weather,' he said. 'Don't you love it?' It was a bluff, while he desperately tried to recall her name.

'Sorry, Tom,' said the girl, as she took them across to Beaumont Street. 'Amanda. You remember?'

'Er . . .' He was not going to remember even if he tried. 'I'm afraid not,' he admitted. 'Did we . . . er . . . ?'

'No.'

'Oh. Good. Well, when I say good, I mean – oh, dear.'

'I know what you mean.'

He was warm and drying off, and in the company of an attractive woman who seemed to know him. Things, he reflected happily, had started going a little better for Tom Cheynor.

In his office, the President chuckled as he looked into the wet face of the young postgraduate on his monitor screen. After a couple of black-outs, Amanda's relay was working perfectly.

'Excellent, my dear,' he murmured, and took a sip of his 1953 Pinot Noir.

Chapter 10

Force Majeure

'Captain,' said Larsen, 'I'm tracing the energy field again.'

Quallem, in the captain's chair, was tapping one finger-nail against her white teeth, and did not appear to have heard him.

Cheynor turned.

'Captain?' he said.

'Range, Mr Larsen?' Her voice was a thin parody.

'Fifteen micro-traks. Closing on vector . . . two-four-nine.'

Quallem swivelled on her command chair. For the first time since leaving Q4, they could hear the rumble of the ship's engines. Cheynor held his breath.

'Evasive action, Mr Larsen.'

'Yes, ma'am.'

The relief was like the snapping of elastic. But something told Darius Cheynor it was not over yet.

'You see,' said Dr Mostrell, indicating the blow-up of his microscope picture, 'the atomic structure has undergone a chemical transformation.'

'As opposed to physical,' Ace said, almost to herself.

Strakk, examining readouts on the other side of the lab, looked up in surprise. 'So the crew-members' cells weren't just aged beyond repair?'

Mostrell replaced his gold-rimmed glasses and waved his pencil at Strakk. 'Precisely. Their bodies must have been *bombarded* with catalytic particles. Quite possibly a form of tachyonic energy.'

'And if you change the chemical structure,' Ace said,

slowly, 'then DNA gets messed up. Corrupt cells aren't replaced.'

'Quite. Now . . .' Dr Mostrell went to his central computer and fed it some of his notes. 'If I enter equations of the *presumed* reaction, we might find out what the weapon was.'

'It's Time,' said Ace. 'Whatever the equations say, it comes down to Time – right? That's what the Doctor would say.'

'Time-breaks,' said Strakk, turning round from the spectrograph. 'That's what he was saying in that message! So when was it recorded – and how?'

'Absolute rubbish,' said Mostrell dismissively, and met Ace's hostile stare. 'This Doctor fellow – qualified, is he?'

'Suitably,' she answered, with ice and lemon. 'What makes you sure you can't use Time itself as a weapon, Dr Mostrell?'

'You can't talk about using something that you're subject to yourself. You get into the most dreadful recursive patterns. Everything must relate to Time.'

'But supposing,' Strakk said, 'that whatever has done this . . . *doesn't*?'

The argument was interrupted by the bleeping of the secondary alarm. The lights flickered once, and dimmed.

'Full alert! What the devil – ' Mostrell checked his power gauges. 'A systems failure!'

The alarm was chirruping through the bridge too, where the lights had dimmed to red.

'Power drain on all systems,' Larsen reported. 'Diverting to keep life-support at full capacity.' He looked to the captain for confirmation, but it was left to Cheynor to give the signal.

'What the hell's happening?' Quallem snapped. 'I didn't order Full Alert – '

'Mr Gessner,' said Cheynor, interrupting her with a rudeness that would have gladdened Ace's heart, 'check the auto-override, find out why the computer has taken us to Full Alert.' He turned to look at Quallem, who was gripping the rail of the podium so hard it looked as if her knuckles would crack. 'The first step in being captain,' said Cheynor calmly, 'is to know your ship.'

'Return to your post, Mr Cheynor.'

The deadlock was broken by Rost, the pilot. 'Losing manual control, Captain.'

'Go to auxiliary,' ordered Cheynor. He met Quallem's eyes with a calmness he knew he could not keep up for long.

She was shivering. He thought he almost saw her smile. Pleadingly.

'Don't take it away from me, Darius . . .' she whispered.

'I'm relieving you of command.'

Her smile was crooked, on another plane of reality. 'You can't do that, Mr Cheynor. I still have Security. I'll place you under arrest.'

'Then do that,' he said. 'It'll hardly matter when we're both dead.'

'Energy field now ten micro-traks,' said Larsen, 'And closing.'

The strain was showing on every face on the bridge. They could hear the tortured engines now, and the comforting hum of the machinery had become a cacophony of squealing and chattering.

Like a thousand restless voices.

Cheynor, taking command, swung around. 'Power in the warp engines, Mr Rost?'

'Less than fifty per cent, sir.'

'Continue evasive. Give it your best shot.' He patched in the intra-ship channel to his console. 'Cheynor to all stations. We have a Full Alert, I repeat, we have Full Alert. Deflectors and weapons crew on stand-by.'

'The ship won't take it!' Quallem screamed.

He swung on her, seeing no salvation now in her twisted, livid face. 'Then given a better order – *Captain*.'

'Energy field on visual,' Larsen reported.

They all saw it now. Like a giant cloak of lights, sparkling and fizzing. Like huge, crackling jaws chewing up Time.

Heading straight for the ship.

On the podium behind Quallem, a shape was starting to form.

The engines of the starship gave one last asthmatic wheeze of flame and died.

Around it, the lights gathered like an army of fireflies, weaving their web. In a matter of moments, the ship was immobile.

On the bridge, the intruder was flickering into being, bathed in green like an effect from a phantasmagoria. It seemed unable to maintain itself for more than a second at a time, as if slowly gathering strength, but with each flicker it grew stronger.

'What is it?' Larsen's voice was barely more than a whisper as he gaped over his shoulder at the entity.

'Monitor your post, Mr Larsen.' Cheynor was at the edge of the podium, sidling closer to the strobing light. Quallem hovered behind him, her body tense.

Cheynor, shading his eyes was attempting to make out the details of the phase-shifting shape at the heart of the column of light. He saw humanoid limbs, a mask like an animal's snout . . . Then the sound of breakers on a jagged shore filled the back of his mind, insidious, yearning. There was something about the light and the sound which he thought he ought to recognize . . .

The voices continued to report. People, doing their jobs as normal, hoping that if they carried on that way it would be part of just another routine survey assignment. And imperceptibly, the reports had begun to address themselves to Second Officer Cheynor.

'Completely immobile, sir. Losing power on all systems.'

'Intruders on Decks E and F, sir,' reported a female TechnOp.

This, at least, was something for which Quallem was trained to react. 'Patrols one and two down, McCarran. Tell them to shoot to kill.'

The spell was broken. Cheynor backed off from the

glowing intruder. 'That's madness. You're sending men to their deaths.'

Survey Corps TechnOp (Second Grade) Rosabeth McCarran was not, by nature, indecisive. But Terrin had been a good captain, a strong leader who gave orders and stuck to them. Now she had come to that crashing realization that hits many in the field of battle, especially those for whom battle is an unfortunate side-effect of what they have been trained for – namely, that her leader was as frightened as she was, and that a strong order was not necessarily going to get them out of this alive. Rosabeth's brother was the leader of Patrol Two. If she punched in Quallem's order, she knew where she would be sending him. Her eyes, unnaturally large against her thin face, were determined.

'I won't do it, ma'am.'

Listrelle Quallem could feel the impact of thirty gazes on her. Her body tingled.

'McCarran,' she breathed, 'Do you want us all to die?'

'Intruders now advancing to Level D, sir.' Larsen heard his own voice quiver. Just keep going, he was thinking, as if everything were perfectly normal.

McCarran was still, impassive, as Captain Quallem stepped over to her console.

One finger stabbed down on the control that McCarran had not wanted to touch.

Deep in the lower decks of the *Icarus*, alarms sounded. Within seconds, the echo of booted feet was clanging along walkways and up ladder-shafts.

'It's over,' Quallem breathed. 'You're finished.'

'No, Listrelle,' said Cheynor. '*You* are.'

She turned, looked into the barrel of his gun. The fluttering began to echo through the bridge again. Pictures flashed into Cheynor's mind, images of hell, images he had seen relayed from Station Q4.

'This is mutiny, Mr Cheynor,' she said with a smile. Quallem was confident she had won now. She knew he had finally gone too far.

'Yes,' said Darius Cheynor. 'I'm afraid so.'

He only pulled the trigger once. The recoil from the Derenna kicked up his arm.

Captain Quallem was still smiling when the shot slammed her up against McCarran's console.

Ace stood under the ladder-shaft, listening.

'It's happening,' she said quietly. 'Whatever it was has caught up with us.'

Dr Mostrell, who was trying to link up the auxiliary power, had a mess of optic-fibres in his arms. 'If I can get this back,' he said, poking around in the electronic spaghetti with a laser-probe, 'we can see what's happening on the bridge.'

The sound of the catch on Strakk's Derenna–24 cut the air like a knife into ice. 'If they get down here ... we'll be ready.'

'Don't count on it, boy wonder,' Ace snapped. 'It kicks Time around the way kids splash in puddles. If they haven't killed us yet, it just means the bastards haven't got round to it.'

Strakk's dose of benzodiazepine was wearing off. 'Are you always such a ray of sunshine?'

The thunder of battle roared again like a tidal wave. And this time, it sounded closer than ever.

It had begun in Hold Five, with flickers like *ignis fatuus* in the darkness, and then the globules had resolved themselves into larger shapes. The walls were no obstacle. Forming details – limbs, helmets, broad-nosed blasters – as they entered the real world, the Time Soldiers leapt, de-phasing, through solid metal. Traces flickered behind them like after-images.

In the dimness of the access tunnel, the echo of advancing feet was distant, yet growing louder.

Tristan Cobain wiped away a trickle of sweat from his nose and glanced along the barricade at his security team. In the red lighting, their faces were drained of emotion. It was the only way, Cobain thought grimly. In his five

90

years as security chief, he'd seen it every time. You had to think of each man and woman as fighting units – as components. They were human beings – Cobain never allowed himself to forget that, and he knew Captain Terrin wouldn't either if he were still here – but you had to forget their human failings. You had to have your team, and orders needed to come from the head, not the gut. Cobain had never believed in instinct. He'd seen three good mates die from relying on it. He looked at the faces once more. No one's eyes could be seen behind their goggles, but he knew they'd all be watching the door to the hold. They were more than just gun-arms. He knew them, although he got little chance to show it. Katja Brintz, nineteen last birthday and two months pregnant. Brad Gillespie – family killed in the Cyberwars. Drew McCarran, whose sister was a TechnOp on the bridge. There were others. They were never just 'you'. They had faces, names, hearts that thumped, families on the Colonies. They had lives and loves and hates.

Cobain did too. He especially hated the silence.

So as he listened to the clangs and shudders from deep behind the metal, he was not wishing them away. He wanted the sound to grow, until it was tangible. He wanted them there.

Tristan Cobain needed to see what he was killing.

The steel shutters burst outwards in a fountain of light-globules.

'Open fire!'

Cobain's order snapped the tension. The air was shredded with blue light.

The invaders, their bodies taking form, did not even attempt to get out of the way. The lasers sliced through them, diffusing as if pushed back by invisible hands. In slow motion, with a fluttering and twittering, the Time Soldiers raised their right arms. Time shrivelled in beams between the blasters and the squad.

Three bodies were hurled against the wall. Two were skeletons, and the third a mass of torn flesh, the bone of his tibia and fibula crumbling beneath him. Cobain was showered with powdered skin and bone. That was Gillespie.

The screams of death were taken up from somewhere behind the creatures' masks, as if in mockery, a banshee parody of the troopers' agony. A cry of battle, feeding off a cry of death.

Cobain fired bolt after bolt. On the invaders came. He yelled at the squad to fall back. It was all they could do. At the portal, Cobain's fist slammed the sealing control. The force wall shimmered down between the aliens and the remainder of his squad.

All but one, Katja Brintz. She had tripped, fallen.

He could do nothing but watch in horror as the invader, floating two metres above her, fired straight into her stomach.

The force-field was splitting open. The invaders poured through like water smashing a dam.

It didn't happen quite quickly enough for Cobain to miss what had happened to Brintz.

The beam had slammed her up against the wall, her skin bleaching. But there was something else emerging from the point of impact. Something with a face, and tiny glistening hands.

Cobain's eyes widened. There was an invader stabilizing just in front of him, and he tasted the coldness in the air now, but he was rooted to the spot by Brintz's screams.

No. They were not her own.

They were the screams of something coming to life, being born into terror, pumped full of accelerated life as it lifted itself . . . towards death.

In the aura of energy, Katja Brintz's hair crisped and shrivelled to death-white. And in the shattered remnants of her womb –

It was the last thing Cobain saw. His head, wrenched from his body by a beam of Time, hit the bulkhead. His skeleton split and fractured in the rays, cracked like fine china.

And on the Time Soldiers came.

They knew there was no need to hurry.

Cheynor slammed the headphones down. 'Recall the guards,' he snapped. 'I've heard enough.' He rounded on Larsen. 'Can we patch in extra power to defences, without losing full life-support capacity?'

'I can try, sir.'

'Good.' Cheynor was gnawing at his finger. He shuffled the events like index cards in his head, ready now to look up the next thing to do.

Quallem, in Strakk's vacated chair, was recovering from the minimal stun-bolt. Cheynor lifted her chin, gently.

'Lieutenant-Commander, can you hear me?'

Her eyes were like polished stone on crumpled cushions. 'I feel like shit,' she said.

'Good. Means I didn't hurt you too much.'

Her voice was gentle, nothing like the metallic tones which Cheynor was used to. 'I can hear the birds. In the morning, over Lac Durenne. Flying against the sun.' She looked into Cheynor's puzzled face. 'Rooks. Their voices are black, ebony-black. And Maman is holding my hand.'

'Quallem...' he murmured, and realized that the woman could not hear him. He cast a desperate look at the TechnOps, who were trying their best with their various tasks on the rapidly draining power. The monitor-screen was blank as well, now, and all communications channels seemed to be filled with the sound of the demonic flapping of wings.

He turned back to her, touched her cheek gently. Her skin was burning.

'Listrelle ... I'm so sorry...'

Her mouth was damp. A smear of lipstick ran from its corner up to her temple, like a bloodstain. Her eyes suddenly cleared, fixed on Cheynor properly, and she gave him a delighted smile.

'*Les oiseaux du temps*,' she said. '*Je les entends. Ils viennent.*'

The birds of Time.

Darius Cheynor was suddenly, inexplicably sad that he had no children.

11

The Riders

'The helmsman steered, the ship moved on;
Yet never a breeze up blew;
The mariners all 'gan work the ropes,
Where they were wont to do;
They raised their limbs like lifeless tools –
We were a ghastly crew.'

(Samuel Taylor Coleridge,
The Rime of the Ancient Mariner)

'Time, Co-ordinator. It's all a matter of Time.'

Helina Vaiq leaned back in the leather chair of her
office and looked at the strange man across several square
metres of mahogany.

'Doctor,' she said, 'the Earth colonies currently have
no major enemies. We're enjoying the longest period of
interplanetary peace since the Cyberwars. Even if I were
to believe that this weapon existed, who is there that
would want to use it against us?'

'I assure you, if my theory is correct, then the period of
peace is rapidly coming to an end,' the Doctor murmured.

Helina slipped out of her chair and went to stand at
the viewing gallery that bordered one side of her carpeted
office. She fixed her gaze on the whirl of stars, and remembered the hologram museum on Earth where she had first
seen it.

'If we ignore you and you're right, Doctor, we are going
to look utter fools. On the other hand, if we take you

seriously and you are a crank, we will also look utter fools.'

'Then maybe you shouldn't decide,' suggested the Doctor, and he felt his two hearts beating with renewed energy. 'Maybe you should wager.'

The woman's eyes opened wide and brilliant white against her ebony skin. 'Wager?'

'You weigh up the potential losses and gains. There are four outcomes. You ignore me, and I'm right or I'm wrong. You take my advice, and I'm right or I'm wrong. Which scenario gives you the least chance of losing, Co-ordinator? Which would you rather be – reviled as a gullible fool, or reviled as a gullible fool and very much dead into the bargain?' The Doctor took out his paisley handkerchief and mopped his brow. 'Are you familiar with the work of Blaise Pascal?' he added.

Vaiq looked surprised. 'I've studied his logic.'

'Charming man.' The Doctor broke off, looked into the distance with slight regret. 'I wonder if he remembers me?' He realized that he had better not pursue that particular line of thought. 'So if you arrange to believe me – what have you got to lose?'

Helina Vaiq sat down, and rested her chin on her hand. Then, as if coming to a sudden decision, she pressed a button on her computer keyboard and the lighting in the office gave a slight flicker.

Almost in anger, she spun the VDU around to face the Doctor.

'My computer says you're telling the truth, Doctor.'

'I suppose I should take that as a compliment. Do you humans ever think for *yourselves*?'

'Yes, Doctor!'

Even the Doctor was surprised by the vehemence of Vaiq's response. 'Go on,' he said.

'I was born on the Aberna colony, Doctor. Thirty-three years ago. We lived under plastic, corrugated iron, anything we could salvage. The plastic came from crashed shuttles. For some reason there were lots of them. So we had plastic huts on mud floors. We had a vidscreen, can you believe it? There was a central relay and everyone had their set tuned into it. Hundreds of sat-channels, and yet our sanitation was a hole in the ground. There were meant to be food drops every week, but sometimes they didn't get through. So when someone died, the family did what was best for the community.' She paused, her face hard with memory. 'You get used to the taste of human flesh, after a while. It's still like that on some of the colonies. You tend to grow up pretty fast in that kind of place. You do think for yourself.'

The Doctor had pressed his fingertips together, and was listening. Someone – he didn't remember who – had told him once that he never liked to listen enough.

'The tanks came in when I was eleven. Our settlement was fire-bombed. They took the survivors. I don't dwell on how I got by, Doctor. If it hadn't been for a major who needed an unquestioning, uneducated secretary, I'd have been roasted on a spit. Or forced to perform unspeakable acts on members of my family, like some of my friends. As it was, he let me go in a couple of years, gave me enough money to get a Corps education. I was the lucky one. So when people call me an unquestioning follower of technology and orders, I don't tend to disabuse them.' She sat back, a little embarrassed by her outburst. 'They feel chastened afterwards.' Helina slammed her fist down on the desk. 'Why am I telling you this? You, a prisoner. Maybe there's something about you makes me think you'd understand that kind of thing.'

'Nothing can equal the cruelty that humans inflict on one another,' said the Doctor softly.

'So,' she shrugged, tapped her fingers on the arm of her chair, 'maybe that's why I believe you. Maybe I think you've suffered too, in the past, and that's why you understand it. Am I right?'

'Maybe.'

'All right, Doctor. So what the hell am I supposed to tell Ballantyne?'

'Somehow, the captain and I have been transported back in time one week. I'm not clear why, or how.

Normally...' The Doctor sighed, remembering. 'Normally I could not interfere to save those who I know will die. But the true path of Time has been disrupted.'

'But how –'

'Don't ask. It's something people like me feel, like the mugginess before a thunderstorm.' He got up, began to pace up and down the office. 'If only I didn't feel so trapped ... and there's something nagging at me. I've felt it ever since I left Oxford ...'

'Which was when?' Vaiq asked, casting caution to the winds. She did not expect to get a logical answer.

'Yesterday. Time flies. It seems like only four hundred years. Co-ordinator Vaiq – what exactly goes on here on Station Q4?'

She shrugged. 'What the hell. If you're a terrorist, you know enough for me to be court-martialled anyway. We're right at the edge of this spiral arm. We're the marker buoy in one heck of a big sea. We've got probes out there at the moment, to tell us what they've found, and so far, it's the usual stuff. Magnetic fields, asteroid belts. Q4 is one edge of Earth's colonial civilization, Doctor.'

'And so anyone attacking this station,' said the Doctor thoughtfully, 'would know exactly what they were doing...' He was whispering now, almost to himself. 'A memory, a suspicion... it annoys me. Like picking through the rubbish in a dimensionally transcendental filing cabinet. Must get it sorted, one of these days.' He looked up at Vaiq again, as if remembering she was there. 'Reminds me. If you should come across a blue box, about two metres high, would you let me know? Unlikely, but it might just turn up. The way these things do.'

'Anything else?' Vaiq was incredulous that she took this man seriously. And yet, she thought, she had to – right? The wager. A fool or a dead fool, take your pick. She had to let him know where she stood, though. 'Doctor, I'm afraid Ballantyne runs this station, not me. And until he has proof he'll do sweet nothing.'

The Doctor leaned on Vaiq's desk and looked into her

striking brown eyes. His face, she noticed, wore its first hint of fear.

'The proof,' said the Doctor, 'might be too terrifying to give.'

Romulus Terrin paced the cell for the hundredth time, his patience in a decaying orbit.

His mind kept slipping away from the anonymous greyness of the cell, back through time. Back to the staring skeletons of the dead Q4.

What kind of creature could leave a whole space-station a husk like that? Like a grape being squeezed of its juice, he thought, dried to a raisin, but worse than a raisin – beyond, to a shrivelled, stumpy blackness.

Terrain had seen death before. Once or twice, he had been too close to it. He wondered, again, what Kenley would have made of it all. Joshua Kenley, his old first officer and friend, might even have been able to get a way out of this blasted cell.

But there had been one thing that even Kenley, the infinitely adept, had not been able to talk his way out of. Berax spores travelled faster than any other bacterial organism, Terrin had known that. He'd also thought the Rho Magnus settlement had been totally sterilized before they got there, but that was a pretty misplaced assumption. It only needed the smallest of cracks in the sterilizing foam and the berax spores, if they were resourceful enough, could pour through it. As they had done. And one thing that berax spores always needed, especially after months of forced, frustrated incubation, was food.

Reinforced plexiglass and gold anti-glare film had been the first food of this particular batch. They wouldn't have liked that, Terrin remembered thinking at the time. When they got through to Josh Kenley's eyes and brains, those would have been more palatable.

That had not been the terrible thing. The terrible thing had been what came after.

Terrin shuddered briefly. He shut it out of his mind, as he could now.

And Kenley would have been a lot more adept at understanding what the Doctor was about as well. Strange chap, the Doctor. He'd accepted all of this time-displacement business as if it was something he did every day.

Terrin had often thought it might be useful to slip in and out of time. And now it seemed to have crept up on him, turned against him.

He sat on the floor with his legs crossed, and tried to be calm.

In St Matthew's, the bell for Hall dinner had rung, echoing across the quads. Bernice saw chattering undergraduates spilling from doors, and she watched them rather longingly from the steps of the Senior Common-room. Rafferty was deep in conversation with Dr Styles, the college President, whom Benny had decided that she didn't like, on account of his pudgy face and narrow eyes. At least the rain had stopped, but it was rather cold, and she wanted to get inside and find out what *asperge maltaise*, quails and new potatoes tasted like according to the St Matthew's College chef.

While she was sure no one was looking, Bernice took out the homing device which the Doctor had given her. To her astonishment, its light was winking a deep red and the readings on its display indicated –

'Are you all right, my dear?'

Her heart missed a beat and she just had time to slip the device back into her pocket before turning to greet the President, Dr Styles.

'Miss Summerfield, isn't it?' he continued. Bernice did not like his silky-smooth affability. 'So glad you could join us.' He lowered his voice slightly. 'James gets very few visitors, actually.'

'Is that so?' They had begun to process into the Hall. Bernice was looking frantically around for her host, desperately hoping that she was not going to be condemned to sit with the President.

'Oh, yes. Since his wife died, you know, he's been quite lonely. Ah, here he is now – '

Thankfully, Rafferty was at her side. He took her arm. In Hall, the begowned multitudes rose to greet the President, and he thumped the table. Bernice watched, intrigued, as an incantation in Latin was spoken by a female undergraduate, and made a mental note to add this to her diary. A few books could be put right when she got back to the 25th century ... It was only when they were actually seated in Hall, with the President a comfortable five places away, that she dared to say anything.

'James,' she murmured, 'you know the Doctor's TARDIS?'

'That old police box he's always fussing over? Yes, I know. Never could work out what the precious equipment was he stored in there, but then that's the Doctor for you.'

Bernice decided that now was not the time to tell him that. As her wine was poured by an attendant member of the domestic staff, she whispered, 'It's here. Somewhere in the college, I swear it.'

'What do you mean?'

'The Doctor gave me a – well, a device. Oh, gosh, I'm going to have to come clean about all this one day. It ... well, he uses it to locate the TARDIS. The box. With me so far? Well, it's currently working its little electronic heart out in my pocket, and the readings show a source less than two hundred metres from here!'

Rafferty met her gaze. He was aware that her eyes were fixed on him in a peculiar, not-entirely sober manner. 'That girl,' he said slowly, 'was talking about a temporal implosion on the front lawn ...'

'Coincidence, James? Why does that word go so marvellously well with Doubt?'

'We'll check it out,' he promised.

On the *Icarus*, the group in the lab had heard nothing after the initial sounds of conflict. Now they were waiting to find out what was happening.

'Got it,' said Dr Mostrell.

The 2D monitor sprang into life.

They saw the ghosts advancing along the cramped walkways, turning their snouts this way and that as if sniffing their route. They shimmered in a haze of green and red, like the lights Ace and Strakk had seen on Q4.

'Party's over,' Ace muttered. 'Ever thought you had difficult neighbours?'

'*Ace, get back!*'

She didn't know what Strakk had seen, but she dropped automatically. Mostrell ducked after her. From the tube of the ladder-shaft, light was pouring into the lab. The air crackled like burning plastic, and something was making Ace's tongue tingle. It tasted metallic.

The shape gathered its wings. They could see the Time Soldiers clearly now, two of them, sweeping their gas-masked heads and their chunky guns back and forth as they advanced, step by step, into the lab.

Strakk was crouching under a metal lab-bench, barely a metre from the creatures.

'How did they get on board?' Mostrell hissed.

Ace felt the answer coming to her. She knew what the Doctor would say. 'They were always going to be on board,' she said. '*We* ran into *them*.'

Cheynor was digging his nails into his palms. It hurt, and he was past caring.

'Mr Larsen, did we get that power to the bridge defences?'

'It's tricky, sir, but I think I have some.'

'Enough for a force-field?' Cheynor held his breath.

'Maximum I can muster is eighty per cent.'

'That'll have to do. Hit it.'

'Yes, sir.' Larsen's hand hovered over the console. He exchanged a desperate look with McCarran, but she flicked her gaze back to Cheynor. 'Sir,' Larsen said, 'it won't hold them for long.'

'I know, Mr Larsen. Do it.'

'Yes, sir.' Larsen flicked the switch. 'Bridge force-field engaged.'

There was hardly any sound on the bridge now, as one instrumental panel after another had flickered out of life.

The soft whimpering was audible to them all. It sounded like an injured animal.

'*Les oiseaux du temps.*'

In the chair in the corner, Listrelle Quallem, her arms wrapped tightly around her body, was crying.

'Slowly. Slowly, Ace.'

'What the hell difference does it make, Strakk?' Mostrell snapped. He was edging his way towards the arms locker.

'Shut up,' Ace hissed. 'He's right. Can't you see? They're blind. They're trying to trace us.'

'That's crazy,' Mostrell muttered.

'But if they move through Time . . . maybe their sensors are bombarded with so much at once that they *can't* see us.' Ace was warming to the theory. 'And that's why we're still alive.'

Dr Mostrell looked, again. The soldiers were passing slowly along the lab benches, hands sweeping through stacks of equipment as if they were not there. Like ghosts or holograms. The halting, careful movements were, indeed, those of the blind.

'They must be passing through our time-phase at some point,' Mostrell said quietly.

'What are you going to do?'

The medical officer already had his hand in the arms locker. 'I don't know what they are,' he said, 'but a Derenna pistol can't miss.'

Ace lunged at his feet, but she was too late. Strakk's cry of 'No!' went unheard above the whine of the weapon. The beam went straight through the nearest Time Soldier and shattered three retorts on the opposite side of the lab.

The soldiers roared. Their eyes burning, they turned to one another and, in a crackle of energy, fused into one. Mostrell, horrified, let the pistol fall. The new warrior, stabilizing now, lifted his weapon in both gloved hands and aimed straight for Dr Mostrell. There was a rush of unearthly wind like the chill from a crypt, and its force slammed Strakk up against his wall and rolled Ace over and over, limbs flailing, till she hit the helium cylinder with unimaginable pain. Time energy coursed from the warrior's blaster, smashing particles into Mostrell. Ace, horrified, lifted her head against the wind and saw Mostrell stagger. Then, caught in freeze-frame, he flickered with energy, his scream echoing in the primitive screech of the warrior. Red fire burst from his hair. His body erupted with light. And slowly, years were stripped from him like mould from an ancient canvas. His white hair darkened. Ace saw a brief image of a thin-faced young man in the blaze of light, and then a frightened boy, before his body, too small to be seen clearly, dropped to the floor in a cloud of clothing.

Light rushed, ripping Time apart, back into the soldier's body, and he swung on Strakk.

Ace staggered to her feet.

'All right, try me, spook!' she yelled.

The outline was changing again. Before their eyes, the Time Soldier was de-stabilizing. Slipping out of phase.

'He's going,' Strakk mouthed, scarcely able to believe it. The light faded, and there was silence.

Except for the hungry, bawling scream of a baby.

In slow and incredulous realization, Ace and Strakk turned as one to look. There was a bump beneath Mostrell's crumpled uniform, and it was moving.

'Christ,' muttered Ace. 'And I thought moisturizer was effective.'

Strakk glanced at the monitor. It was blank.

'Our only chance,' he said, 'is the shuttle bay. Are you with me?'

'You mean we're not going back to the bridge?' Ace was lifting the remains of Mostrell's jacket carefully with the end of the discarded pistol.

Strakk pushed his grey fringe out of his eyes. 'They'll be right in the middle when it hits the fan. You really want to be there? We have to get *off* this ship, Ace.'

Small, frightened eyes looked up at her out of a barely

103

formed face. Two crinkled hands with tiny fingernails reached out for hers.

'And what do we do about the most highly qualified brat in the cosmos?' she asked.

Strakk had one foot on the ladder. 'It's easy,' he said. 'You can bring him, or leave him.' He started to climb the shaft.

'Yeah, thanks for your help, like,' Ace muttered darkly. She scooped up the baby, wrapped in what had once been Mostrell's jacket, but which now resembled a mass of roughspun material. 'Be good,' she whispered, jamming the Derenna into her belt. 'And we may let you meet your grandchildren.' Ace took a deep breath. 'Why did I ever get into this?' She started to follow Strakk up the ladder.

At the top, Strakk checked the corridor, then hauled himself up. Ace passed the baby up to him and he held it. Not awkwardly, either, she noticed.

Ace swung herself up, letting her eyes get accustomed to the even dimmer light here.

'At the risk of being a pain,' she said, holding up her right hand, 'have you forgotten something?' The chunky limiter bracelet on her wrist gleamed under the red lights. 'If I go to the shuttle-bay, I'll be playing Ravel's Concerto for the Left Hand for a living.'

Strakk seemed unconcerned. 'Then you'll have to take your chances on the ship.'

Ace grabbed his spare arm, swung him around with surprising force. The baby started to cry again. 'You're my ticket off this hulk, boy wonder. Get this damned bangle off me, now!'

'I can't. It has a voice-activated neutralizer, and only the captain has access to the code-word.'

'Oh, brilliant. You people think of everything.'

'We might have bigger problems,' Strakk shouted over the bawling of the infant.

Ace looked up and down the corridor. She wondered briefly why the noise of fighting had stopped, and had a worryingly likely theory. 'You know the way?'

104

He nodded.

'Come on, then.'

The baby had big blue eyes, and they were looking at Strakk in awe as he hurried along, keeping close into the bulkhead. 'If you say Da-da, sunshine,' he muttered, 'you're out of here.'

'We have a massive energy build-up, sir,' called TechnOp Gessner.

'Point of origin?'

There was a moment's silence. 'Here, sir.'

The roaring hit them, and the rush of cold wind knocked Cheynor flying. Light stabbed from the ceiling in a dozen places. Two TechnOps were hurled from their chairs by invisible forces. The light, crackling as if alive, was resolving itself into humanoid forms. Cheynor, shading his eyes, saw the wall-to-wall monitor slashed with interference, and the air was filled with the invisible sound of the alien wings. He heard Larsen yell something about the bridge defences, and then in a hail of phosphorescent energy, the figures stabilized.

Cheynor could hear his own breathing.

The only light seemed to come from the crackles of lightning on the monitor and from the red eyes of the twelve gas-masked figures who stood, guns at the ready, at various points throughout the bridge.

Who is in command here?

The voice, like thunder, seemed to come from the tallest of the hijackers.

Cheynor climbed to his feet. He knew that the eyes of the bridge crew were on him. He spread his empty hands wide, in a gesture of peace.

'We are on a mission to survey this sector of the galaxy,' he announced. The desperation in his voice was clearly audible. 'We mean you no harm,' he added.

It was the best he could think of.

Something told him that, on this occasion, his best was not going to be good enough.

Chapter 12

Information Technology

La Cachette was one of Oxford's less frequented restaurants, and Tom wanted it to stay that way, so he never recommended it, but he did often take young ladies there when his industrial sponsorship would allow it. The colour scheme was mainly red and gold, enhanced by the candle in its Chianti bottle which flickered on the table between him and Amanda. It shimmered also in her shades. 'I have problems with light,' she had explained, a little embarrassed. 'I hope you don't mind.' He did wonder what colour her eyes were, and if she would ever take the shades off when he finally got her where he wanted her.

Tom noticed she ate little and drank less. He was disappointed when she smilingly refused his offer of wine, but she explained that it did terrible things to her insides.

He should have known, he thought after his second glass of wine, not to drink on his own. It had been a pleasant meal, but to have a sober companion, like the control half of an experiment, lessened the pleasure. And moreover, he was not quite sure if he had heard what she had just said.

'I'm sorry? St Matthew's *lawn*?'

'Yes,' she said, with a twitch of a smile. 'Professor Rafferty does not seem very worried about it. And I think he should be.'

Tom felt he had missed a vital link in the conversation. 'Surely it's a matter for the gardeners?'

'But not,' said Amanda, sipping her mineral water, 'when we are dealing with dimensional engineering?'

'Sorry,' said Tom, 'you've lost me.' He was rapidly sobering up. What did this girl know about the Department's activities?' He was beginning to feel hints of worry again. Could she be a Free Earth Child or from one of the other New Age peace groups? Tom had assumed they would have the techno-paganists on their side, but one or two of his colleagues had assured him that it was not so, and that various groups were terrified of anyone finding out how the universe actually *worked*. Their fear was that scientists like Tom and Rafferty might, for instance, strip the mystique from the Earth – or discover that pollution and the destruction of the rainforests were necessary cogs in the ecosystem. And so he wondered why Amanda had really sought him out.

'You know the Professor well?' she asked.

'Well enough.'

'Good. Well enough. I like that. Poor Tom, you look so bewildered. I think you don't realize how important you are.'

'Important?'

'To me,' she said softly.

He took a deep breath. 'That's very sweet of you. But I hardly know you, do I? And now I come to think about it, I really can't remember where it was that we met.'

'No,' she said, leaning back lazily in her chair. 'You wouldn't.'

He paid the bill, still bemused and rather unsure what was going to happen. She took his arm as they stepped out into the chill air of the High Street and walked in the Carfax direction. Behind them on the right, Magdalen Tower glowed with spectral floodlights.

'This city rustles with power,' said Amanda. 'You can almost taste it.'

Tom looked at her, a little surprised. 'Yes . . . Yes, I suppose you can.'

'And knowledge,' added Amanda. 'In such a small place . . . so compact. Nearly all the intelligence that matters on this world is here. Don't you think it might explode one day, under the pressure?'

'There are those,' said Tom, 'who would claim it regularly does.' Her use of 'this world' had not escaped him. He stopped, stared at her under the lamplight. 'Why don't you tell me what you really want, Amanda?'

'Yes,' she said, slipping her arms around his neck. 'Why don't I?'

Her wrists felt cold against the back of his neck, and her lips, although moist, tasted faintly of something he could not at first identify.

He recognized it a second later, as her tongue slid around his. It was like the aftertaste from drinking canned beer. A hint of metal.

The coldness on the back of his neck was growing.

As Amanda, smiling, drew away from his mouth, he felt, with a churning stomach, a numbness around his head like an icy helmet. The lights of the traffic smeared, and although he was not aware of his legs giving way, he felt his back sliding against the wall.

She caught his arm. Two young men in rugby shirts were walking past, and glanced at the pair in brief concern. He tried to call out, and found that he could not. He heard Amanda saying, 'His birthday . . . had a bit too much . . .' and then, to his horror, the two lads were walking on with cheerful waves and a shout of 'Good luck, darlin'.'

She looked down, her face pale and cruel. Her left arm had now come back into the light. Instead of a hand, there was now a streamlined, silvery cone, tapering thinner and thinner until it became the sharpest of needles.

It was the last thing Tom Cheynor saw before everything went black.

The data rushed on to the screen of the President's laptop computer. He smiled, snapped it shut and apologized to his fellow dons at High Table. The awkward glances were swiftly quelled. Bringing one's work to Hall was unsocial, but Dr Styles was the President, after all . . .

As soon as he possibly could after his first course, the President gave the time-honoured thump on the table and the undergraduates present at the Annual College

Memorial Dinner rose to their feet with the usual mumbling and scraping of benches.

It was traditional to join his fellow Fellows for dessert in the Senior Common Room, but instead he hurried in the direction of his lodgings, his gown billowing in the evening breeze.

As the group of dons straggled out, hardly anyone paid any attention to the disappearing President – but the hasty departure had not gone unnoticed by the sharp blue eyes of the Professor of Extra-Terrestrial Studies. Rafferty was trapped, though, in a conversation with the new Modern Languages tutor Dr Ellen Rocher, who was berating him about the standard of the Senior Common Room desserts. He decided that agreeing with her about what she called 'stodgy Boy's Own puddings' was the easiest course of action as, with a sinking heart, he saw the President disappearing under the archway into the main quadrangle. He cast desperate eyes around for Bernice, who had vanished from his sight as they left Hall. She was nowhere to be seen. Rafferty smiled at Dr Rocher and said yes, he thought fruit salads were an excellent idea, and left her to the mercies of the Senior Dean's company.

Bernice slipped from behind a pillar with one graceful movement. She had a glass of port in her hand and had clearly been enjoying herself.

'James,' she said with a wine-mellowed voice, 'I do believe you're as curious as I am.'

'I have been called it in the past. I take it you're with me?' His whisper echoed up into the cloisters.

Bernice finished her port in one gulp. 'What's the alternative?'

'Cigars, mints and small talk.'

'Then I'll take danger every time.'

He took her arm. They hurried past the chapel into the quad, which was silent and empty, and slipped under the carvings of ministering angels and into Kent Quad. They were just in time to see the orange glow of the light flick into being on the ground-floor window of the President's office.

109

The President said 'Open,' to the filing cabinet in the corner of his office. One of the most attractive features of the Type 102 TARDIS, for him, was its highly reliable chameleon circuit, while another was its voice-activated lock.

He heard the hum of the mechanism, and, with the laptop under his arm, he strode towards the cabinet. Then he paused. The scuffling under the window-sill had not gone unheard, and he wondered for a second what was the best thing to do. If the observer were innocent, he decided, then he had nothing to fear. And if he had designs, then he would be walking into a trap anyway. Smiling at his logic, the President stepped into the back of the filing cabinet.

Rafferty waited a second or two before climbing through the office window. Such an action was undignified in his long academic gown, but he managed it with the minimum of fuss. Then he leaned out and gave Bernice his hand. He was surprised at how warm it felt, even on this November night. She hopped into the room, flexing her knees.

'Right,' she whispered, 'I wonder where he is?'

Rafferty took a couple of moments to get his breath back, reflecting that the last time he had climbed in a window had been in 1955, to visit a Somerville girl after curfew without incurring the wrath of the authorities. That sort of thing had become much easier now that he was too old for it, Rafferty thought, in fact it had possibly changed in a matter of a few years. He was not at all clear on the well-documented side of the Sixties, for it had passed him by – Rafferty's decade, though, had had its own triumphs. He had a vague idea about Sergeant Pepper being a brand of fizzy drink, and the only Woodstock he knew was a pleasant market town a few miles north of Oxford, but such things mattered little. Those had been the years in which he had first come to know his friend and colleague Ian Chesterton, and when as a postgraduate student he had been taken into the confidence of Professor Travers concerning the matter of a small metallic sphere which was evidently not of this world. He wondered whether the Doctor had told Bernice anything of this history, but reflected that now was probably not the best time to find out.

Bernice was standing with her feet apart and her hands on her hips. Even with the flush of alcohol on her cheeks, her face was alert, intense.

'This floor,' she said, 'is buzzing.'

'Buzzing?' Rafferty listened.

'Vibrating. Can't you hear it?'

He could feel it now. He listened, trying to trace the source, and it did not take him long to look around the back of the filing cabinet. There appeared to be a sort of door, large enough to admit a man, and standing ajar. He looked across the room at Bernice. She made a twirling gesture with her hand, as if encouraging him.

Rafferty hesitated, then hurried to the desk and snatched up the President's external telephone.

'You're not calling the police, are you?' said Bernice apprehensively. 'It'll make an awfully embarrassing scene.'

'Bernice, please credit me with a little common sense.' He tapped out a number with lightning speed.

The telephonist, as he had expected, was brisk. '*This is a UNIT priority number. Please state your name and business.*'

'Rafferty. Get me Alistair Lethbridge-Stewart.'

'*Please hold.*'

He hung on, his heart pounding, for a minute. He kept casting anxious glances at the filing cabinet. Benny was pacing the room with her arms folded. Impatient.

Two and a half minutes. He wondered if UNIT were still there. Coming to a decision, Rafferty slammed the receiver down.

'All right,' he said. 'You win.'

He was quivering with energy, and knew he had to do something.

Steeling himself, he touched the cabinet. He had somehow expected the tingling sensation. He pulled the door open just enough to admit himself.

'Bernice,' he said, 'what would you say if I told you to wait here?'

'It wouldn't be fit for polite company.'

'I thought as much. Sorry. I don't think we should both get ourselves into a mess.' He stepped into the back of the filing cabinet.

She sprang forward. 'James, no!'

The secret door had snicked shut behind him. Bernice was facing solid metal, with no visible apertures or even hairline cracks.

With her heart pounding, she flipped out the homing device. Its red light was flashing wildly. She looked up at the filing cabinet once more, as realization dawned.

The beacon was detecting a time source. Not necessarily the Doctor's.

'Oh, my goodness,' she said.

For a moment, James Rafferty found himself in utter darkness, and his eyes were unable to adjust. Losing orientation, Rafferty decided that this had perhaps been a bad idea. He looked around for the chink of light that showed the way back into the office, and noticed that it no longer seemed to be there.

He felt a rush of air behind his ear. He heard the crack of bone an instant before the pain hit him, and then he lost consciousness.

Bernice was hammering on the unyielding metal of the cabinet.

'James!' she shouted. 'James!'

Silently cursing her current lack of a good blaster, she took a step back from the metal box, and looked around wildly for inspiration.

The shutters slammed down over the window.

Like four guillotines they swished to a halt, thudding into the sill outside. Bernice was at the door in two seconds. It would not budge. She rattled the handle a couple of times, aware that the lights in the room were dimming.

Never one to panic unduly, she swivelled, thinking hard. Sheer brute force over intellect, she thought, and brought a booted foot up hard into the oak door. It boomed angrily, and left her with an aching toe. She gritted her teeth and kicked again. And again.

A familiar voice crackled from the intercom on the President's desktop.

'I really wouldn't attempt any more vandalism, my dear. It's hardly the way for a guest to behave.'

She kicked again. The wood was starting to splinter. 'No,' she snapped in the direction of the desk, 'but then you're hardly the perfect host.'

Two clicks alerted her, and she swung around. Two nozzles like tubular metal flowers had sprung from the floor, and an instant later they began to shoot a yellow gas into the room.

The cloud spread with amazing speed. Bernice flattened herself up against the dented door, wondering if the window might yield more easily. She knew she only had a couple of seconds.

'I think you've had a hard day, Miss Summerfield,' crackled the voice of the President. 'Why don't you turn in for the night?'

'I'm a twenty-four-hour party person, didn't you know? I'd really prefer you called me a cab.'

With one arm over her nose and mouth, she lifted the armchair and hurled it towards the leaded lights. The glass shattered in several places, but the metal shutters clanged, bouncing the chair back into the room. Bernice could feel the gas stinging her eyes. It billowed, swirling like ghosts, injecting her mind with unwanted headiness.

In just a few more seconds, the gas had filled the room.

Chapter 13

Incubus

'I know who's going to win,' murmured Terrin, as he watched low-grav athletics on the interstellar video-link. 'I could put a million on it.' He looked at the Doctor across the pastel hues of their new quarters. 'I'd be a rich man, Doctor.'

The Time Lord was sitting with his hat over his face and his feet up on the perspex table. 'Don't get a taste for it, Captain. You might find the Blinovitch Limitation Effect catching up with you.'

On the instructions of Helina Vaiq, the nameless Doctor and the man who called himself Romulus Terrin were no longer to be treated as prisoners. Compromising with Ballantyne, though, had required that the two 'visitors' be confined to their accommodation until further notice, with an armed guard outside the door.

Although the Doctor still felt uneasy, he was at least more comfortable in the plush lounge. It had an inch-thick carpet of royal blue beneath curving walls, which appeared white but which, if one looked at them for long enough, acquired hints of pastel shades like azure and rose-petal. A circular window looked out on to the stars, and a fountain, fringed with ferns, splashed under green light in the centre of the room. The table was generously laden with coffee, ham sandwiches and various exotic fruits, and the two-metre holoscreen in the corner seemed to pick up an infinite number of channels.

Terrin, though, had obviously been deep in thought while the Doctor had been away. 'Doctor, supposing I tried to contact someone I knew? Supposing I called the *Icarus*? What would *happen*?'

'Did it happen?' asked the Doctor's muffled voice.

'What?' Terrin frowned.

'Do you remember anything like that happening last week? No, of course you don't. Because it didn't.' The Doctor sat bolt upright, and Terrin was unnerved by the compelling light in those eyes of . . . what colour? 'You're part of your own history. What we're doing now already happened. Do you understand?'

Terrin switched off the holoscreen with a wave of his hand. 'Are you saying we can't prevent whatever attacked – will attack – this station from doing so?'

'I'm saying nothing of the sort. Time has been disrupted, Captain. I feel the ripples as you would feel a change in . . . the oxygen level, for example. Somewhere along the line there will be a critical point, a moment where Time diverges from its line of least resistance.'

The Doctor was pacing the room now, and Terrin supposed he was thinking aloud.

'Whatever brought us back here, Doctor,' said Terrin, 'is the same force that we saw . . . that did those terrible things.'

'Yes,' said the Doctor.

'That means it knows what we're doing,' said the captain.

The Doctor turned slowly to look at him, and it occurred to Terrin that he somehow appeared much older. It was as if an ancient thought, a darkness of knowledge, had settled on his features, shadowing them with foreboding. Or remembrance.

'I wondered how long it would take you to realize,' said the Doctor. He tapped his teeth once or twice with his fingernail. Then he approached Terrin and leaned on the arm of his chair, looking unblinkingly at him. 'Captain,' he said, 'why would you want to contact your ship anyway?'

Terrin shrugged. 'To tell myself what I know now? But you just said it wouldn't . . .'

'Captain Terrin,' whispered the Doctor, 'you're a

115

genius!' He clapped the unsuspecting captain on the shoulder and resumed his agitated pacing. 'Of course! How could I have been so stupid? We have to get to a communications unit. And that means I must convince Vaiq once and for all.'

'Do you have the proof that you need?'

'I've had it all along,' said the Doctor.

Terrin was astonished. 'Then why haven't you used it?'

'Because,' answered the Doctor, 'I haven't dared.' He fished in the pocket of his jacket and found the object that had been there all along, and which he had surreptitiously removed from Station Q4 when he had first been exploring with Ace.

Terrin took it. The object was of plastic and metal, about the size of a credit-card, but warped as if left in the sun. It bore the cracked, faded imprint of a Corporation logo and an embossed name.

After a moment's silence, Terrin looked up at the Doctor in horror. 'Where did you get this?'

'From Ballantyne's skeleton,' he answered. 'It's his I.D. plaque. Captain, how would *you* tell a man that you know he's going to die?'

The ghosts of the Time Soldiers appeared more real now, Cheynor had noticed, although still suffused with the same eerie light. The tallest soldier was standing, feet planted firmly apart, in front of him, with its blaster levelled at Cheynor's eyes. Cheynor was wishing something would happen. He glanced down at Quallem and could hardly believe it when he saw how calm she looked.

'It's good,' she whispered.

Cheynor did not know if he dared speak. 'What?' he hissed.

'You had me fooled. We've got to tell them on Lightbase, it's the best one. When did we last have a hijack drill? Years. Years ago.'

Her eyes, he saw, were wide and full of the clarity of madness. He felt no hatred for her now, only pity, and he wanted to reach out and touch her smooth, suede-clad shoulder, to comfort her as he would a child. He wondered if the leader of the boarding party would shoot him if he did.

Prepare, said the voice.

A low throbbing was echoing through the bridge now. Against a far wall, air seemed to twist and fragment.

Prepare for the coming of the Garvond.

A disc of blackness had formed against the white of the wall. It began to grow, like a hole burning into celluloid.

The rushing wind began to ruffle the humans' hair and clothes, and the flood of twittering voices cascaded through the opening like a river from Hell. Only the Time Soldiers remained unaffected, silently watching.

It expanded, blotting out the bridge. The darkness somehow seemed more dazzling than light would have been.

And then the Garvond came.

Like a howl of anguish across the emptiness of space. Like the screams of the dying in the trenches of mud, in fire and in ice. A pinprick of white, like a single star, flickered against the globe of ultra-darkness and then grew.

Cheynor watched in horrified fascination. The white light was the size of his hand now, and he could make out details. Within a matter of seconds, he could see a huge throne outlined in blazing fire, growing now to fill the black circle like a negative image. The creature seated on the throne gave a scream of triumph that sounded like the rending of metal and chilled the air itself. Amid the fire, Cheynor could see two clawed hands clutching the shimmering throne, and the outline of a massive, skeletal head.

For a moment there was silence as the Garvond seemed to swing its skull from one side of the bridge to the other. The fiery outline was like that of a humanoid skeleton, but swathed in a cloak of darkness. The head, if one could call it that, swivelled on a crackling neck of bare bone, and night itself lurked in its hollow eyes.

The eyes which, slowly and inexorably, came to fix their deathly stare on Darius Cheynor.

* * *

The central column of the President's TARDIS rose and fell. Around it, a wreath of red and green lights glowed, pulsing in harmony with the ship. To the side of the console, Amanda stood, waiting.

One corner of the console room was a darkened alcove, barred by three blue beams of light, and sitting on the floor within it was Professor Bernice Summerfield. She had recovered from the effects of the gas, which she had considered a markedly crude method of abduction. She had been captured far more stylishly in the past, and was somewhat disappointed in the President. Now she was watching the President and Amanda with cool indifference. She had already observed the marked differences between this console room and the Doctor's – the colour scheme, for example, was predominantly burgundy-red, with lighting to match. The console was the shape of an upturned cone, flat-topped, with a spiralling central column and smooth touch-sensitive controls. The wall roundels were more compact and closer together. Altogether, the room breathed efficiency and menace.

The President looked up from the console.

'Union,' he said with quiet satisfaction.

He strode to the other side of the control room and descended a small flight of steps to the monitor unit. His hands flickered over the controls for a second. The light in the console room flickered and changed shape as Bernice watched, and suddenly two columns of blue light stabbed from the ceiling. Each held a figure, imbued with the blueness of the light and frozen immobile like a bas-relief in a cathedral. One, to Bernice's surprise, was Tom Cheynor. The other was James Rafferty.

The President opened the communications channel.

'I just wanted to let you know,' he said, 'that you'll come to no harm if you do exactly as I say.'

Tom tried to move his mouth. The President watched with glee as the young man's jaw moved up and down with agonizing slowness.

'Where . . . are we?'

'Now, don't you worry about that. My TARDIS carries

118

a number of spare dimensions, you see. Invaluable. I've trapped you in a stasis field, that's all. A lot less bother than a locked door.'

Rafferty was breathing deeply, trying to gather the right combination of muscles for the vowels and consonants he wanted.

'What . . . do you . . . want with us?'

'Oh, heavens,' said the President with a chuckle. 'I'd forgotten you're such a connoisseur of adventure fiction, Professor. You think that this is where I tell you all the details of my plan, so that when you escape you know exactly how to defeat me. Really.' He tut-tutted, then his voice lost its joviality. 'I have decided to spare you for the moment, that is all. The Garvond will draw strength from your fertile minds when we meet him . . . very soon.'

The President switched off the screen. He turned around, and smiled at Bernice. She was still sitting in her unperturbed pose, hands clasped around her knees. She was determined not to show that the sight of the imprisoned Professor and Tom had upset her.

'I suppose it's equally trite,' she ventured, 'to tell you that you'd better not harm them?'

The President chuckled as he re-entered the main part of the room, and swaggered over towards Bernice's prison. 'Trite indeed, my dear, but I should have been most disappointed had you not said it.'

'Oh, good. I'm glad we've got that out of the way. Can we clear something else up?' The President, engrossed in the console, did not seem to be paying her any attention, but she carried on anyway. 'I'm not your dear, nor anyone's, as it happens. Terms of endearment cut very little ice with me.'

The President tried to raise an eyebrow, failed, and settled for raising both instead. 'Really, my – Well, you must have been spending too much time with the Doctor.'

'And what is that supposed to mean?'

Strolling past the immobile Amanda, the President approached Bernice's cage and leered down at her. 'He doesn't make close friendships, does he? Most conspicu-

119

ous by their absence, in his file. Although I dare say you've noticed, attractive girl like you. No, there's only one lady the Doctor has any time for, as far as I can tell, and that's his creaky old Type Forty. Which I am going to find!'

'The Doctor's terribly resourceful,' said Bernice apologetically. 'It can be quite embarrassing at times. You know – never uses a simple solution where a tricky one will do. Although you look like the sort of chap who'd cheat at Patience, given half a chance.'

'I hope your sense of humour holds out, Miss Summerfield, until you meet the Garvond.'

'Yes, now, you mentioned him. Your boss, is he? Or maybe your agent? Mister ten per cent?'

The President straightened up and nodded quietly to himself. 'Before long,' he said, 'you will know the Garvond very well indeed.'

'I hope this works,' murmured Strakk.

'It had better,' Ace said. 'I don't know about you, but I'm not quite ready for breast-feeding.'

Strakk took a last look at the peaceful form of the five-day-old Ferris Mostrell, whom he had just placed in the soft hollow of an incubator in the ship's medical unit. He checked that all the tubes were attached correctly, while Ace watched the door, and then he closed the cover of the incubator over the new infant. 'Sweet dreams,' he said quietly. 'If you're lucky, we'll be back for you.'

Ace checked the corridor. 'Clear,' she said. 'Most of the spooks must be on the bridge.'

'That would have been their target,' Strakk agreed grimly. 'All right. Let's see about getting off this ship.'

They kept close in to the dark bulkheads, Strakk first, then Ace covering the rear.

'You sure the brat's going to be okay?' she muttered.

Strakk grinned over his shoulder. 'You sound almost concerned. Don't worry, I know about babies.'

'Yeah?' Ace was interested.

Strakk paused at a junction and seemed uncertain. He

listened. No sound. Not even the engines. The ship was dying.

'Yeah,' he said. He looked at Ace, briefly, and waved a hand as if it were unimportant. 'There was a girl from the Academy,' he said. 'She had a kid. Mine. We were hoping I'd get a cushy station job on one of the Colonies, so we could set up home together.'

'What happened?'

He shrugged. She couldn't see his eyes. 'They died,' he said. 'In a skimmer crash. One of those things. It was three years ago.'

'I'm sorry. I didn't know.'

He took the left-hand junction, and answered her, keeping his voice flat and emotionless. 'Most people don't.' Suddenly, his arm shot out and pushed her back against the wall. 'Hellfire. We've got one.'

Ace looked out of the corner of her eyes. The Time Soldier was emerging from the floor about twenty metres ahead of them.

'Back,' she said.

From behind them, a primal screech let them know that the creature had picked up their trace. They ran for the nearest door. Shimmering through Time, the soldier did not need to follow them. It began to re-form just a few metres from them, in a blaze of green.

'The door,' Strakk yelled. 'The rec-room.'

Ace slammed her fist on the door control.

Strakk knew the Derenna would do no good, but his training triggered reflexes. He unleashed three pulses of energy. The soldier howled. In triumph, not in agony.

'Come on, Strakk!' Ace shouted, and grabbed him. She pulled him through the opening door as a beam of accelerated Time pulverized the wall where he had been.

And sliced into his hand.

The skin was blasted and withered like an autumn leaf. He screamed, doubling up as the door slammed down behind them again.

Ace was controlling her panic. She assessed the room. There were silvery, reflective tables set up for chess and

121

backgammon, and a number of inert computer and VR terminals. No one was off duty today.

The door was wobbling.

Strakk's agonized face met hers. His hand was wrapped in his jacket and he didn't dare look. Ace pulled him further into the room, none too gently. He slumped against one of the leather sofas, breathing heavily.

'It can come through walls,' he said in desperation. 'All it has to do is flick out of phase – I'm right, aren't I?'

Chess pieces were scattered from one of the tables in a shower of luminescence. The Time Soldier, feet first, was beginning to rematerialize in the centre of the rec-room.

Ace took his hand carefully. It was crooked, arthritic. The skin was speckled with liver-spots and the fingernails were brittle.

'Does it hurt?'

'It's numb. The muscles don't work. Ace – '

'I know. Keep still. Remember? It may be able to skim back and forth like nobody's business, *but that's its flaw.* It's like trying to locate one air-molecule.'

The Time Soldier was stepping forward, its flickering arms spread out in front of it.

'We can't escape it,' Strakk hissed. 'It's going to find us before long.'

Faster than thought, a time-ray smashed into the sofa, which hit the wall in a shower of ragged leather and foam.

Ace and Strakk ran. The shriek of the Time Soldier seemed right on top of them. In desperation, Ace kicked over the backgammon table and pulled Strakk behind it, just as the soldier channelled its next beam of particles.

The accelerated Time smashed into the mirrored table and charred it.

They didn't see the energy bounce back at the same angle and hurtle, inverted, into the Time Soldier.

It staggered and screamed. This time, the death throes of the hunter. A tortured, thrashing sound mingled with almost human screams of pain. Strakk lifted his eyes from his arms, in disbelief. Green fire was blazing from the body of the Time Soldier, distorting its outline. The creature writhed in a ghastly dance of pain, its screams neither male nor female, almost animal, mingling with a terrifying din that sounded like the whine of a saw-blade into sheet metal. As they watched, the creature twisted and spiralled into a vortex of light, growing smaller and smaller, until it finally blinked out of existence.

The silence was deafening.

Ace pushed the scarred table aside. Dust that had been backgammon pieces trickled to the floor. She stood up, looking around. There was no sign of the Time energy, nor any of its products.

'What the hell happened?' Strakk breathed.

'Physics,' said Ace, with a satisfied smile. 'Spook City scored an own goal.' She kicked the remains of the table. 'What are these made of?'

'Hylerium,' said Strakk. 'It's used everywhere.'

The look that passed between them spoke volumes.

'Can you walk?' Ace asked urgently.

'I'll try.' Strakk was aware that his arm was turning numb, and an internal chill was making him shiver uncontrollably. 'We have to get a message to Lightbase. Tell them everything we know.'

'Lean on me,' Ace said.

He took her arm. 'Thanks. Sorry I blew it.'

'We're still alive. That means we're winning. So far.'

With Ace supporting the weakening Strakk, they made their escape from the rec-room.

You will reveal the code for the starship's warp motors.

The voice crashed through infinity. It was mediated through the leader of the Time Soldiers, and was addressed to Cheynor. The soldier's eyes pulsed with their hypnotic red as the barrel of the gun was pressed between the officer's eyes. It felt icy cold.

'Why?' Cheynor whispered in bewilderment. 'With all your powers. What possible use could this ship be for you? All we want is to return to Earth –'

You will not return to Earth. You will become one in

*union with the Garvond, harvested from the fields of Time
as many were before you. Reveal the code.*

'I don't know what you mean.' Cheynor wondered how
long he could keep bluffing.

*The access code for the warp motors is neurologically
embedded in the minds of the ship's three senior officers.
We can extract it, but it will be painful and will leave you
of no use to us. It will cause you far less inconvenience if
you choose to tell us.*

He knew the crew were waiting for his move. They had
lost Terrin. They had lost Quallem in all but body. Darius
Cheynor was the last hope of the Survey Corps crew, and
he did not know what he was going to do next.

'My security force outnumbers you.' It was the best he
could think of.

*Your guards have been eliminated. All humans except
those here on the bridge have been eliminated.*

A skeleton crew, thought Cheynor, and wished he
hadn't.

'I can't do it,' he said. 'If I give you control of this ship,
I have betrayed my fellow human beings.'

The Garvond pulsed with energy. The skeletal jaws
moved in their curtain of fire, but no words were heard.
Invisibly, a command was sent, and Cheynor saw the leading Time Soldier glow briefly as it was received.

His arms were pinned from behind. The gloved hand
of the leading Time Soldier descended over his face. A
second later, it felt as if the cold and grasping hand
reached into his mind and tugged at it. Cheynor was dimly
conscious of being forced to his knees.

He saw dark ravens, pecking at the rubble of his mind,
and a swollen sunset over a polluted river. The skull of
the Garvond burst from the sun and hurtled towards him,
its yellowing teeth savaging Cheynor's memories. He was
a small child, running as fast as he could across the rubble,
slipping in filthy mud, gashing his leg open as he fell.
Above him, a helicopter chattered and twittered, descending, coming in for a strafing run. Fountains of mud burst

on either side of him. Shattered rocks exploded as the helicopter hurtled through the skies.

He heard the triumphant screech of the pilot, saw its face of ragged flesh and cracked bone. He was rolling, down, down the slope, deeper into his mind. He wanted to scream, *No, not that way*, but he could not.

There was a boy in the river. He was screaming, sinking. Something underneath was pulling him down. Down to the caves beneath. He wanted to call his name. The name of his brother, Simeon. The mud clutched at his ankles now, and the cold sunlight stabbed his eyes. He reached for Simeon's hand.

The floor of the bridge came up to meet him.

Cheynor crouched, clutching his stomach, feeling the pain recede. He could hear his own breathing, ragged and harsh. He blinked rapidly and the glare faded to yellow, then red. He was hauled to his feet, and in the haze his vision came back to him. He focused on Quallem. She was hugging herself and looking fixedly at the Garvond. Other faces swam into view, familiar faces that he had seen every day for the last two years – Larsen, Gessner, Rost, McCarran – all perspiration-slicked, all frightened, all watching him.

The Time Soldiers released their grip, and once more the Garvond crackled with excited energy.

You will tell us, Darius Cheynor. Willingly or otherwise, you will tell us.

There was silence on the bridge, except for a soft sound just at the edge of Darius Cheynor's hearing. It was gentle, melodic, and unsettling.

He looked down, knowing what he would see, at Listrelle Quallem. She had started, very quietly, to sing.

Chapter 14

Cracks

'Du musst herrschen und gewinnen,
Oder dienen und verlieren,
Leiden oder triumphieren,
Amboss oder Hammer sein.'
('You must either conquer and rule or serve and lose,
suffer or triumph, be the hammer or the anvil.')

J. W. von Goethe

The President of St Matthew's College was playing chess
against his TARDIS, and losing.

As the pieces flicked across the scanner, pushing his
queen deeper into an unforeseen trap, he allowed his mind
to wander. It was ironic, he thought, that he should have
escaped the routine into which Gallifrey had fallen, only
to acquire a taste for the sedentary academic life. It had
been a dynamic world once, a powerful world, the home
of the Time Lords. But the man who now called himself
the President was far, almost immeasurably far, from the
Ancient Time, from an era when even the exploits of
famous renegades had become legend.

Among the Time Lords, he had been nothing. Known
at the Academy by the code of Epsilon Delta, he had
become a mere attendant to Gold Usher, with mundane
duties and no real responsibility. That, despite a respect-
able double beta in cybernetics, was where he had ended
up, a robed lackey wasting his brilliant mind. He had had
another name, then – a longer one – a different face, and
certainly no title; but his lowly position had given him

unforeseen advantages. For one thing, no one expected Epsilon Delta to have any kind of scientific knowledge, and so it did not occur to anyone that he would have either the means or the inclination to adapt a spare TARDIS to his own palm and voice prints, under the guise of official inspection.

Nor did many other Time Lords have any idea of the progress in the cybernetics faculty of the new, advanced Academy. His creation, a totally new model, had been the result of a combination of factors. The first had been his own under-estimated skill in electronics. Another was the enormous amount of time during which nobody really cared where he was and what he was doing, time which he often spent in the Panopticon archives, reading, preparing. Some files had restricted access but he broke into these, and became something of an expert in the much-discouraged doctrine of weaponry systems.

Over that time, which by Earth standards could be measured in decades, his hatred and resentment grew. He watched the colourful displays in the Panopticon, nodded respectfully to the elders in their heliotrope robes, while inwardly he seethed, sought escape from this mindless life and yearned for his revenge.

One night, Epsilon Delta had left. The primed TARDIS was waiting, and creations were planted inside, ready to let him in. He picked up security transmissions from Gallifrey on a coded channel. It was the crowning irony for him that the disappearance of a Type 102 was noticed far more quickly than his own absence, and indeed was awarded a far higher level of importance by the High Council.

He read, in the data banks of his TARDIS, of those other, legendary renegades, black sheep whose histories had been suppressed and who seemed to revel in ridiculous titles. Prominent among these case histories were those of three escapees who had passed through the Academy. 'The Rani' he had heard of, as her experiments had been notorious even in his day. The name of 'The Master', too, had been mentioned in the hushed tones of rumour, although he gathered that little had been heard of that troublemaker on Gallifrey for quite some time – many doubted, indeed, that he was still alive. It was the third renegade who intrigued him, a Prydonian who called himself 'The Doctor'. He, too, had stolen a TARDIS, but according to the files, that had been a minor offence in comparison with his interference on numerous planets. Twice this Doctor had been put on trial for his actions, and both times he had actually come out of it quite well. There seemed to be a subtext contained in the report, a kind of grudging acceptance of the Doctor's existence and, indeed, of the occasional necessity of his intervention. All of this intrigued the new renegade, and he determined to find this other Time Lord as soon as possible. Somehow, Epsilon Delta had an instinct that here lay the key to his much-needed revenge.

He had time. By Time Lord standards he was quite young, the equivalent of three hundred and fifty Terran years. He saw the gas sculptures of Remmosica, the Leisure Hive on Argolis, the pyramids in the sands of Earth . . . An unfortunate encounter with some belligerent Sontarans forced his first regeneration, and the body he was left with was, by no stretch of the imagination, as handsome as his last one. Time Lords were not meant to worry about their external appearance but Epsilon Delta had learned that it was important in other parts of the Universe and he was decidedly unhappy with the tubby, ageing figure that he now presented. Still, nothing could be done – he wasn't about to waste a regeneration for the sake of vanity.

He set himself up, for fun, in several different roles on various planets. The one he enjoyed the most, though, for which he had had to fabricate academic credentials with the utmost precision, was his existence as President of the largest and richest of Oxford's colleges. Sometimes it occurred to him to pop into the Science building on Banbury Road and casually mention where they were all going wrong, but he had resisted the temptation so far – it was not really his scene. Earth was a useful hideaway, and plentiful supplier of good wine and smoked salmon sandwiches.

It was at about this time that he began to notice something very odd about his TARDIS. Although it had all the facilities of the Type 102, adapted to his own needs, and a fully functioning chameleon circuit, there was something wrong. The time machine, although dimensionally transcendental, was *finite*. And its energy was being drained. This was something of a shock to Epsilon Delta. He had the computer run the scan again, and discovered that the craft was, in fact, shrinking. He had sudden, horrible visions of Space-Time folding in on itself in parody of the Great Crunch, until only the console room was left, until ... He had shivered, gathered his wits and set off on foot to locate the interface.

He remembered, now, his first sighting of his destiny. He had walked through the corridors lined with greyish roundels for something like an hour before he found what he was looking for. The anomaly appeared to be a wall of lights, barring a corridor deep beneath the replica of the Royal Albert Hall that he had programmed in at some point during his travels. The lights ate up the roundels as they advanced, and it was then that Epsilon Delta had heard the voice in his head for the first time.

Do not fear, Time Lord, it had said. *You shall have your revenge.*

After that, it had been so easy. The Garvond had promised him not only the domination of Earth, but also a vast source of energy, to achieve with his TARDIS feats never attempted by Time Lords, even those from his advanced epoch. They would travel together to a period of 'crystallized' time, a thousand-year period in the history of Earth. As the President knew, these stretches of immutable Time were rare and possessed a huge inertia, making them difficult to tweak and disrupt. Any minor change – like, for example, the assassination of a Government minister – would release a vast amount of energy ...

He broke off from his reverie as Amanda stepped smoothly back into the console room, fresh from recharging. Her body, still supple and humanoid, was tinged very lightly with a moon-silver colour.

She touched the console with her fingertips, smiling down at the President.

'He has you beaten,' she said.

'I know.' The President irritably stabbed at the key that toppled his king. The red and green whirl of lights at the heart of the time rotor pulsed with victorious energy, and an audible roar of power coursed through the console room.

It had not been so long ago, he reflected, that the Garvond had reached out and touched his mind. He had come to know what the Garvond was. Where it had come from. And everything, like the perfect detective mysteries of Colin Dexter which the President admired, had come together, and he had chuckled at the irony of it all. Through the creature, the President (as he now liked to call himself, following the Gallifreyan renegades' tradition of adopting titles) learned the pleasure of true malice. Of taking Time in one's hands and –

'I did not locate the Doctor's time machine.'

Amanda's voice registered, and he turned to her wearily.

'What's that you say?'

'The Type Forty. It evaded me. There is a mark on the lawn, and yet I detected nothing.'

The President waved a pudgy hand. 'The Doctor's using trickery. These Type Forties are rather resilient. We must have it, though. The Garvond has drawn all it can from this model, and the Doctor's is part of the plan – an essential component of the time reconfiguration. At least we have the Time Focus.'

'And the others.'

'They entered unannounced,' said the President with a shrug, and he got up and began slowly pacing the console room. 'I could hardly invite them in for tea and muffins, could I?' He scowled – not at Amanda, but at the fizzing knot of lights in the time rotor.

130

'I don't know,' offered Bernice from her alcove. 'Nothing wrong with being reasonably civilized.'

The energy crackled and flickered.

Despite herself, Benny shivered. It looked angry, she thought. Like a wasp trapped under a glass.

'It would revolutionize his new paper to Berkeley, I admit,' the President continued. 'But we can't have anyone wandering in and out of TARDISes, no that won't do at all.' He was talking more to himself now. 'Quite out of the question.' He stopped, then smiled directly at Amanda. 'But yes, you are right . . .' His brow creased once more. 'To complete the equation, we do need the Doctor.'

'It needs me,' said the Doctor broodingly. He put his feet up on the table again and assumed an expression of intense concentration.

Helina Vaiq, who had joined the Doctor and Terrin in their quarters, frowned at him.

'So, Doctor, you think you know something about this mystery . . . attacker?'

The Doctor looked slowly up at her, and his features darkened with foreboding. It chilled her like nothing had done since that day back home, when they had heard the napalm-tanks coming over the rise towards their shanty town.

'Oh, yes,' he said grimly. 'I think I almost know too much.'

The silence was broken by the bleeping of Vaiq's intercom. She gazed at the wrist-device in astonishment for a second. 'That's the priority channel.'

Terrin and the Doctor exchanged concerned glances as the co-ordinator took the call at the holo-terminal.

'Vaiq here.'

Ballantyne had hovered into view. Behind him, they could see the control centre, bustling with agitation.

'Where the hell are you, Co-ordinator? We need you right away in Sector 20!'

'I'll meet you there. Ten minutes.'

131

'That's not all, Vaiq. Get four guards and bring those two prisoners down with you. I want to see them with my own eyes when they explain this.'

The hologram snapped off.

Vaiq, dumbfounded, turned to face the Doctor and Terrin.

'Well, you heard him,' she said.

Sector 20 was one of the station's gigantic loading hangars, criss-crossed by fragile walkways and spindly stairs. As the Doctor and Terrin were marched at gunpoint along one of the bridges, the Doctor glanced down, saw steel stretching away below him and hover-vehicles scuttling across the floor far beneath them. To their left and right, huge crates, coloured vermilion or emerald, lifted themselves silently on antigrav beams, but below, the loading bays echoed with the creaks, clangs and shouts of continual activity.

They were frog-marched along another walkway, underneath another vaulted ceiling, and the Doctor involuntarily widened his eyes. These people knew what they were doing, he thought. Their construction engineers were respected throughout the known galaxy, and with good reason. To think that it could all crumble to dust. Just one slip. One mistake now, and it would be ended, the lives of thousands hurtling to their end in an instant. He shuddered. It could not be allowed to happen.

'Doctor,' said Terrin quietly, 'I picked up the supervisor's badge.'

The Doctor darted a warning look at him. 'Say nothing, Captain. Leave it to me, do you understand?'

'Doctor, I know what a philosopher would do. I have always thought there must be truth in death. Philip Larkin said – '

'Be quiet, Romulus.'

Terrin looked crestfallen, but drew breath sharply as they were brought to a halt.

A small, concerned knot of people had gathered on one of the antigrav levels. With Vaiq leading, and the guards

132

behind, the Doctor and Terrin stepped into the diagonal column of light which led to the floating floor.

At the top there was Ballantyne to greet them. His face was set in a kind of hardened whiteness, like a mask of clay. The Doctor thought he looked frightened. It did not take long to find out why.

The body had been cordoned off by a domed force-field, and lay against one of the crates like a broken doll.

'Why don't you have a closer look, Doctor?' said Ballantyne in a low, threatening voice. 'This is, after all, something which you will know about?'

The Doctor was moving forward to lean over the body, and no one stopped him.

The name-plaque, which could still be read, identified the man as Crewman Cal Pagett. The Doctor peered through the haze of the electronic shroud. The man's face was deeply lined, the eyes staring sightlessly from paper-thin flesh. At the chin, the skin was ripped like cloth, and yellowed bone showed through the gash. The man's uniform, almost in tatters, hung limply on a wizened body, and two cracked hands had been laid across what remained of his chest.

The Doctor did not move. He had seen death in many forms, and it always angered him, but this time he was trembling. He felt Ballantyne's breath on the back of his neck.

'Pagett was twenty-six,' murmured the supervisor.

The Doctor, calling on his hundreds of years of experience, somehow gathered his resolve and turned to face Ballantyne.

'It's started,' he said. 'Do you doubt me now?'

Ballantyne's jaw stayed clenched, and a nerve had begun to twitch in his cheek. He was not meeting the Doctor's eye.

Vaiq had stepped forward. 'You knew this was going to happen, Doctor?'

'Yes,' whispered the Doctor, and his voice was hollow.

'This is the attack which you spoke of?'

'This?' The Doctor rounded on her. 'All *this* proves is

that the Time barriers are being breached. Very slowly, maybe, and in limited spatial relation, but still breached.' He raised his voice so that everyone on the platform could hear him. 'This is . . .' He waved a hand as if to dismiss them all. 'This is a mere calling card.' He turned his back on them, and nobody stopped him when he went to the edge of the platform and sat there, his legs swinging over the edge.

He might have been angry or deep in thought, but without seeing his face, Helina Vaiq could not tell. She looked anxiously at the supervisor.

Ballantyne did not alter the determined set of his jaw. 'He knows more than he's telling.' He glanced over at Terrin. 'And this one . . . his DNA sample says he's Romulus Terrin. But how easy is that to fake? Pretty simple for a professional, I'd have thought.'

Terrin met the hostile stare with dignity. And all the time his fingers were gently rubbing the edge of the twisted identity-plaque in his pocket.

Helina Vaiq had joined the Doctor, just out of earshot. 'Doctor?'

He did not answer.

'Doctor, you're the only person here who seems to have any idea how Cal was killed, and I want to know.' The Doctor was still silent. 'I'm human too,' she went on, and anger was creeping into her voice. 'I'm the one who has to tell his wife and his three-year-old son. And it would make it easier if I knew. It would make it better if you didn't have to – to treat us as if . . .' She broke off, for the exact words that she needed failed her now.

The Doctor turned suddenly, and his face bore a sad smile. Standing up, he touched Helina's elbow, awkwardly.

'I'm sorry, Miss Vaiq. I don't mean to. It's just that I wonder . . . if there will ever be an end to it, one of these days.'

'An end to death? I hardly think so, Doctor.' Her voice held the bitterness of suffering.

The Doctor sighed. 'This isn't my job. I don't get paid for it. I don't get any kind of reward.' His eyes were deep, hypnotic, but his voice was cracking like old wood. Helina found herself wondering, for the first time, how old he could possibly be. 'I've never asked for any. Sometimes there are some. The smile of the baby child. The first sunset on a soft and new-born world. The taste of the purest spring water, untouched by any pollution of Man's making . . . But it's not enough. I'm tired, Miss Vaiq. Do you understand me? No, of course you don't. A child of less than forty Earth summers. How could you possibly understand?'

Helina could have said that she had once thought that she would never see another summer. That she had imagined her existence as leading up to a meeting with a fireball that would lash her skin, flaying it to the bone. Just like her sister's life. But she chose not to. Instead she asked:

'You're some sort of detective, aren't you?'

The Doctor smiled. 'In a way. Although I sometimes wish I could be more of a teacher. It's all very well to give a hungry man a fish . . .'

Helina frowned. 'I'm sorry?'

'Oh, an old analogy.' The Doctor gazed at the distant floating crates. 'One I picked up on Earth some time ago. There's a hungry man whose crops have failed, although he lives by a river. In one day he's visited by two missionaries. The first brings a basket of fish and tells him he can eat as much as he likes. The second, though, gets a pole, a thread and a piece of wire, and teaches the man *how* to fish. Who has performed the more useful service?' The Doctor clasped his hands behind his back and began to walk away from Helina Vaiq, no longer looking at her. 'Sometimes,' he said, 'I'm just expected to have an endless supply of fish.'

Ballantyne and the guards were blocking his way.

'And now where do you think you're going?' asked the supervisor coldly.

For a moment the Doctor, dwarfed by the tall, thin supervisor, looked as if he did not have an answer. Then he smiled.

'Well, Supervisor. Do you want my help, or not?'

Ballantyne did not answer.

'I'll take that as a yes. If you want to keep an eye on me, I suggest you come with me, and bring your philosophical friends along too.' The Doctor nodded to the impassive guards. 'Miss Vaiq, I need to send an important communication.' He gestured to Terrin. 'You too, Romulus. Come along.'

As the station guards resumed their position by the body of Crewman Pagett, they did not notice the slight shift in the shape of the electronic shroud.

A twist of red and green light crackled to itself, spurting above the man's body like St Elmo's Fire. For a moment, a gas-masked head reared up, its eyes burning bright, and sleekly muscled arms began to form in the shimmering air above Pagett.

The figure hovered for a second, trying to stabilize, then snapped out of existence like a deactivated hologram.

Quincy, the central computer of Q4, squatted like a queen bee at the heart of the station's communications complex. Its network of fibreoptics, inlaid into the station's infrastructure, told it everything it needed to know. Other computers, in the past, had embraced their host stations. Quincy held Q4 together. Deep within Quincy beat the equivalent of ventricles and aureoles, sending the cells of data along the uncountable capillaries.

At 16.30, Central European Time, one major artery of Quincy was monitoring an emergency transmission, and a tiny fragment of one of its brain cells was storing it. For the operator of the terminal on this occasion – he identified himself as 'Theta Sigma', but the transmission was backed by Co-Ordinator Vaiq's priority override – had requested that the message, although of primary importance, had to be recorded, and beamed on all frequencies in precisely one hundred and sixty Earth hours. Moreover, during its week of storage, the message was to be kept in a protected cell, preferably encased in a concentrated force-field.

Quincy performed without question. Had its artificial intelligence included curiosity, it might have wondered how Theta Sigma could know that a call on such an important distress frequency would be required in one week's time.

'And there it is,' said the Doctor. He flicked off the holo-recorder, and emerged from the communications booth which he had been assigned in the Control Centre. 'Now let's play it back, shall we?'

Ballantyne's 3D starmaps twisted and split, became instead a blue-tinted hologram of the Doctor's lined face.

'Attention, Earth vessels. This is a recorded message, on a priority channel, intended for the crew of the Starship *Icarus*, currently patrolling the fifty-fourth sector of explored space.' The Doctor was seen to pause, look aside. 'The identifying tag is – codeworded "Daedalus".' The image jumped slightly, indicating the pause the Doctor had made here. He was in greater close-up now, his eyes as large as beach-balls and full of dark warning.

'Lieutenant-Commander Quallem, this message is for you. This is the Doctor. You must trust me, and do as I say. Captain Terrin is with me, and he has given me the relevant code-word. This, as I understand it, is his personal signal to you that no compulsion has been exercised, and that he is not being forced to misinform you under duress. Your ship must not, I repeat must *not* be allowed to come into contact with alien forces between Q4 and Lightbase. If my theory is correct, you are running into a trap – set by one of the deadliest powers ever to inhabit the dimensions of Space and Time. You must change course to avoid this grave threat – I repeat, avert your current path and advise Earth of your situation. You must believe me – me, and your captain, who is still very much alive. Someone is causing disruptions – the most serious time-break. We have very little time ourselves. Listen to my warning. It's the only way, Lieutenant-Commander, to prevent the terrible catastrophe which you saw on the space-station – an anomaly that was never meant to happen. Please do as I say – for the sake of Humanity.'

The image broke into shards and seemed to fall like rain to the floor of the centre, before re-forming into the standard tracking holograms.

Ballantyne had been watching, and now he strode down to meet the Doctor, Terrin and Vaiq. 'Very good, Doctor,' he said, and there was neither warmth nor trust in his voice. 'I hope, for your sake, that this little game turns out to have had some purpose.'

'I hope so too,' said the Doctor. 'For *your* sake.'

Ballantyne appeared unperturbed. 'Miss Vaiq has now made herself entirely responsible for you. I've done all I can,' he said. 'I think you'll agree.'

'I trust the Doctor,' said Helina Vaiq.

She and the Doctor exchanged a smile.

Ballantyne looked from one to the other. 'If I'm wanted,' he said, 'I shall be in my office. I have a number of administrative tasks.' He left the centre.

'I met many like him,' said Terrin softly. 'I could have become one all too easily.' He shook his head as if shaking off memories. 'So, Doctor. What now?'

'We wait,' said the Doctor grimly. He was perched on the floor, oblivious to the bustle of the centre, consulting what appeared to be a small leather-bound book. 'Are you diary people?' he asked, 'Either of you? No, I doubt it. Wrong century. No one writes like Samuel Pepys these days. Observant fellow, I recall . . .' All the time, he was furrowing through the pages, as if trying to locate a particular reference. 'And then there was Francis Kilvert . . . I gave Arthur Young a couple of tips when I was in France, too. Aha! Here we are.'

'Don't tell me,' said Vaiq sardonically. 'You might just be going to explain something.'

The Doctor did not seem to have heard her. 'I was right, then. The ravaging of the fields of Time. Just as recorded in the Future Legends. And yet no one . . .' His eyes were looking inward now. Into the past. His own past. 'No one could have liberated such an immense power,

138

unless . . . Yes, yes . . . And it would explain why you and I, Captain, were brought here unscathed. Brought back one week in time, rather than consumed, like those . . .' He seemed to remember suddenly where he was, to take in the fact that the centre was full of bank after bank of monitors and holo-consoles, and the young and concentrated faces of their operators. 'Like them,' he said, and to Vaiq it sounded as if he had tried to choke back the words. He got to his feet, and took one last look round at the room full of technology. 'I must be alone,' he said. 'I need time to think.'

'I'll come – ' Vaiq began.

'*No!* You have no idea at all of what it all might mean. If I'm right, then . . . someone . . . is tampering on a scale that could never have been imagined. Leave me alone for an hour.'

'I hope you know what you're doing, Doctor,' said Vaiq softly.

The Doctor rubbed his eyes. 'So do I, Helina.'

And he was gone.

Terrin, as if coming to a sudden decision, unclenched the hand that he had been keeping at his side for the past five minutes, and forced what he was holding into Helina Vaiq's damp palm. 'I've decided something important,' he said. 'Take this. You may understand. I hope, for all of us, that you never have to.'

He left without another word.

She looked at the I.D. plaque. The corporation logo, flaking and bent. The barely legible name.

She felt cold. Lost, and uncontrollably shaking, as she had done that time she had lain in the bunker, watching as her sister's flesh was burnt to ash by the giant flame-throwers, and carried to the heavens while the soldiers laughed among themselves. She felt the bile rise in her throat. The past. None of them could escape the past. And now, it looked as if their future had been decided too.

Chapter 15

Echoes

The Doctor found himself free to wander at will among the officers and technicians in Q4's brightly-lit corridors. He even got friendly smiles from one or two of them, and raised his hat in return.

The lounge deck was adorned with hanging plants, thick carpets and chrome tables. The Doctor looked around the central bar as he strolled nonchalantly into it. Above him, the domed roof stretched up, beyond which the galaxy's spiral arm could be seen twisting away into infinity. In the bar one or two officers were slouched in chairs, and some overalled engineers were playing cards in the corner, but otherwise the atmosphere was calm and anticipatory.

The barmaid was a petite young woman in a high-collared tunic, with cropped claret-coloured hair and a single crescent-moon earring. Beneath an illuminated notice that read OFF-DUTY CREW ONLY, she was polishing glasses, her cherry-red mouth wearing a slightly wistful smile.

The Doctor perched on one of the bar-stools, placed his hat down in front of him, then rested his chin on his hands.

'Quiet in here,' he said.

She shrugged, threw him a coy glance. 'Okay for me,' she said. 'You gotta take time out to smell the roses, as someone said. What'll it be?'

'A glass of water, please,' replied the Doctor moodily.

She laughed as she siphoned it. 'Want lemon in it? Lime?'

'No, just water.'

'Sorted. You can't be drowning many sorrows.' She set the glass in front of him. She rested her own chin on her hands in a slightly mocking attempt to meet his eye. 'Right?'

'Wrong,' said the Doctor. 'Sorrow floats.'

'Well, that don't bother me,' she said, pouring from a bottle of cherry brandy. 'Rumour says there's something on.' She sipped. 'There's a buzz. Something in the air you can sense. Sweet, and it leaves a sour taste. Sour because it means half your mates are going to die soon.' Her mouth drooped at the corners. The Doctor studied it intently. 'Oh, I've had it before. Never been wrong. Why d'you think I'm here and not flying shuttles no more?'

'It's a hard life,' the Doctor murmured, 'but it goes on. Things change.' The Doctor met her eyes for the first time.

'Yeah. *Slàinte mhath.*' She took another gulp of brandy.

'Have you ever . . .' The Doctor hesitated, 'made a mistake?' he asked. 'One you weren't aware of until the consequences became clear?'

'You *joking*? I've lost count. I get holo-cables from my mistakes. I wake up next to them. I wear them. I drink them and throw them up again. Hell, it's not the end of the world.' She breathed deeply and gulped another mouthful. 'Why? What have you done?'

'I'm not sure.'

'All right.' The girl wasn't deterred. 'You're having an affair.'

'No, no.'

'Well, maybe you should. Maybe that's your problem.'

'I doubt it.'

'Okay. Touchy, ain't you? How old are you?'

The Doctor looked past her at the rows and rows of bottles on the chrome shelf.

'I honestly don't recall,' he said eventually. 'I used to be sure. Too old, that's the answer.'

She leaned forward a little further. 'Trust me. It'll work out. Things do.'

Somehow, there was more than just blind hope in her voice, more than glib comfort.

'I should spend more time thinking,' said the Doctor softly. 'And looking.' His face became a little brighter. 'I should come to these places more often. Village pubs, space station bars. The only way to learn what *really* goes on in the wider institution.'

'Too right. But I shouldn't be doing this, y'know? Drinking on the job. Shooting my mouth off.' She laughed. It was a brandy-washed laugh, deep and rich. 'Always do, with older men.'

'I see.' The Doctor, a little uncertainly, broke his gaze away from hers. 'My life,' he said, 'doesn't allow me to . . . stop, very often. Work things out.' He sighed, shrugged. 'I don't . . . make close friends all that easily. And sometimes when I do, I hurt them. Under pressure, usually.'

'Don't worry,' she said with a grin. 'You're all right. I wish they could all be as nice as you.'

When he looked back down at the bar, he saw that she had moved her glass so that its rim was touching his.

'I often wish I could be as nice as me,' he said. 'Thanks for the talk.' He flipped his hat back onto his head and jumped down from the stool.

'Any time.' It could have been weariness that made her voice listless, or disappointment. 'Sorry. I wasn't much use.'

'Oh, but you were.' The Doctor's face creased into a fleeting smile. 'I like to be listened to. Touching. Gets you right *here*.' He tapped his chest, on both sides, then gave her a parting wave. With his hands plunged into his pockets, he wandered back towards the antigrav-tube. He did not look back.

'Hey!' she called. 'Come back soon, when things are better!'

As she watched the little figure saunter away, ducking and weaving between the tables and the enthusiastic plants, she realized she did not know if he had heard her last words or not. After a few more seconds, he was gone from her sight.

Strakk's legs were still supporting him, but Ace could

sense him growing weaker, and felt more and more weight on her own shoulder. She wondered how long she could keep it up.

Eventually they had to stop, at yet another of the junctions. Ace had been on many freighters and battlecruisers where one level looked much like any other, but the *Icarus* was the worst of the lot, with its cramped corridors and its smudgy lights that made you squint. The girl checked the power in her pistol while Strakk, wheezing and coughing, slumped against the wall by one of the service-ladder shafts.

'Not carrying any morphine, I s'pose?' Strakk asked, gritting his teeth.

'Sorry, not my scene.'

'Thought not. Worth asking. You know, those things are bound to be guarding the shuttle-bays.'

'Not necessarily. They probably think everyone's dead. Or they haven't bothered to check.'

'I'm cold,' Strakk muttered, 'but it's just my age, I reckon. What about you? Feel all right?'

She looked down at him, surprised. 'Yeah.'

He nodded, wincing as another stab of pain went through the rheumatic joint of his shoulder.

Ace snapped her gun shut. 'We've got to keep going, soldier boy.'

He shook his head. 'Got . . . to rest . . .'

'Come on!' She grabbed him under his good shoulder, pulling him with all her newly honed muscles, but he resisted. 'Sit there and you'll never claim your pension.'

'I wanted to die,' he said quietly, 'once. When they took me to identify Anji's body. As for Mikaela – my daughter – there was nothing left. Too small, you see. Burnt to a crisp. But they let me look at Anji.' He glanced at Ace, trying to focus on her with his weakening eyes. 'It was enough. I wished I'd been in the skimmer with them.'

'I'm sorry,' Ace said. She hoped she truly was. She heard a voice reminding her of something deep within her soul, her weaker, more vulnerable younger self. 'A friend of mine got in a fire. It wasn't an accident. The smell of burning freaked me out for months after.' She was fingering the restrainer-bangle on her wrist, longing to rip it off.

Strakk, recovering his breath, looked Ace up and down properly for the first time. 'Look, when I saw you and the Doctor on Q4, I just thought you were just scavs. For metal, maybe. You're not, though, are you?'

Ace leaned against the bulkhead, gave him a languid smile. 'You gonna get up, Albion?'

'What *were* you doing there?'

'You'd never believe me. Just call me a troubleshooter, all right? As in, I shoot and it causes trouble.'

Strakk grinned incredulously. 'Captain Terrin used to make a joke like that.' He shook his head, gazing into the distance. 'Poor bastard.'

'Hey, c'mon. He might not be dead.'

'No I meant – it was his only joke.' He slumped back. 'It was thanks to him that I got myself a life. Y'know? After Anji and Mikaela . . . Well, I kind of went to pieces. I had a kind of job on a samizdat network, but it sort of fell through. Didn't have anywhere to go. One night, I found myself in a bar on some hole of a moon or other, with a load of off-duty Survey crew. One of them was a girl called Tanja Rubcjek. I guess we just . . . got on well. The way people do.' He shrugged. Ace smiled indulgently. 'She suggested the Corps to me. I laughed it off, but in the end I went for it. Three months later, I was on Terrin's crew.' He smiled bleakly. 'And I end up stuck here with you.'

'Some guys would give their right arm for that.'

'Not funny.'

'Wasn't meant to be. Come on, we'd better move.'

Ace reached out. She realized, though, that Strakk was not concentrating on her words, for his eyes were looking past her at the corridor wall. With her heart thudding, she followed his gaze.

A ghost. Flickering against the wall. Ace backed off, the pistol levelled with both hands. It won't do any good, she thought, but it feels better. Strakk gathered his strength and moved back with her. They could feel the cold wind, and the ghost, flickering with light, took form.

At first Ace wondered if it was a trick of her mind. Then, as she looked into the face she knew so well, she took a step forward.

She felt Strakk's hand on her sleeve. 'Don't move, you idiot. It's a trick. A projection.' He, too, had recognized the familiar crumpled suit, the fedora with its paisley hatband matching the tie, and the face with its lines of wisdom.

The pale image of the Doctor lifted his chin slightly as if listening. Then he stepped into the corridor, smiled, and raised his hat in their direction.

For a moment, Time seemed frozen. Neither of them heard, until it was too late, the spectral fluttering. Ace saw the ghost of the Doctor walk into the bulkhead and shimmer into nothingness, just as the rushing hit her from behind, and she swung – too late. Strakk cried out as he was pinned to the floor by a Time Soldier.

Ace saw the gas-masked snout solidifying right in front of her, felt the chill on her lips as it raised its gun.

The Time Soldiers, flickering like candle-flames, turned their heads from side to side as if scanning the air for orders. Then Ace and Strakk both heard the echo of the voice.

Bring them, said Garvond. *Bring them to the bridge.*

The Doctor, alone in the lounge on Q4, was deep in thought.

He knew he should have acted when he sensed the disruption in the air in Oxford. He had checked with his diary – the eighteenth of November, 1993, had most definitely been a Thursday in the Earth calendar, a day when the streets should have been bustling with students' bicycles, minibuses, hurrying shoppers. And yet the traffic had been Sunday traffic. The couples strolling through the Botanical Gardens had been people enjoying their leisure day. And that newspaper . . .

'The TARDIS,' he muttered to himself. 'If only I could get back there . . .'

There was a brief trilling from the direction of the door. He ignored it, but it sounded again five seconds later.

Vaiq's voice crackled through the intercom.

'Doctor? Are you all right in there?'

Irritation flitted across his face, and then he relented. They could not be expected to understand, not with limited information. He pressed the lock-release, and let them in.

'You're going to be needed,' Vaiq said, as she and Terrin entered a little sheepishly. 'Ballantyne's called a briefing, to decide what we ought to do.'

The Doctor made a contemptuous sound as he stretched out on the sofa, just as Terrin was about to sit down. 'Meetings, briefings, conferences – can't people *think* and *act* in this century?'

'You said something about the "fields of Time", Doctor,' said Vaiq cautiously, as she poured herself a glass of nectarine juice from the decanter. 'What exactly did you mean?'

The Doctor sat up very slowly, and looked from one to the other. As representatives of the human race, he thought grimly, they were not the ones he would have hand-picked to hear this first. But they were better than most, and they were prepared for anything now.

'There is a book,' he said, 'a book which only a few pairs of eyes on my world have been permitted to see. The reasons are obvious enough. It is called *The Worshipful and Ancient Law of Gallifrey* –'

'Gallifrey?' said Terrin. 'But that's just a myth itself. All the stories of Time Lords and Guardians – no one's ever proved –' He was quelled by the Doctor's impassive gaze. Terrin knew that nobody had ever looked at him in quite that unearthly way before.

'You told me once you were broad-minded, Captain,' said the Doctor chidingly. 'Kindly allow your mind to be stretched a little further.' He sat cross-legged on the couch and closed his eyes. 'The book,' he said, 'has many properties. But it tells in part of the coming of a creature, a being more powerful than Time itself. It has been given many names. Garavond, Garivont, Garvond. Its names – there are several thousand – are corruptions of the Old High Gallifreyan *gjara' vont*: "of darkest thought". It can feed, you see, on fear, buried suspicions and mistrust.' His eyes snapped open and he saw he had their rapt attention. 'We cannot let it take form. Time will no longer have a winged chariot, but rather a carriage of death, guarded by demons.'

'Doctor,' Terrin put in, 'if this creature is just a legend – '

'Believe me, Captain, it's very, very real.'

'But how can it gain enough power to do this, assuming it's been dormant until now?' he asked, baffled. 'Surely if it's been unheard, unseen all this time – '

'It has been dormant – deep in the Matrix.' The Doctor was almost thinking aloud now. If his help was to be useful, he reasoned, it was better for them not to be ignorant of what they were dealing with. 'Part of the Matrix is the Panotropic Net, the sum of all Time Lord minds, living and dead, from the great Rassilon himself to the lowliest of orderlies. According to the legends, the Garvond was held imprisoned by that power, the power of Time Lord minds. But the creature could feed off the very hate and fear that was keeping it captive.'

Vaiq slammed her glass down on the table. 'Doctor, what you've said up to now seems to have been borne out. But how the hell do you *know*? How do you even know that this – this – Gara-vont creature really exists?'

The Doctor's voice was sombre. 'Because apparently,' he said, 'I created it.'

Chapter 16

Into the Vortex

'The innocent and the beautiful
Have no enemy but time.'

William Butler Yeats

The bridge was like a nightmare. Ace saw, out of the corner of her eye, the young lieutenant being brutally pushed to the floor by his Time Soldier captor, and she bit her lip. Her eyes, though, were drawn in horrified fascination to the swollen globe of darkness on the Captain's podium. With a crackle of light, the creature within reared up to watch the arrival of the new prisoners, and gave a purr of satisfaction that rolled across the bridge on a wintry chill. Shuddering, Ace found herself behind Cheynor, in the centre of the ring of Time Soldiers.

'Hi again,' she said without much enthusiasm. 'Thought we'd crash your Hallowe'en party. Sorry we didn't bring a bottle.'

Cheynor hardly seemed to have heard her, but Quallem had unfurled herself from her ball like a hedgehog, and stared at Ace.

'*Nous allons mourir*,' said Quallem gently, as if to a child. '*Nous allons tous mourir*.' It was as if she had found the still point in her hurricane of madness, to lie at its centre, oblivious of the pressure which was crushing her.

Ace turned to Cheynor in horror. 'What's Boadicea under? Or don't tell me, she finally flipped?'

'I have relieved Lieutenant-Commander Quallem of command,' said Cheynor levelly.

148

'And the spooks relieved you,' surmised Ace. 'Brilliant work, Major Tom.'

His face was bleak now, she saw, the tanned strength like a pantomime mask. She wondered what he had seen, what had happened since she left.

'Is there anybody else?' he asked in a whisper.

'Alive? We didn't see anyone. The place is empty.'

'Mostrell? What happened to him?'

Ace wondered quite how to put it. 'He ... won't be on solids again for a while.'

You will listen, if you wish to live.

The voice echoed from every surface on the bridge. They looked into the Garvond's heart of darkness, some fearfully, some, like Ace, more resolute.

When you have revealed the access code, thundered the Garvond, *this ship will be ours in which to destroy all hated life. Our time-ship will sail the Vortex, consuming all in our path.*

'It's my ship,' said Listrelle Quallem quietly.

Cheynor and Ace were not near enough to stop her. She had climbed to her feet and was facing the Garvond with anger in her eyes.

'It's my ship!' she screamed. 'Mine! You can't do that. I don't want to play with you. Get out of here. Get out!'

The Time Soldiers were sizzling with excited new energy. Ace saw the dozen pairs of red eyes burning with a lust for new life-force, and could only watch in horrified fascination. It was strange how Quallem had regained a haunted beauty and nobility. Lifting her head on its slender neck, she met the Garvond's stare without flinching. Looking death in the eye, as only the truly brave or mad can do.

Time energy burned on the Garvond's claws. Its words were borne on a hiss of delight.

Then you ... command this vessel? Fascinating.

Quallem's face was glowing under the alien lights. 'It's my ship,' she murmured, swallowing. 'It's my ship and you're not to hurt it ...'

Three of the Time Soldiers had surrounded her in a crescent, like attendant angels of death.

Ace knew what was going to happen. And there was nothing she could do to stop it.

The flash of light filled the bridge. Dazzled, thirty-one humans flinched. The Time Soldiers did not even appear to have fired, merely to have extended their aura in three fluctuating beams, which converged on Quallem. The woman was frozen in a parody of surrender, her arms high above her face. The light poured from her, scattering, and her mouth opened in a silent scream as her back arched, her legs withered.

Ace lifted her eyes from her hands and looked into the flames of Time. She saw, dimly, the face of Quallem shrinking on the skull like a toffee-wrapper shrivelling in the fire, and molten flesh pouring from her body. Her red-gold hair burned with whiteness.

Ace blinked. There was a greenish after-image on her retina. It was a second before she was aware of how quickly the light had snapped off.

Where Listrelle Quallem had stood, there was something that was still just alive. One half of the skull was dented and blackened. The jaw was working, trying to cry out, and wisps of white hair were blowing in the breeze. Bone gleamed under the lights. The apparition's legs were cracking to powder. As they watched, the husk of Quallem crumbled and fell. Her skull, brittle as chalk, smashed into pieces and the shards were scattered across the floor. The report echoed up into the highest reaches of the bridge, reverberated in their minds, stamping something there which their nightmares would always be able to summon.

The Garvond rippled with a pulse of energy. Another command, like a mental finger-click. The Time Soldier next to Cheynor rammed him up against the nearest console and held him there.

'Let him go,' Ace snarled.

Everyone turned to look at her.

150

Now Ace, too, met the creature's empty eye-sockets, and shivered involuntarily.

'I always hated Trick or Treat,' she murmured. Then she raised her voice. 'I suppose if you had a brain I'd be able to see it. What are you on, bonehead? The X-plan diet?'

The Garvond's head seemed to lift from its body, looming up in the globe of darkness, over Ace. It appeared fascinated by her.

Ace folded her arms. 'You see that plastic skeleton in the ghost train? That's *you*, that is. That's what you do for a living.'

It was far enough. The Time Soldier wrestled her arm in a no-compromise grip, and then the floor of the bridge connected with her face. She could feel numbness in every muscle of her body, and realized with a shock that she was quite unable to move.

She heard Cheynor speak.

'This is unnecessary. You're murderers. Barbarians – '

The Garvond's voice was almost visible, a black cloud hovering in their minds. *A primitive human idea. We have evolved beyond any form of barbarism. Humans resent those who are superior. And in the end, they realise that there can be no opposition.*

Ace could not move her head, but from its forced angle she could see Strakk, similarly held by a Time Soldier, the creature's gun jammed tight against his cheekbone.

The code, Captain. Or these two humans are next.

There was a horrible, crisp silence.

She could also see Quallem's shattered head, where it had fallen. The jaw forever caught in a scream of agony. Something ridiculous came unbidden into Ace's mind, a song she'd heard on one of her visits to the Sixties, about dying before you got old. She closed her eyes.

You have three seconds, Captain.

She could hear the ragged breathing of the creatures, like the flapping of enormous leathery wings. The sound marked time. She could not see Cheynor. She felt the Time Soldier's cold blaster tightening against her jawbone.

151

Two seconds.

Numbness. Blackness. She wished she could have been with the Doctor and Benny, here and now, at this pointless end. And still there was no sound from Cheynor.

One.

Ace's eyes snapped open. She fixed her stare on the smashed skull.

Skulls. Death. Ending.

'For Christ's sake, Cheynor!' It was Strakk.

Time seemed to hang like an executioner's blade. And then, unbelievably, she heard Cheynor.

'It's my I.D. number.'

The Garvond exhaled with deep satisfaction.

Something made Ace realize that the pressure had gone from her back. Slowly, life began to seep back into her cramped limbs. She sat up, unbelieving. She was alive.

Cheynor's plaque was ripped from his uniform by the Time Soldier, who crossed, as if already knowing what to do, to the first officer's console.

'So much for double-bluffing,' murmured Cheynor.

Ace, dizzily, looked at Strakk. 'What does he mean?'

'It was supposed to be too obvious,' Strakk answered bleakly, clutching his withered hand. 'Something as easy as one of their I.D. numbers.' The disgust in his voice was evident.

Someone had slipped to Ace's side as she watched the Time Soldier entering the code at the terminal. She looked around. The young operator would have been pretty but for her exceptionally hollow cheeks and tight, starved-looking skin. She looked as if she hadn't eaten a decent meal in days. Her I.D. plaque gave her name as McCarran, R.

'Are you all right?' she asked gently. 'What happened to you and Strakk?'

'It's a long story. What's the cabaret all about?' She nodded at the skeletal intruder.

'It calls itself the Garvond – '

Before McCarran could continue, the lights flickered once again, and then blazed with fresh, orange light. Every

152

terminal on the bridge came back into chattering action. And beneath it all, there was the sound of the engines. Roaring, deep in the heart of the ship.

'The warp,' said Strakk. 'They've got it.'

Through the Bridge echoed the cavernous laughter of the Garvond.

A light was winking on and off on the console of the President's TARDIS. Amanda spotted it first. Her whitish-silver finger stabbed at a control, checking the readout, as the President held a glass of claret up to the light.

'The Garvond has achieved warp power,' she reported in her flattest tones. 'The ship is entering the Vortex.'

The President smiled, and took a sip from his glass. 'Oh, splendid. Cheers!' he added, in the direction of Bernice.

She, leaning against her alcove, looked away from him. 'I hope your liver's enjoying this too,' she answered.

'And now?' Amanda asked. Benny could have sworn she saw irony and contempt in the android's face.

'Well, now,' he said, and beamed at her across his florid countenance. 'It's time for the Doctor. Over to you, I think, my precious.'

The Vortex howled with tangible energy. Through a corridor of light, the *Icarus* streamed, blazing with unearthly power like a metal phoenix.

The ravaging of Time had begun.

Chapter 17

Come as You Are

Many of the gigantic crates brought into Q4's loading bays went straight down antigrav elevators to the food stores. Here, in the refrigeration section, thermal-suited crew members worked a rota, constantly supervising the stacking of new containers and the removal of empties.

Storage Monitor (First Grade) Emmi Dasselle had been dispatched to check an apparent weight imbalance in Hold B. As Dasselle patrolled the gangways between the towering food silos, she shivered slightly, and wondered at the sheer amount that could be consumed in a short space of time by an outpost with a permanent crew of two thousand and a constant flux of traders, ambassadors and others.

Dasselle flipped out her catalogue and read the LCD. With a sinking heart, she realized that the imbalance could not be pinpointed, and she was going to have to check the thermal readings on every attack.

She made her way through to Hold B's second hangar, her footsteps loud as gunshots.

I'm twenty-eight, she thought with mounting resentment. I've worked hard, been promoted twice. So why do I still get the shit jobs?

She blinked at the LCD readings.

They had changed in the last minute.

Emmi Dasselle had a very bad feeling when she found the freezer. It looked like one of theirs, certainly – a cube of about ten metres, featureless except for the serial number and thermal monitor on the side – but there was something wrong.

She clipped her hand into her gauntlet, and touched the surface of the freezer. Even through the thick PVC, there was a perceptible *tingle*.

She'd seen enough. Emmi opened her communicator and sent a call signal.

A gentle humming cut into the silence of the hold. Dasselle's pistol was out and ready in a second. From the side of the freezer, a red light was spilling, as the access portal opened of its own accord.

The intruder, Dasselle saw, was a female humanoid. Tall, dark-haired, with mirrorshades on her eyes. It might have been the light, but her skin seemed shiny, like that of a metallic fish.

The dark-haired girl had a pistol slung in a silver belt on her dress. Dasselle had fired a warning shot as soon as she saw the hand move. It glanced off the girl's elbow. Dasselle backed off, panic rising in her stomach.

Casually, Amanda shot her down. Dasselle jerked, smashed against the crate on the opposite side of the silo and slid to the floor.

Amanda, ignoring the body, strode over to the elevator and programmed the floor she wanted.

As the lift ascended, she adjusted her belt-buckle, and in response her skin faded to grey, then white enough to pass for humanoid, before acquiring a healthy pinkish tinge.

The President's other accessories were more primitive. Like black-plastic tailor's dummies, they were identical, and their movements lacked grace and, often co-ordination. They could, however, perform routine tasks, like bringing Professor Rafferty and Tom Cheynor through the dimensional corridor to the console room.

Three of the black androids guarded the prisoners now. Rafferty, Tom and Bernice stood in a line as the President walked up and down past them, savouring his power.

'You know, I never trusted him, Bernice,' said Rafferty, as if the President were not there. 'Not since the day he served plonk in a 1967 Sauternes bottle at High Table.'

'Sixty-seven?' Bernice glared at the President's jowls with renewed hatred. 'Have you no shame?'

The President, with his hands clasped behind his back, appeared to consider the question as a serious one. 'No,' he answered eventually, with a smile.

'And we all wondered why we never saw you,' Tom muttered. Bernice glanced at the young man. His hair was tousled and he was looking rather pale and haggard – obviously he was less used to unusual experiences than either herself or Rafferty. She rather wanted to give him a quick hug, but she was unsure how James would take it.

'Do you know,' the President said suddenly, 'how tricky it is to exploit a TARDIS in the wine-trade? I mean, antiques, fair enough. But there's no point getting good claret from the Twenties and bringing it back to sell to the Oxford Wine Company at inflated prices. I mean, when it's only just been laid down, it might as well have come from yesterday!' He beamed, as if they should all find this fascinating. 'Anyway,' he said, and the smile was suddenly switched off, 'it's nearly time for you to meet your new master.'

'And what's his conversation like?' Tom snapped irritably.

The President narrowed his eyes. 'Engrossing, Mr Cheynor. Positively unmissable!'

Coloured swirls cascaded on to the main monitor on the bridge. Ace knew what they were – attempts to depict the impossible, the ship's sensors' interpretation of the Vortex. They were travelling in Time.

The soldiers were glowing with new energy, flickering agitatedly as they stabilized. The Garvond's huge eye-sockets were fixed on the screen and the bridge was filled with the creature's rhythmic breathing. All in all, thought Ace, it was quite chillingly impressive, but she wondered why they had not actually done anything else yet.

She looked at the faces that were bathed in the unnatural hues. The tense, drawn faces of an exhausted spacecraft crew: Cheynor, Strakk, McCarran and the others. She wondered if here, now, after all that she had lived through to get here, these were the people with whom she was finally destined to die. Shattered into atoms in the Time Vortex. She realized that she really had no idea exactly what the Garvond intended to do with them all. Her gaze fell on the close-fitting helmet of the nearest Time Soldier, on the red eyes burning behind its visor. She wondered what the creature looked like. If it had been properly alive, once. She shuddered. It didn't do to think about these things too much.

'It's gaining power,' Strakk murmured, breaking the silence among the humans. He was looking intently at the Garvond, squinting slightly at the unnatural whiteness of the creature's bones. 'Every second. As if it's feeding off the time travel itself.'

Ace realized he was right. 'It must have to reach a certain point. Gain enough power to break out. And their attention's taken up . . .'

Rosabeth McCarran looked at Ace with something akin to admiration. 'If you're talking about fighting these things,' she murmured, 'I'm with you. They killed my brother.'

The girl was young, intelligent, but her lean and hungry look made Ace uncomfortable. Ace paused – perhaps a second too long – before she turned towards Lieutenant Strakk. 'What about you, boy wonder? Got the strength back?'

'Count me in. I'm itching for a fight.'

Cheynor unfolded his arms and turned on her with evident concern in his face. 'Now, wait a minute. You saw what these things did to Listrelle – '

Strakk met Ace's eyes. The two of them had built up a kind of rapport since their escape from the lab, and he was following her thoughts. 'What've you got in mind, Ace?'

'The bonehead needs the warp engines to give it juice, right? Without them, it can flit in and out of time, but never aim for any particular point and break out.'

'That's just speculation,' Cheynor hissed.

'*Informed* speculation, Major Tom,' Ace reported. 'So where are these engines, anyway?'

'Level A-zero,' Cheynor said. 'This is beginning to sound dangerous.'

'It's not exactly been a tea-party so far, has it?' Ace snapped. 'What else do you suggest we do?'

Cheynor met three accusing stares. He did not know what he should say. His memory was still full of the horror of the first boarding, and of what the Time Soldier had made him see. The wasteland; the death and destruction; his brother, sinking slowly into the mud. His eyes, haunted and confused, came up to meet Ace's.

'We have to try,' he said.

A week earlier in real time, and not far away in space, Amanda was counting the seconds. She knew where she was headed.

She met no one as she marched along the sweeping white corridors of Q4's accommodation block. And when she found the door she wanted, she swivelled to face it with mechanical efficiency.

'According to the legend,' said the Doctor broodingly, 'the Garvond is a gestalt, a mental composite.' He was pacing up and down in the plush lounge, and not looking at either Terrin or Vaiq, who were both doing best to follow his logic.

'And that,' Terrin asked slowly, 'is how it gains its power?'

'No, no. Power is something entirely different from life-force. The creature is *made up* of mental energy – the intellects it fed off in the Time Lord Matrix.' He looked up, and there was a hint of slight amusement in his face. 'Including the paradox. The woodlouse in the woodpile. The one I thought I had erased,' he said. '*My own.*'

Terrin and Vaiq exchanged glances.

'Your ... mind?' Vaiq asked slowly.

'Well, influence. A print. A poor copy, if you like – oh, don't worry.' The Doctor waved a hand airily and resumed his pacing of the room. 'It's a little like having one share out of millions in a corporation. But it did help in one respect,' he added, leaning over Terrin and looking him intently in the eye.

The Captain found the Doctor's direct gaze a little disconcerting. 'Really?'

'Yes. It was focusing on that part of the entity – although I had no definite idea what it was at the time – that allowed me to travel through it unscathed. To use it, rather than be used by it. And that, Romulus, was why you and I ended up transported back here and not consumed like those other poor devils. I communed with the entity.'

'Doctor,' said Vaiq bemusedly, 'I'm very glad you didn't try and tell me all this when you first arrived.'

The Doctor straightened up and gazed into the fruit-bowl, remembering. 'I was sure I'd felt something, a tele-pathic tug. I'm quite familiar with a number of mental techniques that came in useful. And it gave me a suspicion as to what we might be dealing with.'

'But what about me, Doctor?' Terrin asked. 'I came through the vortex, or whatever it was, *after* you.'

'Yes,' said the Doctor thoughtfully. 'That disturbed me for a while, so I was wary of you. You have to imagine that I opened a tunnel, so to speak, and it hadn't closed before – '

A thump at the door interrupted the Doctor and he whirled round. They were all staring at the door when the second punch came. And it split the thick metal of the door right down the middle as if it were made of nothing stronger than wood.

The Doctor narrowed his eyes. Terrin and Vaiq were flanking him. The co-ordinator had her gun levelled before Amanda had even stepped over the threshold, but the Doctor held up a hand to stay her.

'No, Helina! Not this time. Keep back.'

Metal shards cascaded into the room. The android advanced at a steady pace, her eyes fixed unmistakably on the Doctor.

'Who are you?' Vaiq yelled. 'What do you want?'

Amanda, as she had been programmed, ignored the other humanoids and addressed herself solely to the Time Lord.

'How pleasant to meet you, Doctor.' The voice was steely but seductive. 'We're talking a little trip, you and I. And the captain may like to join us.'

One thought was making itself rise above the others in Helina Vaiq's sharp mind. The Doctor, the one man who had any idea of what was going to happen to Station Q4 and the thousands of people on it, was about to be forcibly removed. Somehow, the girl had to be stopped.

'I'll come,' said the Doctor. His face betrayed tightly controlled anger. 'If it's me you want – or your master wants – then I'm here. Leave these people alone, let them get on with their lives.'

The Doctor was not to know how effective his words to Amanda would have been. Vaiq's well-aimed kick, fast as it was, could not overtake Amanda's reflexes. The co-ordinator's booted foot was grabbed by the android, who hurled Vaiq against the table, sending glass and crystal crashing to the floor. Her head hit the corner of the holo-console.

The Doctor and Terrin were very aware of Amanda's raised gun.

'Follow me,' the android ordered. 'Now.'

Vaiq was groggily trying to sit up.

The Doctor nodded to Terrin. 'Let's do as the lady suggests, Romulus,' he said, and raised his hands.

Terrin, with a despairing glance at the dazed Vaiq, followed suit. Amanda marched them from the room.

The shattered door wobbled in front of Helina Vaiq, and she realized she was not going to make it, let along get a clear shot at the intruder. She got as far as the communications panel on the wall, and slammed her hand against the emergency alarm.

The computer read her palm-print and activated the klaxon. Within milliseconds, it was echoing through every deck of the station.

160

Chapter 18

Focus

The President grinned across his brick-red face as the prisoners were marched into his TARDIS.

'Captain Romulus Terrin,' he said, shaking his hand of the bemused captain. 'Well, I am pleased to see you.' He stopped pumping Terrin's hand up and down and turned slowly to look down at the other silent prisoner, whose face was impassive beneath his white fedora. 'And ... the Doctor? My goodness me – the Doctor!'

Aware that he was being mocked, the Doctor looked past the President's shoulder, across the reddish-hued console room of the Type 102, and raised his eyebrows at those in the room whom he knew. 'Hello, James,' he said. 'Hello, Benny.'

Bernice had turned pale when the Doctor had entered, and still had not recovered herself sufficiently to greet him properly.

'Quite a little gathering you have here,' said the Doctor, looking up at the President. 'Dr Styles, isn't it?' The President opened his mouth. 'Yes,' sneered the Doctor, 'at least I suppose that's what you choose to call yourself here on Earth. Who are you really?'

'I am Epsilon Delta of Gallifrey. Furthermore, I am the President of St Matthew's College, Oxford, one of the most respected academics in the world.' He nodded to Amanda, who led the Doctor and Terrin over to stand with the others.

'Doctor,' said Rafferty politely, trying to ignore the dark android whose hand was still clasped to his elbow, 'wonderful to see you again, old fellow. I don't suppose you'd tell us what's happening? You're always so good at that sort of thing,' he added a little lamely.

'Why don't I leave that to our friend here?' suggested the Doctor, who had been watching Epsilon Delta very carefully ever since he had mentioned the name of Gallifrey.

The President smiled benignly. 'All will become clear soon enough, Doctor,' he said.

'I should have known there were other Time Lords lurking in those ancient colleges. What a perfect place to hide away. What kind of President did you make, I wonder?'

'He wouldn't allow parties after 10 p.m.' volunteered Tom Cheynor in a thin voice.

The Doctor's brow clouded as his gaze fell on the exhausted-looking young man for the first time.

'This is Tom, Doctor,' said Bernice helpfully, although still without quite meeting the Doctor's eye. 'He helped me out in Oxford.'

Amanda was at the console. 'We are headed for Earth,' she announced flatly. 'Arrival imminent.'

The President smiled as he walked past his little row of five prisoners, surveying them, enjoying the power. 'We have some minutes in hand. Splendid. Let me entertain you. Are you impressed by my androids, Doctor?'

The Doctor wrinkled his nose. 'Technology is a means to an end,' he said, with an audible steeliness. 'Whether it impresses one or not depends on the use to which it is put.'

Bernice raised her eyebrows. 'Fifteen-love,' she whispered in amused admiration.

'Very concise, Doctor.' said Epsilon Delta. 'Very gnomic. I see I have not been mistaken in looking forward to meeting you.'

'I'd imagine that for you, as a common or garden megalomaniac, the most important uses are threats, killing, other brutality. All the menial tasks which you find too tedious to carry out yourself.'

'Thirty-love?' Rafferty wondered aloud.

162

'He's quite deranged,' offered Bernice as an aside. 'There ought to be a club for them, really,' she added, more to herself. 'A society, you know. Where chaps like him can go along to play Conquer-A-Planet and shoot people. Would spare an awful lot of antagonism.'

'But then, I suspect it already it a game to him,' said the Doctor, scowling up at the President. 'Wouldn't you think? Playing with lives. Experimenting. All for fun.'

'A lot of it about,' murmured Bernice, not quite low enough under her breath. If the Doctor recognized her allusion to recent events on a parallel Earth, he did not let it show.

'So, what's it to be?' he said, looking challengingly up at 'President' Epislon Delta. 'My time is valuable, you know.'

'You've got to hand it to him,' Terrin muttered to the others. 'I think he knows what he's doing.'

Bernice gave the captain a withering look. 'Known the Doctor long, have you?'

'Less than a day.'

'I wish I had your proselytic faith.'

'Time, Doctor?' Epsilon Delta was saying, with an ironic smile. 'Time indeed. You see, you are a key element in a vast and beautiful plan. Amanda over there,' he nodded to the android, who was impassive at the console, 'started it all off for me. She rather spectacularly assassinated – or should I say, will have assassinated – a prominent member of Earth's current government. An event which sent ripples of unimaginable power out through the sub-strata of crystallized Time, and into the Vortex.'

'That kind of disruption,' the Doctor muttered, 'would create anomalies. Warps in Time.'

His adversary smiled. 'Do go on, Doctor.'

'Breakthroughs from an alternative universe where what you wanted to happen – *happened*. Small things. Like dates changing their days. Like phantom newspaper headlines. But Time springs back into its *natural* shape, releasing huge amounts of energy. Something I saw happen in other circumstances, not that long ago. How

163

am I doing?' The Doctor's voice held simmering anger. 'And creating a considerable source of *power* for anyone with the means to exploit it.'

Bernice updated her running total. Match point . . .

'Excellent, Doctor, excellent!' Epsilon Delta clapped his hands with a sound like the kneading of dough. 'Why do I surround myself with fools, when you and I could have such a stimulating discussion?'

Whoops, thought Bernice. Forty-fifteen.

The Doctor smiled. 'I really don't know. But I imagine the company of androids is reassuring – when you have the difficult task of finding companions with less imagination than yourself.'

And that's style, added Bernice to herself in satisfaction. Serving an ace to win the game.

Epsilon Delta turned away from the Doctor and strode over to the console. When he looked up from the readings, his face was triumphant.

'We have arrived, Doctor. And now you will see the culmination of our plan.'

The Doctor was far from surprised when he saw that the androids had silently taken the forms of twentieth-century human police officers.

'Oh,' the President said with a sudden smile, 'you may wonder, Doctor, how one stabilizes a time-break of this magnitude.'

'The thought had crossed my mind.'

'It's very simple. One needs a lens, so to speak. Time passes through a focus when it's being concentrated, just as light does. The focus has to be something or someone with a link to both time-zones.' He smiled. 'I chose mine very carefully.'

The Doctor did not need to follow the President's self-satisfied gaze. He already knew that it was directed towards the young man called Tom.

'All right, Vaiq. This had better be good!'

A medical attendant was massaging Helina Vaiq's bruised forehead with a cell-rebuilder. She had been lifted on to the sofa in the guest quarters, and her headache would have been gently abating, were it not for the fact that Ballantyne was pacing the carpet in front of her and shouting very loudly.

'A woman took them,' she said quietly, each syllable sending flashes of colour through her aching brain. 'Looked human. Couldn't have been.'

What do you mean?'

'Strength,' Vaiq muttered, closing her eyes. 'Strength of ten.'

'And I don't suppose you've any idea where they might have gone?' asked the supervisor with heavy sarcasm.

'Off the station.' She waved the medic away and sat up, slowly and carefully. 'Sir – go to full defence alert. Send a message to P4 for back-up.' She risked opening her eyes for a second and focused on the blurred figure of Ballantyne. She kept thinking of the cracked I.D. plaque that was sitting in her jacket pocket. 'It's going to happen.'

'You think I've been idle, Helina?' Ballantyne barked. He shook his head, sighed. His voice became momentarily softer, kinder. 'I've already beamed requests for assistance to P4 and Q3. It'll be hours before they reach them, you know that. And I've got all security units on stand-by. We still don't know what killed Pagett, I haven't forgotten. And furthermore, Dasselle's been found dead in Hold B. The work of our intruder, it seems.' He paused. 'What more can we do?'

Vaiq slumped back into the cushions. 'All right,' she said. 'I need a drink.'

The warp engine had reached a thunderous pitch. The Garvond was swollen now to twice its former size and breathing with lustful anticipation.

Cheynor wondered how much more the *Icarus* could take, but he knew McCarran was waiting for his signal.

He nodded.

Rosabeth McCarran doubled up with an agonized scream, clutching at her abdomen. Strakk and Ace each took one of her shoulders, and Cheynor met the blank stares of the two Time Soldiers who were turning to face the little scene.

'Please,' he said, 'this woman needs to be helped.'

McCarran was pale, her breath coming in ragged gasps. Ace exchanged a look with Strakk. They were both wondering the same.

Cheynor extended a hand towards the Time Soldier. 'Please. Let us take her to the medical centre.'

What affliction has this human?

Cheynor rounded on Strakk, whose mouth worked soundlessly. Don't look at me, said his face.

'Can't you bloody understand anything about us?' Ace yelled. 'You need us all alive, right? She's got multiple contusions of the – of the placental – arteries. It's the first symptom.'

The Time Soldier's head bent slightly. It was watching McCarran. The woman let out a scream and redoubled her agonized gasps.

'For God's sake!' Strakk was joining in now. 'That means she's YXY-antibody deficient. The disease is contagious in oxygen-rich environments. If we don't get her out in two minutes, she'll infect the whole crew.''

You cunning bastard, thought Ace admiringly.

The Time Soldier flickered with inlaid messages from the Garvond. It seemed to waver, then turned away from the humans with sublime indifference.

Is that it? thought Ace, her heart leaping with thoughts of revolt. *Maybe we're so unimportant that they just don't care any more.*

'The lift,' said Cheynor.

Ace's heart was thumping. They carried McCarran over to the elevator door – she was horribly light – and Ace felt the tingle up her spine. She remembered Quallem. The broken skull. She could hardly believe it when they got inside the capsule. For one moment she thought that the Garvond was going to have them all killed there, in that tiny space. The creature, though, was shaking among its tendrils of black and white, its entire concentration seemingly given over to communing with the computers of the *Icarus*.

They were going to get lucky.

The door slammed shut and the elevator began to descend.

In a spontaneous, uncharacteristic moment, Cheynor thumped the wall and let out a yelp of delight. 'Well done, everyone. Good stuff!'

'Rosabeth.' Strakk was not smiling.

Ace looked down. The young TechnOp was slumped on the elevator floor, still pale and sweating. Something seemed to kick Ace hard, inside. She suddenly knew. They had all been very stupid.

'Too ... bloody ... convincing,' McCarran said, gritting her teeth. 'Right?'

Strakk's hand was under her chin, and he lifted it gently so that he could see her eyes.

'What was it?' he asked.

McCarran's hands were pressing her stomach, creasing and twisting her uniform. 'Catressium,' she muttered, and swallowed hard.

'Oh, for God's sake!' Strakk let her go in disgust.

'Strakk!' Ace was angry. Angry with herself, for letting McCarran do it, letting her think simulation would not be enough. Angry with Albion Strakk, for not seeming to care.

'What's the matter?' he snapped. 'Catressium's a mild emetic. You get god-awful stomach cramps for ten minutes and then you vom. After that it gives you a slight high.' He glanced briefly down at McCarran. 'She'll live. The stupid idiot.'

Ace closed her eyes as the relief hit her in waves.

She heard the elevator door swish open. Instinctively, her blaster was up and ready. She wondered why she and Strakk had not been stripped of their weapons, but supposed the Garvond knew they were useless.

They were in one of the ship's lowest tunnels, dim and uninviting, with only just enough room to stand.

'Wait,' Cheynor said. 'McCarran, are you going to be all right here?'

The girl, still kneeling, nodded with an effort.

'Right.' The acting captain's eyes were bright with a zest which he had kept hidden till now. 'Let's get in there.'

The bulkhead door was a hundred yards ahead of them. They ran for it, Cheynor leading, then Strakk, with Ace bringing up the rear. Their booted feet sent echoes bouncing around them, clanging like bells in a chamber.

Cheynor was breathless when they reached the end of the tunnel. He held up a finger to Ace and Strakk.

'You know ... that ... when they realize what we're doing ... they'll send one of them down?'

'Then we'd better be quick,' said Ace. 'Get back.' She was tapping out something on the keyboard at her wrist. 'This'll have a friendly chat to your door,' she said. 'Persuade it to have a nervous breakdown. I was going to slap some multi-nitro on it, but this is less messy.'

Strakk grinned. 'Are we going to keep her on, sir?'

'Possibly.' Cheynor, his hands ready to clap over his ears, was staying deadpan, and Strakk wondered what was really going through his mind.

The opening-panel flickered twice before detonating. The report was surprisingly quiet. The bulkhead slid upwards.

But they all heard the next sound.

It was the roar of the engines, but magnified, twisted, as if the technology were being devoured by demonic forces. A part-organic, part-mechanical scream of rage, of primal hatred. Thundering out of the engine-room, down the tunnel towards the elevator.

Cheynor gave a low whistle. 'Not quick enough.'

'*Get in there!*' Ace yelled.

Strakk leapt through the gap. Cheynor was wavering, looking from Ace to the doorway and back again.

'It's sensed us, Ace. The Garvond *is* the ship. If it wants to stop us – '

She lifted the blaster. Both hands, steady. A matter of centimetres from Darius Cheynor's forehead.

168

'If you wimp out on us now,' Ace breathed. 'I swear I'll kill you. *Get in there.*'

Cheynor gave her an anguished look, and followed Strakk into the engine room.

The noise was unbelievable. The room, a simple greyish sphere of a dozen metres' radius, throbbed with it. Beyond a hazy screen the vast arena housing the warp-engines themselves could be made out in the greenish light. Panels of touch-sensitive keys covered the walls.

Strakk whirled round, helplessly. 'So what now?'

'We destroy it.' Ace looked from one of the officers to the other. This was where she needed them. This was where the plan truly, finally became her own. 'We smash the whole lot!'

McCarran felt better. She'd had precious little that was solid inside her anyway, having lived on pills and water for the past week. When she had known for sure that her brother Drew was dead – how long ago? hours? – she had gone into autopilot. She was a survivor. She needed strength, she realized, like that girl Ace. The one who'd started as a prisoner and now she was running the fight from the inside.

Whispers rippled down the corridor. Ghostly voices. Dozens, scores of voices, all of them agitated, as if awakening to find their nest invaded.

Rosabeth McCarran gripped her blaster. Like others before her, she knew it was useless, yet somehow could not bring herself to do without it.

The walls were bulging.

She had only just noticed, but now that she saw it, she realized how logical this would be. The spinning recklessness controlled her head, and everything suddenly seemed so much better that it was.

The whispering grew to muttering, groans, and the air bled angry light.

'All right,' she said. 'I'll be with you, Drew.'

Rosabeth blinked. She knew she just had to remain co-ordinated for long enough, to hold them off until the second stage hit her. The psychedelic in catressium tabs was a slow one, she was sure of that.

In a shower of light, a Time Soldier leapt.

She saw its teeth.

For the first time. The snout, which they had all assumed to be a gas-mask, ripped apart by a scream of hunger. The hunger for life. For the life of Rosabeth McCarran. It blazed with the Garvond's fury as it raised its gun-arm.

'Get them, Ace,' McCarran murmured. 'Just get them for me.'

Then she kicked out from the tunnel wall and leapt into the whirlpool of Time energy.

Ace lifted her booted foot, ready to kick in the main panel. She suddenly became aware of cries from Cheynor and Strakk, and saw them hurled against the panels by an invisible force. A second late she lost her own balance and crashed to the metal floor with the breath knocked out of her.

Hissing and crackling had begun to fill the engine control room. She turned over. Metal snakes were uncoiling from hidden positions on the walls, spitting sparks.

'Oh, gods,' Strakk breathed, sliding himself slowly up the wall with as little movement as possible.

'What are they?' Ace yelled.

'Security probes! Designed to home in on illegal access. They must all be under the control of that monster!'

The slithering probes seemed to unfurl themselves from the wall and undulate across the room. Ace saw that they were inlaid with glistening circuits, like lines on their silvery skin. The nearest began to snap and bite within inches of her face.

She risked a quick look around. Cheynor was pinned into the corner, Strakk trapped by one of the serpentine probes that had coiled itself around his leg.

'It's playing with us,' Ace snarled. 'Unoriginal, bone-head. If you want to kill us, why not do it properly?'

'Don't encourage it!' Cheynor's face was a mask of sweat, his eyes darting between the probe and the door.

'All right,' Ace murmured, as her right hand began to wander stealthily towards her left wrist. 'Keep them talking, boys . . .'

The first blast, a half-second long, slammed McCarran backwards. She twisted like an autumn leaf. She was fifty-five when she hit the elevator wall and broke her spine.

She smiled up at the Time Soldier as it approached, silent, swift as thought.

The next blast lasted a second. It jerked her limbs into a brief, scarlet-blazing motion. When it released her, she tried desperately to gasp air into her eighty-seven-year-old lungs.

The creature had stopped, with its bristling gun-arm immobile, its lascivious breathing clearly audible behind the helmet. *Behind the helmet.* The old woman tried to force her mouth into a smile. She had seen what she had suspected. And she knew what the Time Soldier was seeing, as well. Two blue eyes, burning still with love and hate, with power to live, with the unquenchable spirit of a human fighter. In her ravaged face there was something which the Time Soldier had once understood. Which it could no longer understand.

Her voice was like a dry well. She could taste the blood in the back of her throat as she spoke.

'You aren't just a thing. A monster with a gun. Are you?'

The Time Soldier remained still. Its eyes were burning brightly. The broad gun was trained on Rosabeth's head.

'You understand about pain. About the human race. You're not just killing us for nothing.' Her face, scored with lines and yellowish-white, was exultant. 'I know who you are!'

The hissing breath gathered itself into a recognizable sound. It cascaded through many resonances before settling on one. The voice that issued from the ghostly mouth was not that of the Garvond. It was, for the first time, the soldier's own.

'How . . . long . . . do . . . humans . . . live?'

171

The words were uttered with vampiric pleasure, steeped in the adoration of death.

Rosabeth almost grinned with the blackened ashes of her teeth. 'You mean . . . you don't know?' She lifted her chin, still proud.

She was looking the Time Soldier straight in the eye when the third blast ripped through her body, shattering her bones to splinters.

Chapter 19

The Link

'What though the field be lost?
All is not lost . . .'

Milton, *Paradise Lost*, Book I

The sunlight was glittering on the river as the St Matthew's First Eight reached the home strength. Pulling in synchronized motion, the sweating rowers were a length ahead, spurred on by the cheers of their supporters.

No one noticed a whisper in the air as a grey haze formed itself on the bank behind the spectators, just in front of the pub terrace. It solidified with a trumpeting sound into a sleek black Porsche, on which the sunlight did not seem to reflect.

It sat there, waiting.

The Doctor and Epsilon Delta watched the rowers on the scanner. The self-styled President rubbed his hands with glee at his team's evidently performance.

'Splendid! Some things never change, even in one's absence.' He was now attired in a fur-trimmed cloak with a broad-brimmed hat and a walking cane. Now the President took a mirror from his pocket and began to admire himself at arm's length. 'Unfortunate,' he said, 'the way that your friends wandered in here unannounced. Now you must admit that so far I have been tolerant. Most tolerant.'

The prisoners and the androids were waiting in an anteroom – the Doctor had seen them led away. He and Epsilon Delta had the console room to themselves.

'Don't waste your words, Epsilon Delta. Just tell me what you want. And don't try to make your threats stylish. It grates.'

Epsilon Delta leaned down until his eyes were on a level with those of the Doctor. Neither Time Lord flinched.

'I want,' said Epsilon Delta, 'your co-operation, your respect, and your TARDIS.'

'Unlikely, inappropriate, and impossible. Now, if you'll excuse me, I have a time-line to save.'

'You think I am not serious, Doctor.'

'I think you're trying too hard. You know the location of my TARDIS. Yours is tuned into it.' The Doctor's voice was uncharacteristically harsh.

'But I need you, Doctor, to give me access to the capsule. Now let me remind you – my androids have an immense capacity for destruction. Their hands can be programmed to crush lead and platinum, so I doubt whether a few puny human bones would cause them more trouble.' He straightened up, swaggered across to the anteroom door. 'Shall we go and see who they could start on?' he inquired, leaning on his stick with manorial arrogance. 'Professor Rafferty, perhaps? He would crunch easily. Or Bernice? More of a challenge, but I'd imagine she's no less brittle than any other human.' The flippant tone vanished and the renegade narrowed his eyes. 'Your TARDIS, Doctor. If you want your friends to live.'

For a moment the Doctor stood with his face betraying nothing. Then he bowed his head and walked over to join Epsilon Delta.

'I'll show you,' he said quietly.

Ace was conscious of every muscle in her body.

She could hear her breathing, and Strakk's and Cheynor's, above the haunting whispers and howls from the engine room. Hovering centimetres from her face, the probe crackled with energy. She could almost smell the Garvond in the machine, taste the decay and death. She thought of baby Monstrell again, in his incubator, and the husk of Quallem lying in fragments on the floor of the bridge.

Ace, moving her finger to one key at a time, punched in the icebreaker that she needed.

Then, flat on the steel floor, she resorted to something that she didn't often do.

She prayed.

The end of the day was quite beautiful, noted Bernice, and the sun was dappling orange on the river. There was a pleasant sense of old-fashioned charm about the boat crews' supporters with their tea and scones on the pub terrace. It would all have been most agreeable if she could have ignored the unbreakable grip of a Gallifreyan android disguised as a woman police constable in the British Metropolitan Police Force, and the utterly defeated expression on the face of the Doctor.

'Couldn't we have got a closer fix?' complained President Epsilon Delta in annoyance, scanning Magdalen Bridge with a telescope.

Amanda, her shades reflecting the activity on the river bank, cupped her hand to her head as if listening to something. 'Negative. Danger of energy field disintegration.'

'Oh, very well.' The President, presumably conscious of the stares that the eclectic group was getting from the spectators, snapped his telescope shut and nodded to the police-androids. 'Let's go.'

Bernice saw Captain Romulus Terrin looking around in wonderment. 'I hope someone is going to convince me this is real,' he said faintly. 'It looks frighteningly like twentieth-century Earth.'

'Open mind, Romulus,' said the Doctor. 'Open mind. Be a good chap and keep quiet, would you?' And Bernice imagined he would have dug the captain gently in the ribs, had he been a little nearer and unmenaced by the coldness of Amanda's pistol on the back of his neck.

Bernice, Tom, Rafferty and Terrin were led away first,

firmly propelled by their fake police. Then came the Doctor and Amanda. The android towered head and shoulders over the Doctor, who looked like a man being taken to execution. The President, quietly chuckling, brought up the rear.

It took a couple of minutes before Bernice realized they were getting encouraging shouts and laughter from both sides of Oxford High Street. She turned to Captain Terrin, but he was too engrossed by the broad, sweeping street with its thundering traffic to be able to utter anything coherent.

'What is it?' she cried to Tom Cheynor as they were marched past delicatessens, barbers and novelty shops.

'I think we might have been mistaken for a Rag parade,' he admitted a little embarrassedly. 'If anyone throws money at you, don't worry.'

The Time Soldiers were waiting in Radcliffe Square.

Two of them, feet planted firmly apart, shimmering in the evening light. They hovered just above the cobblestones, little more than outlines in a greenish mist. The domed Radcliffe Camera could be seen through their bodies, its gentle yellow soaking the dregs of the sun.

The party halted. Bernice could feel her heart thumping, and she heard the Doctor draw breath.

The President stepped forward to greet the ghostly figures. His face glowed with exultation and smugness, and he whirled to face the party of prisoners with his cane held aloft. Its tip came to rest just short of the Doctor's nose.

'We have our escort, Doctor. Now – where are we headed?'

For a moment the Doctor was silent. Behind them, the evening traffic roared. Bernice heard bells ringing somewhere near, voices and laughter on the other side of the square – ridiculously joyful sounds. She wondered if the Doctor was going to astonish them all again.

'St Matthew's College,' said the Doctor. 'Front quad.'

The probes screamed.

'Up!' Ace shouted. 'Get up!'

Cheynor and Strakk were on their feet. The metallic snakes thrashed in agony at the bombardment from Ace's attacking program. Like wounded beasts, they squealed in pain and fury, lashing out at whatever was in their path. Sparks leapt from control panels. Screens smashed to pieces. The shrieks from the Garvond's gestalt mind grew in volume, piercing hatred and terror into their brains.

It hurtled towards Ace from the door of the engine room. Blotting out Strakk and Cheynor. More tangible than darkness, deeper than thought. She knew what was happening as the noise and blackness hit her. This was the Garvond's fury. Its attack against those who had deceived it. Ace tried to scream that it needed them. It has always needed them. That was why it hadn't killed them. Right? But now it was punishing them. In the way it knew best. Through the mind.

They reached to her like hands from water, dragging her down. Faces swam in the blackness. The Doctor, only half-seen like a child's tracing. There was Death, in his cloak of darkness, and behind him, in a vast and undulating train, the armies of the dead, marching through Time with a slicing, rhythmic beat. The scythe whirled, came biting down at her like a wind, and in that split second she remembered the many times she had faced him before, and lived. And the others, who had not been so lucky. Mike. Shreela. Jan. Souls screaming with the ship as it hurtled to destiny through the Vortex. She tried to lift herself with her palms flat on the floor. Death's blade skimmed her hair, slicing a lock from it, which split into fragments, each falling and becoming a droplet of blood.

She could see outlines in the darkness now. Wooden, creaking. In the corner, a stuffed bird, watching her with swivelling eyes. *Creepy.* That old word. Rustling noises spiralled around her, trapping her. Roundels had begun to form on the wooden panelling, and now she knew this place for what it was. Not that house, Gabriel Chase; not some mystic land of her fears; not the TARDIS. None of these alone, but the darkness of all together, like a potent

177

mandragora stealing away her life and dragging her down into oblivion. Where the Garvond lay.

And above her, the accusing eyes, the lost eyes, of the face she wanted to love. The face of Audrey, her mother.

Then Ace, falling towards death without absolution, saw the Doctor.

And the Doctor, smiling, watched her fall.

She opened her eyes.

A familiar sight greeted her. The low, circular room with its dim lighting and the captain's dais. Still sitting there, trembling with power in its own aura, was the Garvond. The frightened, useless TechnOps held at their posts by the Time Soldiers as the space-chariot sped on through an endless night. Somehow, she was back on the bridge.

Leave them, said the Garvond's voice in her head. *They are unimportant now.*

'We failed,' said a voice she knew.

Her vision still blurred, Ace swivelled her head to the right. Albion Strakk was picking himself up from the floor by the elevator doors.

'How the hell did we get back here?' Ace hissed.

Strakk slumped beside her. 'Just be thankful if didn't attempt anything more amusing.'

Cheynor was back in his seat, next to them, gazing blankly at his palms as if seeing them for the first time in his life. He looked up, carefully, squinting in the orange light of the Bridge, and his eyes met Ace's.

'I saw my brother,' said Darius Cheynor faintly. 'It used him against me, like a weapon. Like before.' He shuddered. 'And I felt something else, too. Something I senses when these creatures first boarded, as if I should *know* more about them. Like I'd been through all this before . . .'

'And you?' Ace hardly dared ask Strakk.

The lieutenant's eyes were a long way away. 'I saw Mikaela and Anji burning. Their death, over and over.'

The silence was like ice. *What are we dealing with?* Ace thought. *It knows everything. It burrows into our minds*

178

like a worm, chewing our fears and hates, spitting them back at us.

'Okay,' she said. 'The rabbits got pulled out of the hat. Next time we'll be sawn in half.'

The cheeriness of her words was hollow, like a waiting coffin. She didn't ask Strakk what he thought had happened to Rosabeth McCarran.

She was thinking about death, and the shadowed face of the Doctor.

Somehow, the Garvond had delved to the place even she did not actively dare to confront. The part of her soul which flowed with the fire of mistrust.

Mistrust of the Doctor.

On the lawn of St Matthew's, the ill-assorted group had circled the flattened square of grass like mourners around a grave. Luckily, the college was closed to visitors that afternoon – except to those accompanied by the President, of course, no matter how strange they might have looked. The two Time Soldiers had simply vanished outside the Porter's Lodge and re-formed themselves silently on the lawn.

The Doctor, sensing that everyone was waiting for him, held out his hand to Bernice.

'Is this really the time?' she asked.

'Give me the homing beacon.'

'Nicely,' she reproved him.

'Give me the homing beacon, nicely.'

She thumped it on to his palm and turned away in annoyance, arms folded. The Doctor, almost without looking, unscrewed the device and prodded inside it for several seconds. Then he looked up, his face impassive.

'I hope you're ready,' he said to Epsilon Delta.

On the bridge of the *Icarus*, the Garvond blazed in anticipation of its new power.

They all heard the voice.

At last, it said. *The final connection. The ship of Time. Then, we can emerge from the Vortex . . .*

* * *

Behind the Doctor, unseen by anyone, Amanda smiled. And her finger tightened on the trigger of her blaster.

Chapter 20

Location and Dislocation

One moment the square of grass was there as before, and then, in less than a blink of an eye, the TARDIS sprouted from it like a square blue tree.

Bernice was impressed.

'Gosh,' she said, 'you know, I'd almost accuse you of being theatrical.'

'Almost?' the Doctor raised an eyebrow.

'You'd take it as a compliment.'

Epsilon Delta stretched out a pudgy hand to stroke the paintwork. With a sinking heart, Bernice realized she could hear another of those melodramatic chuckles growing steadily in the back of his throat.

'So where was it?' Rafferty asked in wonderment.

'Here,' said the Doctor grimly, 'but not *now*. You see, when we first arrived in Oxford, the ship sensed the Garvond's intrusion, and activated a rarely used system. It's called the DITO – Defence Indefinite Timeloop Option.'

'Which means?' asked Tom eagerly. He was determined, even more so than his mentor the Professor, to follow all this. Now that he was beginning to think rationally after the initial shock, he was realizing that it might all have some bearing on his future studies. He wondered how the soldiers would react to his taking notes.

The Doctor turned to Tom and looked him squarely in the eye. 'The TARDIS,' he said, 'was always a millisecond in the future. Wherever you were looking for it. That caused the imprint on the lawn, because the ship had always *just been there*, a millisecond ago. An infinite loop is child's play to create. It's only the application which

181

is – ' The Doctor shrugged and almost smiled, 'redolent of genius.'

We have heard enough.

The voice whispered around the quadrangle, echoing from the stonework and the ivy. Like a ghost of Oxford. Only they knew it was no ghost. All eyes were on the leading Time Soldier as its eyes flickered in harmony with each syllable.

You, Epsilon Delta, will now stand aside. Your time and your usefulness are at an end.

The President looked slightly put out, but even Bernice was impressed by how quickly he recovered. He gave an obsequious bow. 'Very well. As your master decrees. I trust,' he added, 'that Gallifrey, as we agreed, will be handed over to me before the Ravaging?'

We made no deals with you, said the Time Soldier.

The silence in the quadrangle was tense. Everyone was rather interested to see what would happen next. Everyone except the Doctor, who was nonchalantly unlocking the TARDIS.

Epsilon Delta let out a hearty laugh, which stopped rapidly when he realized that no one was joining in.

For the first time, he looked frightened.

'What do you mean?' he asked.

The android will complete its task, said the voice from the Time Soldier. *For the disruption to be brought full circle, this must happen.*

Amanda, responding now not to the President but to another, greater power, flexed her gun-arm.

The second Time Soldier emitted a shattering blaze of green radiance, shards of light slicing the evening air like knives. Before anyone realized what was happening, the android and the President were swallowed up.

An after-image, just a blur of purple light, lingered there on the lawn for a moment, and then there was silence.

The Doctor looked up. 'Hmm,' he said, 'I wondered when he'd work that out.' He pushed the TARDIS door open and smiled sadly up at the Time Soldiers. 'We'd better get this over with, then. Come on.'

Bernice could not believe her ears. 'You're going to let them into the TARDIS?'

'I'm not letting it do anything. Merely saving your life. All your lives.'

'Doctor,' James Rafferty said in astonishment, still gazing at the place where the green flare had been. 'What happened to the President and Amanda?'

The Doctor paused for a moment before meeting the gaze of his old friend.

'History,' he said sadly.

In Heathrow, it was as before. Only this time, Amanda was on roller-skates.

She skimmed along the smooth floor of the terminal, her body silver and black, the briefcase once more by her side. She knew the position of the blue-uniformed guards, of the target. Dodging the travellers and their trolleys, she sliced past one check-in desk after another.

Target thirty metres and closing.

The voice crackled in her ear as it had done on the dress rehearsal. Or maybe that had been the real thing, and this was the dress rehearsal. It didn't much matter to Amanda. The effect was to be much the same. Only this time the commanding voice was ghostly, inhuman. It was the voice of the creature of Time, the anomaly from the Matrix and the intruder in the Time Vortex, the dark angel of pure energy that called itself the Garvond.

The Last Call light was flashing there, as it should have been. She saw it. Now she was at the security gate. She tightened her grip on the reflective briefcase.

The data rush identified the target. Visual confirmed it. The face under the thinning grey hair was the right one. He was reaching for his boarding pass. She threw the case vertically into the air and the target swivelled round to face her as he became aware of the movement. The case landed on her outstretched palms and Amanda looked along the sleek nozzle of the laser blaster.

Before she fired she looked at him for the last time. The face of a man who delighted in his several lives, the face of a connoisseur of wine, a purchaser of expensive suits and an incorrigible bore. The face of Epsilon Delta, former assistant to Gold Usher – alias Dr Styles, President of St Matthew's College, Oxford – alias the Home Office Minister of Great Britain.

He was slammed up against the barrier with three red circles staining his jacket.

Someone screamed. People hit the floor of Terminal Two in panic.

Excellent, said the voice of the Garvond.

And now Amanda knew her work was done.

'I enjoyed that,' she said to the world in general. 'One would think I'm almost becoming human.'

The deactivator was located in her head, so it was her face that blew out in smithereens, leaving a gaping gash of metal. Then the briefcase smacked to the floor, blasting the SwissAir counter with a couple of rogue shots. Amanda disintegrated. The fractures began from the neck down, the metal of her body crumbling like parched earth, and the cracks grew wider and wider as they spread to her limbs and torso. Cracks and holes linked, bursting open gashes in her metallic body. In a matter of seconds the torso had caved in, and with a crash, the remains of the android collapsed in a shower of fine dust on the floor of Terminal Two.

One by one, people were starting to pick themselves up off the floor.

Three seconds later, the target achieved critical blood loss and died.

Four pools of dust, tinged blue and silver, were also rippling in the wind in the front quad of St Matthew's College, Oxford.

Bernice, Tom, Terrin and Rafferty had turned as one when they felt the androids' grip relaxing. The disintegration had been spectacular, but Bernice somehow knew it didn't indicate a victory. For one thing, the Time Soldiers were still very much present, and for another the Doctor's

184

expression had not changed. She was angry now. He had not told her what was really going on.

'You knew that would happen,' said Bernice. 'Didn't you?'

The Doctor shrugged. 'They were instruments. When the Garvond no longer needed them, it disposed of them.' He looked meaningfully at the shimmering Time Soldiers. 'The real enemy doesn't make deals.'

Enter the TARDIS.

'Very well.' The Doctor surveyed the quadrangle one last time. 'This should give the American tourists something to talk about. Benny, Tom, you're needed, I believe.'

'Me?' said Tom Cheynor, who had been wondering when he could go for a strong pint in the Turf and pretend it had all been a very misguided Rag Week stunt. 'Why the hell me?'

'You are the link with the past and the future.' The Doctor glanced at the Time Soldiers. 'Isn't that right? The Time Focus. A door, so to speak.'

The soldiers were silent. The Doctor gave them a knowing smile and stood back to allow Bernice and Tom past.

Benny stopped and looked deep into the eyes of the man who so often had put her life in danger. And who then saved her, only to throw her into yet another life-and-death struggle. It had always been challenging, up until now. It had even sometimes been fun. Living the past was even better than digging it up. But quite what the Doctor had dug up now she didn't care to speculate. Especially after last time.

'I've just got this awful feeling that people are going to die again,' she said quietly. 'And you know it.'

'If I could stop people dying,' said the Doctor sadly, 'I'd not be here now.'

'Ace understands you even less than I do, you know.'

'I know.'

'Where is Ace, by the way?'

'Safe.'

The Time Soldier crackled threateningly. Bernice glowered at it, then gave one last, meaningful look at the Doctor before she entered the TARDIS.

Tom was looking at Rafferty. 'Professor, tell the Doctor I can't go. Tell him we've got a tutorial together on Wednesday. Anything. Please!'

'Tom.' The Doctor's voice was quietly commanding. 'You're no longer safe in Oxford.'

And Tom Cheynor realized that this was the first thing the Doctor had said which made sense. He looked the police box up and down, shaking his head, and then walked inside.

The Time Soldiers, moving faster than Rafferty or Terrin could see, closed like a sea of energy around the TARDIS and the Doctor. Their hissing voices clearly indicated who was supposed to remain behind.

The Doctor looked from one to the other. 'Professor,' he said. 'Captain. You still have a part to play. Remember the river bank.'

The wall of green light around the TARDIS was thickening. The Doctor was vanishing into the fog like a phantom, and like some kind of fluid, the blur of the Time Soldiers swept after him. Rafferty and Terrin stood back, watching open-mouthed. The light began to fade, taking the outline of the TARDIS with it. There was a loud, trumpeting noise in the quadrangle, echoing from the walls of the Hall and the Chapel. It lingered long after the TARDIS had gone, whispering away into nothingness.

Rafferty and Terrin turned at the sound of running footsteps from behind them.

The astonished face of Harry, the porter, was gazing at the lawn where the TARDIS had been. Slowly he turned to look at Professor Rafferty.

'I suppose it's a Faculty thing, Professor?' he asked, with a strangely glazed expression. 'If it's a Faculty thing, I won't be asking, like.'

Harry had seen a lot of odd things in these past few days. It seemed almost normal that Rafferty should be accompanied by a tall man in what looked like some kind of futuristic military uniform, who had adopted a posture owing not a little to the martial arts.

'Is he on your side, Professor?' asked Terrin.

'What? – oh, yes, calm down, old fellow.' Rafferty patted Terrin on the shoulder as the latter straightened up, relaxing. 'I must apologize for my friend, Harry,' said Rafferty in a conspiratorial voice. 'He's from the twenty-fourth century.'

'Ah,' said Harry, who was wondering whether he ought to be relieved about this. 'I'll, er, leave you to get on, then.' He nodded to the Professor and the Captain, and plodded back in the direction of the Porter's Lodge, where the Dean of Decrees was looking for his mail and a congealing tea was waiting to be eaten.

'All right, Professor Rafferty,' said Terrin levelly. 'I suppose I have to accept that I am where you say I am. Now what are we going to do?'

The human capacity to focus on the relevant can sometimes be amazing. Two time-displacements in one day – the second considerably greater than the first – might have been enough to send a lesser man scurrying for the safety of a corner where he could gibber in peace. Romulus Terrin, whose mind truly did try to be broad despite the occasional high-banked channel of prejudice, had assessed the situation and decided not to let it worry him. His immediate thoughts, as before, were with the inhabitants of Q4 and the crew of his own ship – despite the fact that they were all four hundred years in the future. It was a concept he was happy enough not to try envisaging. He settled for thinking of them as merely distant, and now the need for action was manifesting itself in every cell of his body.

'You heard the Doctor,' said Rafferty with quiet satisfaction. 'That machine we arrived in is still parked on the banks of the Cherwell.'

Terrin took a large gulp of air. He wondered if all Earth air tasted of fossil fuel or if it was just this city. 'All right, Professor,' he said. 'Let's go.'

They ran to the porter's lodge, and turned sharp left.

As they dashed along the busy pavement, Terrin was impressed with Rafferty's pace and control of breath. Maybe twentieth-century man has something going for him after all, he thought.

Rafferty knew where he was going. They kept an even pace along the traffic-clogged Broad Street, till they jogged into Turl Street beside the Paperback Shop. Groups of students were gossiping beside their bicycles at the entrances to Exeter and Jesus – Rafferty hoped very much that they were none of his. Except for exams and formal Hall, he rarely wore his full academic subfusc, and did not usually make a habit of dashing about the streets in it.

He suddenly noticed he had lost Terrin, and looked wildly around for him in panic. In a city like this, you could get lost for ever.

He was there, gazing raptly in at the window of the bookshop behind them. Rafferty raised his eyes in a helpless and unaccustomed appeal to the heavens, and jogged back to the Captain.

Terrin was pointing. 'An original A. S. Byatt,' he was saying in wonderment, 'on *paper*. And the Larkin letters. Have you any idea how much these would fetch in my century?'

Rafferty was rather heartened, but something was yelling in his mind, telling him to get a move on. 'Literature has a time and a place,' he said. 'Come on.'

And he almost had to drag Terrin away. The Captain had a kind of wistful melancholy about him, James had decided, almost as if he were obsessed with recapturing the past, but right now they had no time to stop and think.

They ran the length of the street, and caught their breath at the corner.

Terrin was gasping. 'You know... Professor Rafferty...'

'James, old chap ... Call me James.'

'James ... I really ... must get myself back on that fitness course ... when I get back to the ... ship. Some more ... fencing with my ... first officer.'

188

Rafferty straightened up. His heart was beating at a healthy rate, he noticed, and he was really quite enjoying himself. 'You're doing very well for someone not used to our atmosphere,' he said kindly. 'When all this is over, you and I are going to have a good chat. What makes it all the more fun is that you really shouldn't be here at all, of course.' He grinned disarmingly, like a man twenty years younger.

Terrin, breathing deeply and bent almost double, managed a smile. 'Don't worry. I'm not going to go treading on any butterflies.' A thought suddenly occurred to him. 'James – are you going to know how to operate a Space-time capsule?'

It took Rafferty a second or two to realize that the question was meant in deadly earnest.

Chapter 21

Control

'A wanderer is man from his birth.
He was born in a ship
On the breast of the river of Time.'
                          Matthew Arnold, *The Future*

Shadows.
His mind intrigues me as I draw my strength through the telepathic link. So much of it is half-hidden, like a spiral staircase into a dark tower.
Where do these images come from?
Where do these thoughts come from?
I know things I once did not know. I feel things I once could never have felt. I am almost part of the real world again. With each death, with each bite into the substance of the Vortex, I grow in power and vision.
But do I gain more from these humans than I had at first realized . . .?
Soon, all of creation will be mine.
I have no time for such idle philosophy.

'I've got a headache,' muttered Ace.

Strakk, slumped with her against the navigation console, shot her a brief look of sympathy. 'Don't worry. Pretty soon it won't matter any more.'

Some of the crew had been overcome by exhaustion and were slumped in their chairs or across consoles. Time Soldiers hovered, restless, near every one of them. Cheynor was the only human still standing up. Ace was beginning to wonder if strain and tension were his bread of life. She didn't think she'd seen him let up even once so far, but she supposed it was his ship now, and that he felt responsible.

The Garvond throbbed with energy. Ace wondered what the creature was thinking.

Its tangible darkness seemed to have spread tendrils into every corner of the bridge now. Chattering and rustling swept through the circuits of the consoles, fizzed in the air like radioactivity. Its skull burned with anger.

'It's heading for something,' Strakk muttered. 'Building up its strength.' He sighed. 'Wish the Doctor's message had been clearer. I suppose the transmitter on Q4 was just totally fragged. Shame.'

Ace was stony-faced. 'It wouldn't have helped. He's going to get us all killed, whatever happens.'

Strakk grinned weakly. 'Sounds to me like you and the Doctor have a great working relationship.'

'We did have. Something went wrong. I'm still trying to understand it. I think that's what the Doctor wants. For me to understand him.'

'And how are you doing?'

'He doesn't realize I know him too well. And that it doesn't make things any better.' She shook her head, as if trying to clear it of such thoughts. 'Sorry.'

The ship juddered, bouncing them up and down. Larsen, shaken from sleep, stirred above them with a groan, and they heard the crackle as a Time Soldier moved to cover him.

'Ace,' Strakk muttered, looking over his shoulder. 'I think these guys are edgy.'

'I reckon you could be right.'

They exchanged a glance.

The ship thundered on through the Vortex.

Approaching it now, in the realm where Time and Space were meaningless, came a blue police box.

Within the TARDIS, the Doctor had his hands poised at the console, but appeared not to be doing anything.

Bernice and Tom were seated in armchairs which had somehow appeared underneath the scanner screen. The time rotor rose and fell with a rhythmic breathing which was not that of the TARDIS, and the red glow which had earlier suffused Epsilon Delta's Type 102 cast devilish hues over everything. The Time Soldier guards were little more than smudges of light hovering above the console, but for the Doctor, Benny and Tom it was unsettling enough to know they were there.

Bernice cleared her throat, wondering if the Time Soldiers could hear her. 'I don't suppose you're actually in control any more, Doctor?' she asked, with her eyes wide and her chin poised on one finger.

'Control?' The Doctor looked up, his expression still bleak. 'It takes more than just observation of the moment to tell who's controlling whom.' He cast a wary glance at Tom Cheynor. 'Isn't that so, Tom?'

The young man appeared confused. 'I suppose so.'

They sensed the redness shimmering. Laughter, as if from a fissure into Hell, boomed in the console room. And then they heard the voice.

I know your weaknesses, Doctor. You forget, your mind is pitifully open.

'This creature can read your mind?' Tom was astonished.

'It *is* my mind. At least partly.' The Doctor did not meet Tom's eye. 'It's routing its power through the TARDIS' telepathic circuits.'

Bernice was struck by a thought. 'What did you do with the cross-check circuit you were talking about? The link with Ace?'

The Doctor put his hands behind his back and looked a little shifty. 'There was one?'

'Yes! You put a telepathic link into her mind, and the TARDIS wouldn't trust you, only her. You have a very convenient memory sometimes.'

'And so does the TARDIS.' The Doctor glanced up at the blur of the Time Soldiers, as if wondering how much he dared say. 'I was – reconfiguring – while we were in

Oxford – some of it in unorthodox ways. That circuit was one of the first to go. I smashed it.'

'You did *what*?'

'Don't worry. It's all been selective, constructive vandalism.'

Bernice looked horrified. 'I thought you were trying to realign the TARDIS with the old pattern. Well, the new pattern. You didn't tell me you'd taken a hammer to the poor thing!' She shook her head in despair. Only the Doctor, she thought, could get himself into so much complicated trouble during what had been, for her, an absence of less than a few hours. It was suddenly brought home to her, in a sudden, shocking jolt, that a whole multitude of happenings in other places and times could have separated the Doctor's departure from Oxford and his reappearance in the President's TARDIS. And he still hadn't really explained what he'd done with Ace. Benny was not even really sure she wanted to know.

The Doctor shrugged. 'I had other things on my mind. Besides, destruction can be a dynamic force. And you only perceive it with hindsight.'

'So – ' Bernice looked from the console, to the Doctor, to the incandescent Time Soldiers. The implications of the Doctor's action were simmering in her mind. She could feel that when they came to the boil, someone or something was going to get hurt. She decided not to put the question she had been considering, and instead asked, 'So where are we going?' She received no answer, and slumped back into the chair with a sigh. She glanced at Tom. 'Doesn't all this make you wish you'd read Sociology instead?'

Your efforts mean nothing, Time Lord.

The Doctor glared defiantly at the lights above the console. 'We're not finished yet, Garvond. Don't fly too near the sun.'

It was then that Bernice felt a familiar chill grip her as the sound she had heard in Oxford rippled through the console room. Twittering, like a thousand angry birds in a cavern.

And with the sound, the time rotor began to slow.

Rafferty and Terrin hurtled down the path towards the black Porsche, ignoring the stares from the pub terrace.

The police constable – a real one this time – who had been hovering by the car for the past ten minutes looked up expectantly as the two men careered towards him.

'Now then,' he said, poised to pounce. 'Which of you gentlemen is the owner of this vehicle?'

Rafferty and Terrin glanced at one another. The Professor was uncomfortably aware of their eccentric appearance.

'It's mine,' said Rafferty. 'I, ah, didn't realize this was a no-parking zone. Terribly sorry.' He shrugged, and gave his best after-dinner smile. He was aware that Terrin was slipping round the other side of the car. Please, James Rafferty was thinking, just let the door be open. I'll do anything as luck's payment. Even the first-year calculus revision class. Even another Faculty drinks party.

The policeman sighed. The look he gave Rafferty was a mixture of disdain and despair as he unfolded his notebook. 'Name, sir?'

'Look, tell you what – I'll get my licence. It's in here.'

And he grasped the handle of the jet-black door.

In less than a second, the policeman had seen the twin flashes of movement. The door slammed in his face. He hammered on the tinted window, shouting angrily.

Then he straightened up.

Lateral thinking, he said to himself, with a smile on his face. That was what the Sarge always said. They couldn't sit there forever.

He grinned at the setting sun.

It was reflecting very beautifully in the car's glossy exterior. Nice looking motor, he thought in approval. Shame it's driven by a joker.

He was still engrossed in such thoughts when a mechanical screeching began to emerge from the car's bonnet. Shocked, he took a step backwards.

A few seconds later, it was perhaps fortunate that there were no witnesses to the young constable's expression.

Tension hummed in the Doctor's TARDIS. The Doctor, pacing around the console with his hands clasped behind his back, paisley handkerchief trailing from one finger, would occasionally glance up at the still time rotor, and then at the nimbus above it. Each time, his expression showed deep contempt.

'Doctor,' Tom asked, 'what are we doing?'

'Waiting,' said the Doctor. 'For a signal.'

Tom slumped back into his armchair. 'Why does it need to wait?' he muttered.

'Perhaps it's tea time,' Bernice suggested. 'I could murder some scones myself, actually.'

The Doctor had directed his unnerving gaze at Tom once more. 'I doubt there'll be honey still for tea. No jam either, not today, not tomorrow. Never, with the Garvond.' He rounded the console till he was level with Tom, and narrowed his eyes as he looked down at the young man. 'Myself, I'm fond of almond slices. I don't have much time for anyone who doesn't like almond slices.'

'Oh, I adore them,' said Tom somewhat uncertainly.

'Of course you do,' said the Doctor, whose tone had not changed. He straightened up and resumed his circling of the console. The nimbus throbbed for a second, then resumed its shimmering. Shadows grew in the corners of the console room. 'Of course,' the Doctor continued, to no one in particular, 'toffee is the most useful confectionery for analogies. Have you ever seen a mechanical toffee-maker?' He whirled round to face them, looked from one to the other. Bernice and Tom appeared equally bemused. 'It stretches the toffee in one direction,' the Doctor spread his hands wide, 'then slaps it together again.' His palms came together with a resounding smack. 'Then it stretches the two-layered toffee,' he said, his eyes wide and bright, the Time-energy nimbus reflected in them. Bernice was beginning to wonder if the Doctor had spent a little too much time indoors on his own recently. 'And so on,' he concluded, gripping the edge of the console with both hands. 'And if you have sufficient resources – and sufficient stupidity – you can do the same with Time. Points which start close together can end up far apart. Aren't you familiar with Smale?' This last comment was thrown at Tom.

'Of course,' the young man said, relaxing a little at the mention of a mathematician whose work he had studied. 'The chaos of dynamical systems. Squeezing and stretching space until you're left with something multi-layered and unrecognizable . . .' He broke off, going very pale. 'Doctor, are we going to stop this?'

'It's possible,' said the Doctor darkly. 'But if you want the right answers, you have to learn to ask the right questions.'

'Or vice versa,' Bernice put in.

The Doctor glowered at her. She smiled placidly back. The non-verbal exchange could have meant a multitude of things, and Bernice, behind her smile, could tell they weren't going to get many of them sorted out much before this was over.

The familiar twitterings of the Time Soldiers filled the console room. As they watched, the nimbus grew to a dazzling intensity before splitting into two Time Soldiers once more. Almost solid, they hovered above the console like angels of death, then slowly floated to the floor, their red eyes glowing with hate.

Above their restless noise came another sound, which for Benny was even more familiar: the low hum of the TARDIS doors opening.

Vaiq was sitting in her office, with her hands curled round a chilled glass of fruit juice.

Her intercom buzzed. Wearily, she took the call.

'Vaiq here.'

'Helina?' The voice was that of Ballantyne. 'You're never going to guess what we've detected.'

'Surprise me.' Her head was aching again. She closed her eyes briefly, and saw images of fire.

196

'It appears to be a rogue energy source. Approaching, but not on any scheduled flight path. And if I were you I'd come to the control centre, because there's something else I'd very much like you to explain.'

Something told Helina Vaiq that the Doctor's words were about to start turning into reality.

'Look!'

The voice was Cheynor's. As Ace, Strakk and one or two others leapt to their feet, the Time Soldiers clustered defensively around the oblong shape that was forming next to the Garvond's throne. Their blasters covered a wide arc. Ace swallowed.

Silent, veiled in green light, the TARDIS shimmered into solidity on the bridge of the Survey Ship *Icarus*.

Ace's fist clenched at her side and something welled up inside her, a mixture of dread and excitement.

'He's here,' she said. 'The Doctor's here.'

As the glow faded from the TARDIS, the Garvond gave a deep-throated roar of triumph. It billowed through the clouds of Time and shook the bridge, and they felt it rock the floor beneath their feet.

Bernice was the first to emerge. She shoved her hands into her pockets and sniffed. 'Bit stuffy in here.' She glanced around. 'Hello, Ace. Glad to see we haven't mislaid you.'

'Yeah. Cheers.'

'You know this person too, right?' was Strakk's contribution.

Tom was behind her. He stopped, blinked a couple of times. 'Oh, well,' he said eventually, in a very small voice. 'In for a penny . . .' He stepped out on to the podium, giving the Garvond very nervous glances, before he descended to the main floor of the bridge.

Darius Cheynor's incredulous gaze had been on him from the very first second.

The Doctor had emerged. He nodded to the Garvond. 'Oh, very pleasant,' he spat in its general direction. 'Very theatrical. Only a couple of millennia out of date with your cultural references, but not bad.'

He looked around the room. Ace hoped he was seeing what she would. Tiredness, hunger, the hostage look. Faces of people coming to terms, people getting a grip. She hoped the Doctor appreciated it all, what people went through.

There was silence on the bridge, except for the distant thunder of the engines.

The Doctor descended the Captain's podium and none of the Time Soldiers stopped him. He nodded to Strakk. 'Lieutenant.'

Strakk acknowledged him wearily. 'Hadn't forgotten you, Doctor.'

The Doctor gave a smile as dazzling as it was brief. 'Sorry I couldn't return the favour.' He turned to Cheynor, who was still staring intently at the third occupant of the object that had materialized on his bridge. 'Acting Captain Cheynor, I believe. Captain Terrin sends his regards.'

Cheynor's eyes widened. 'You mean . . .?'

The Doctor nodded silently.

He looked at Ace. She could sense he was trying to read her again, to see her reaction to this latest reunion. 'We have to go on a journey,' he said softly.

It was perhaps unwise that Ace chose that particular moment to look over the Doctor's shoulder at the looming skull of the Garvond.

And remembered the darkness.

Falling, with the Doctor standing over her.

'Yeah,' she said, and the inside of her mouth felt dehydrated. 'Tell me about it.'

All eyes were on the Doctor. He turned, slowly, to face his adversary.

'So,' he said, 'here I am at last. We have had fun and games, haven't we? There must be simpler ways. Couldn't you simply have challenged me to a game of chess? Or ping-pong?'

You over estimate your own importance, Doctor.

'I think not.' The Doctor had somehow gained a radius

of floor-space around him. Ace realized he had done it again. That great attention thing. He leant on the dome of the tracking console and met the Garvond's empty stare. 'Remember, there is some corner of a Garvond's field that is forever – ' The Doctor tapped the side of his own head. 'Doctor.'

The Garvond's hiss was electric. The three nearest Time Soldiers blazed dangerously in harmony with their master's anger. Ace met Benny's gaze across the bridge. She knew they were both thinking the same. If he pushes it now –

'I thought I had put right my error,' said the Doctor softly. 'I broke a rule, but then you know that. A rule that no other Time Lord dared break. Or at least I will. Will have done. And I erased my own print from the Panotropic Net in the Matrix.' He drew breath. 'I knew you'd come. A creature of legend, oh, but so true. So real. Ever since that time I saw the *Ancient Law*, back when I was dealing with that Skagra business. I saw my part in your creation *and I destroyed you!*'

Something very odd was happening to Tom Cheynor.

The Garvond's breath was like audible fire, like the clouds gathering before an electric storm. It grew in size and brightness, its throne filling the black globe and rising now, like a bubble lighter than air.

The humans cowered. Even Ace, trying to stand her ground, felt her feet pull away. She saw the shattered skull in her mind again, heard the screams and the exploding of bone after bone. All life, all death, passing in an instant. With power unimaginable.

She felt an arm steal round her waist. It was Strakk. Whether giving comfort or seeking it, she did not know. She held him anyway.

You may have thought me destroyed, once. The Garvond's voice was like clashing rocks, booming in an underworld where demons rose from ancient sleep. *But now . . . I am reborn!*

Tom Cheynor had turned to face them all.

'Doctor!' Bernice cried. 'He's – '

'The Time Focus,' the Doctor growled. 'Back! Everybody back!'

The TechnOps needed no second bidding. They surged away from the looming Garvond.

As they watched, the creature gathered itself like a cloak of night, its bubble distorting into a new shape. A finger of fire and darkness reached out towards the crowd of humans. And then, in one sudden inrush, it happened. A javelin of black light hit Tom between the eyes and he stiffened in silent pain. For a second, his body was surrounded by a halo of possession, the time energy's deadly sparkle.

No longer under its own control, the body of Tom Cheynor turned to face the assembled crowd. His eyes were burning with green fire. There were lines around them. Lines etched by age and pain which had not been there before.

The ships of Time. The Garvond. And the Focus. The parts were all assembled, the power surging into the Vortex. Detonation was imminent.

Surrender, Doctor.

The mouth which moved was Tom's. But the voice was still that of Garvond.

The control centre of Station Q4 was filled with the babble of TechnOps and the hum of holo-units.

Helina Vaiq blinked when she saw the two figures standing with Ballantyne on the other side of the Itopian Helix display. One she recognized as Romulus Terrin, looking slightly more controlled but also more haggard than when she had last seen him. The other was an extraordinary sight. The striking, intelligent face of a fit-looking man in his fifties was rather undermined by the outlandish clothes he was wearing – a black costume with a butterfly-shaped tie at the neck, adorned with what appeared to be a broad and baggy-sleeved black cloak with a fur hood. The man, whose arms were folded, glowered at her defiantly as she looked him up and down.

Eventually, Vaiq turned to Terrin.

'How did you get back here?' she asked.

'Oh, you'll like this,' muttered Ballantyne as he strode past. 'You'll like this a lot. Orbit stations!' he yelled, striding towards the far end of the centre. 'I want that data-shot in twenty seconds!'

Terrin scratched his nose. 'The same way we came, actually. That machine was pre-programmed to return to its last destination, as James here found out rather haphazardly.'

'I knew what I was doing, old chap. I am a friend of the Doctor's, you know,' the man called James reproached him.

'Anyway,' Terrin said, 'one of your security thugs met us in the lift. Charming people. This is James Rafferty, by the way. He's a professor at Oxford. Or at least, he was, some time in the 1990s.' Terrin was obviously enjoying himself.

James Rafferty gave a brief bow. 'Delighted.'

'I see,' said Vaiq, who had decided that she had better appear to have grasped the situation. 'And where might the Doctor be?'

Terrin and Rafferty looked at one another in a rather guilty manner.

We control the Time Focus and your TARDIS. You have lost. Surrender, Doctor. Or I shall blast the years away from these humans one by one. Their ages withering, peeling from them like onion skins.

'It's horrible,' Bernice whispered. 'He's not that creature. He's a human being . . .'

'We are both old, Garvond,' whispered the Doctor. 'With age should come wisdom. There's more beneath the skin of an onion than you think.' He spread his hands wide. He gave a slow, melancholy smile. Then he tipped one forearm down slightly.

The key of the TARDIS came sliding out of his sleeve and into the outstretched hand of the Time Focus.

'You win,' said the Doctor softly. And he raised his hat to the ghoulish husk of a human before him.

He turned back to face his companions and the shreds of the *Icarus* crew.

'People have died,' Ace said, her voice low and threatening. She broke away from Strakk and faced the Doctor. 'People have died, and that's all you can do? To tell it that it's won? We all fought for our lives up here! All of us! *Where the hell were you*?'

The Doctor did not answer. Ace turned away from him and slammed herself up against the wall, fighting her emotions.

Strakk's hand rested awkwardly on her shoulder. She looked once. Saw the twisted flesh, the joints blasted by Time. She shrugged it off, with powerful anger.

The rustling and twittering began again as the Time Soldiers shed the last of their instability. Becoming whole, they screeched in deadly symphony, their outlines filling to opaque forms now. The tallest, the one who had killed Quallem and threatened Ace, swept to the first officer's chair and took the controls with consummate efficiency. On the screen, the swirls of the Vortex were beginning to stabilize.

Benny, outwardly more calm than Ace, was still full of confusion and questions. She could see the whole thing slipping away. It had started with mystery, and the company of James. She felt she could see it ending in horror once more. Soon, she thought, I have to do something about these glamorous illusions of discovering the universe.

She watched the Doctor, across the shadowed bridge.

She could hardly believe it when the Doctor caught her eye with his compelling stare, and then slowly and deliberately winked.

Chapter 22

Ships of Time

'I want visual!' Ballantyne was shouting. 'Visual, you idiots!'

Rafferty glanced down at Vaiq. 'It's awfully good of you to let me look round your century,' he said politely. 'I shouldn't really do this sort of thing, you know.'

She gave him a brief smile. 'If you're a friend of the Doctor's,' she said, 'then I wouldn't put anything past you.'

Romulus Terrin was staring at the central holo-globe.

As were many more of the unoccupied faces in the arena of the control centre.

A mother will pick out her own child, no matter how young, from the crowd in a kindergarten. And Romulus Terrin, Captain of the *Icarus*, had no difficulty recognizing the battered hull of his own ship slowly approaching Q4.

It took him just a little longer to realize what Ballantyne's next logical step might be.

He joined the supervisor at his console.

'Ballantyne. Whatever you do, don't shoot it down!'

The supervisor looked down at him with a withering expression. 'That action would be rather precipitate, Terrin.' He drew breath through his teeth. 'However, as it is on impact trajectory, I would suggest that we have to do *something*.'

Terrin shook his head. 'What the hell's been going on up there . . .? Didn't they get the Doctor's message?'

On the bridge, Bernice had sidled up next to the Doctor. He did not acknowledge her.

'What were you doing there?' she muttered.

'Surrendering, Benny,' answered the Doctor. 'As the Garvond ordered.'

Benny looked hard at him, or rather at his profile. 'Material isn't everything in the game,' she said. The Doctor remained impassive. 'You gave the Time Focus the TARDIS key. That's not a surrender, that's a sacrifice. Skewer movement. A clever pinning of the knight.'

There was the very slightest flicker of the Doctor's eyes towards her. She got the idea he might just have been impressed. 'Rodzynski versus Alekhine,' he murmured. 'Look it up some time.'

'I will,' Bernice answered quietly. 'If it works.'

The face which had once belonged to Tom Cheynor was blazing with energy. The hand of the Time Focus stretched out towards the Doctor and beckoned him towards the police box.

Come, Doctor. The time is now.

'Doctor,' said an urgent voice at his elbow. It was Lieutenant Strakk. 'Doctor, there's something I've got to tell you.'

'It'll keep, Lieutenant.'

Strakk was glancing nervously at the Time Soldiers manning their stations. 'I'm not sure it will, Doctor –'

But the Doctor had stepped forward to the TARDIS. 'Ace,' he said quietly.

She turned from the wall, faced him as if bracing herself to attack. Her face was cast downwards, lost in shadow.

The Doctor nodded sadly, as if something he knew had been confirmed. He paused at the door to the TARDIS, beside the Time Focus.

'Best of luck, everyone,' he said, and stood back to let the creature into his time machine. There was a rush of green light as the humanoid form blurred and slid through the doors like liquid. The Time Soldiers, chattering with excitement, glowed from within.

Strakk cast a worried look at Cheynor.

The acting captain did not appear to notice. He was

still gazing at the point where the young man had been standing, the young man who had so resembled him.

'I thought I'd seen this all before, Strakk,' he said. 'When it started. You realize what this means? It wasn't me that had lived it before. It was him.' Cheynor nodded towards the blue box. 'My ancestor.'

Strakk stared at his senior officer. 'Are you sure you're all right, sir?'

'No,' Cheynor murmured. 'I'm not. That's how those creatures were able to get such a precise fix on the *Icarus*. The race memory. The link between us . . .'

'Don't worry,' said the Doctor softly. 'The show must go on. They would always have found someone.' He raised his hat to the assembled crew, gave one last smile to Bernice and entered the TARDIS.

Ace moved so quickly that even the Time Soldiers were not there to stop her. She pushed Cheynor and Strakk out of the way, and with a determined leap she was inside the TARDIS as the doors slammed shut.

Bernice, Strakk and Cheynor slowly turned to look at one another.

The Time Soldiers were still absorbed in guiding the ship through the Vortex, and did not appear to have noticed, or did not care. The flickering lights and low twittering of their communication continued, above a confused babble from the TechnOps. Cheynor waved an absent hand to calm them down.

'I just hope she knows what she's doing,' Strakk muttered.

Benny shook her head. 'I don't,' she said. 'If she's not going to get the Doctor into trouble, then I hope she's got no idea at all.'

She fell.

In the first instant, the sickening wrench had grabbed her stomach and she knew she was plummeting through blackness, the dimensions losing shape around her. She felt the rush of air, steeled her body for an impact, hoping the combat suit would absorb it.

Dizzying lights, red and green, swirled around her.
And Ace, at high velocity, tumbled towards nothingness.

Chapter 23

Architecture and Mortality

The TARDIS had been watching, waiting. It had recoiled from the sentience whose power had coursed through its library, but it could do nothing to reject it. Even sending a warning was not necessarily a good move. For this TARDIS, plucked from a world where its owner had died a shattering death, did not trust this man who called himself the Doctor. How could it?

Many things had happened which it did not understand. And now its dimensions, over the last few weeks, had been twisted and turned like the layers of that multi-coloured cube which the Doctor used to enjoy playing with. It had even felt parts of itself taken away, sensed the patches of blackness and pain when they died.

It knew there had to be a reason.

And it sensed the reason had something to do with the creature whose tendrils it now felt gripping it once more.

The TARDIS shuddered as its dimensions undulated anew. Rooms lay scattered like confetti upon the waters, and now, more flotsam and jetsam came, riding the waves.

Ace felt herself smack into water and carry on falling, enclosed by chill, slowing. She floundered, unable to tell in the blackness if her eyes were open or closed. Then she felt her shoulder being grabbed, and her body hauled from above by a great strength.

She spluttered, moving to rub the water from her eyes as she straightened up.

She was dry.

The Doctor stood opposite her, watching her intently

and with a hint of concern. She spread her hands, looking uncomprehendingly at him and into the blackness beyond. She wondered whether she ought to say that there appeared to be nothing supporting her feet – or would she fall when she said it, like Bugs Bunny when he looked down and saw that he'd whizzed off the edge of a cliff?

The Doctor grabbed her hand. 'I might have known you'd try to follow. Don't you realize you could ruin everything?'

Ace was astonished. He appeared genuinely angry. She almost said that she hadn't been going to do anything so rash. That she just wanted to smash his world apart in fury when she saw him give the TARDIS key to the thing that used to be Tom Cheynor, after all they had done, after the hijack, and what had happened to Quallem and McCarran and Dr Mostrell. That it had only been something deeper, primal, an emotion wrenched out of her by the struggle with the Time Soldiers, that had made her want to act. To be where the solution was. She still wanted to scream at him that she had nearly died once too often.

Instead she kept her voice level. 'So what the hell's happened to the TARDIS?' She shook off his hand in undisguised irritation.

'A lot of things. But when I left Oxford with the Time Focus on board, I knew the risk I was taking.' He looked at her almost pleadingly. 'I'd set the architectural reconfiguration in motion some time ago. Now, I just triggered it to randomize. If there's anywhere I can trap the Garvond *eternally* . . .'

Ace went pale. She grabbed the Doctor by his sleeves and almost shook him. 'And what about us? Will we be trapped here too?'

The Doctor gave her that look she knew so well. The one which meant he couldn't or wouldn't answer directly. He appeared ghostly in the blackness. Like a Time Soldier. Ace shivered, with a sudden mental image of herself, too, transformed into one of these inhuman dimension-riders.

'It all depends,' the Doctor said softly, looking out into the blackness. 'When you're dealing with non-Euclidean space . . .' He winced and shook his head. 'I don't even know how many effective dimensions the TARDIS has – '

Ace was rapidly beginning to regret her curiosity. '*Effective* dimensions?'

An unearthly screaming shattered the void. Ace, her heart thudding, looked up. Discs of white were whirling above her like the lights in a nightmare ballroom. They were more than light, though; they had solidity, depth . . . Now they were starting to fall from the sky like autumn leaves.

They looked familiar. Ace suddenly knew why. They were surrounded by falling TARDIS roundels. She felt the Doctor tugging her hand, and now they were running, running with the Garvond's screeches of anger in their ears.

A staircase extended in a corkscrew under their feet, growing with each footstep. It swirled below them, like cream in black coffee. Ace saw that the Doctor was occasionally glancing at a device she recognized as his homing beacon, although she did not know how it would help. She just hoped he knew where he was going.

Strange objects, half-real, floated past them. Ace glimpsed a pair of shoes spinning off into infinity, and a couple of parchment scrolls on which she read, in Gallifreyan, the words, 'Certificate of Dimensional Engineering'. After them fluttered a paper bird, which she saw was actually a 'Viz' Christmas Special. Her head reeled.

The Doctor stopped, panting, making Ace come to a sudden halt behind him. He was making frantic alterations to the homing beacon.

Something made Ace turn and look up the staircase behind them. With a roar that seemed to shatter the space of the void, a figure loomed over the crumbling edge. Ace saw something glowing green and red, pulsing with energy, like a humanoid but now much taller. It bore the face and limbs of a man, vaguely familiar, but suffused with a deadly radiance. And the mouth . . . As it threw back its head for another triumphant roar, Ace saw, with astonishing clarity, the vicious teeth and the blackness that lay beyond.

'Doctor – '

'Quiet, Ace – '

'But Doctor – '

'Give me your computer!' he shouted, and hurled the homing device over into the void.

'What?'

'It's the only way to locate the library. If you give me your wrist-computer I can home in on the TARDIS circuits and get some order into this mess. Come on, Ace!'

His fingers shook with impatience. Above them, the Garvond/Time Focus was rearing up to pounce.

Ace realized this was no time to argue. She unclipped the computer from her arm and practically hurled it at the Doctor.

Ballantyne, Vaiq and Rafferty were all watching the same blip on a massive three-dimensional grid.

Behind it, dominating the control centre, was the huge and shimmering slab of the *Icarus*, the picture which the blip represented.

Rafferty was chewing at the inside of his lip. Doctor, he thought, this time you may just have taken too many chances.

Bernice Summerfield had been talking in a low, urgent voice to Lieutenant Strakk.

'Inverted the energy?' she whispered in fascination. 'And it was totally destroyed?'

Strakk shrugged. 'As I say. The beam got reflected.'

'Like judo,' Benny murmured. 'Turning your enemy's own strength against him . . .'

Strakk glanced over her shoulder at the vigilant crew of Time Soldiers. 'It's not a trick I'd like to try pulling off a second time. We were lucky to get away with it once.'

Benny thumped a fist angrily on the bridge floor. 'If only we could have told the Doctor.'

'I tried,' said Strakk helplessly. He rubbed his crooked

hand, wincing as another stab of rheumatism cut into him. 'So what are we going to do?'

'We have to get a message to Q4!' Cheynor was suddenly filled with one of his intermittent bursts of zeal. 'Tell them that these creatures can be destroyed.'

'What are they meant to do?' Strakk asked. Fear made his tone sharper than he would normally have dared. 'Get the windows at the right angle to set up the Galaxy's biggest heliograph?'

Bernice looked at the huddle of TechnOps, whose expressions ranged from fixed terror to uncaring exhaustion. They weren't going to get much help there. Then she swivelled to take in the shimmering Time Soldiers, each in a crew position, all working in harmony. All, if she had understood correctly, formed a giant entity with the ship and the Garvond. And were concentrating so hard that they had let Ace go . . . They could try sending a message. But what would it say? Think big, Bernice said to herself. She remembered the adrenalin rush of a fulfilled ambition. Think big and you get there. And suddenly, as if a curtain had been raised, a mad idea, inspired by a half-remembered article, took a bow inside her mind.

Bernice grabbed Strakk's arm. 'Lieutenant. Space stations can operate simple molecular deflection for asteroids, space debris and so on, can't they?'

Realization dawned on Albion Strakk. 'You know, she's right, sir.'

Cheynor had already started to shake his head. 'Impossible. To enclose the whole structure – to deflect a beam of accelerated particles – I'm no physicist, but the energy required would be phenomenal.'

'They can only try!' insisted Bernice. 'But we have to send a message to them without this lot – ' she jerked her thumb towards the Time Soldiers, 'getting an earful of it! I don't know about you chaps, but I've got very little desire to be turned into Miss Havisham for my pains.'

'There is a way . . .' Strakk murmured. He grinned suddenly, like lightning in a grey sky. His tired eyes were alight with their former fighting spirit. 'What the hell,' he whispered, flexing the fingers of his seventy-three-year-old hand. 'Who wants to live forever?'

There was a door hurtling towards Ace, like a train on invisible tracks. An old, oaken door with metal hinges. She grabbed it as it floated past.

'Doctor!' she yelled.

He whirled round on his step, still punching calculations into the computer. His eyebrows lifted. High above them, the Garvond roared.

'The library,' he said. 'It worked!'

'So are you coming, or what?' Ace wrenched the door from its frame and reached for the Doctor's arm.

They both vanished inside.

The Time Focus gathered itself and with a screech of triumph, leaped across the chasm.

The Doctor and Ace were hurrying between high banks of shelves. Ace was not especially surprised to hear the ghostly wind flutter the pages of the books, but she hadn't expected snow. The flakes fizzed and melted on the hot surface of her combat suit. Unbelieving, she looked down and saw that her boots were churning through at least twenty centimetres of crunchy whiteness. The thick spines of the books, within touching distance, were covered with a uniform, crisp layer of rime. So were the gravity pads, which floated just above the snow.

The Doctor, readjusting his tie, swivelled in a full circle. A book caught his eye on the shelf, and he pulled it out with a frown, rubbing the frost off the dust-jacket. 'I had no idea this was here.' It was called *200 Poems on The Transit System*. He threw it aside. 'This way,' he said, indicating an endless tunnel of bookshelves. 'Mark my footsteps!'

Ace nudged up the bodytemp regulator on her belt. Kicking up snow as she followed behind, she covered their rear with the Derenna pistol. Like Strakk before her, she thought there would be no harm in trying. And if old zombie-features showed his skull, Ace was going to be ready.

'Where are we going? And why?' It was as good a time as any to ask.

'The focal point,' said the Doctor, advancing slowly. 'The eye of the dimensional hurricane. The Garvond's like a vulture lured by fresh meat, only what it wants to peck at is the power of the TARDIS. Tied in with the *Icarus*, that would make it invincible.'

Ace, sweeping her gun in a wide arc, was finding it hard to keep her footing. Snow was covering her head and shoulders. 'Yeah,' she said. 'That's one thing that got me. If the bonehead can travel through time –'

'Yes.'

'And use Time as a weapon?'

'Yes.' The Doctor stopped and ran his hand along a row of frozen books.

'Then why,' Ace asked, coming to a halt, 'did it need to hijack the *Icarus*? It doesn't need a ship to travel in.'

'No. But it needs a circuit to complete.' The Doctor was studying readouts on the LCD screen of Ace's computer. He looked up at her through the snowflakes. 'The *Icarus* arrived in direct response to the situation on Q4. Now the Garvond's using it to create that situation. It's the kind of paradox that appeals to its twisted sensibilities.' The computer bleeped. 'Ah!'

A section of bookshelf swung out, and books scattered on the snow. One of them fell on Ace's foot, and as she picked it up she saw the title clearly: *Communications Networks and Temporal Rectification* by Prydonian Chancellor Parjtesa-Kalayethzor Rodan.

Junk had followed the books – balls of string, papers . . .

And, slowly toppling, a rusty pushbike.

The Doctor shook his head sadly. 'Entropy.' He turned and, for a moment, fixed Ace with a deep and compelling gaze. 'I never worry too much about it, you know. Dissipation produces a complex system of conflicting motions. Eventually the behaviour of many dimensions is reduced to one.'

'Is that good or bad?' Ace was edgy, still covering their tracks with the Derenna, and trying not to look at the fallen bicycle. She knew only too well what it brought back.

The Doctor blinked.

'Come on,' he said, and stepped into the opening.

The Time Soldiers' excitement was mounting. Their leader, seated now in what had been Terrin's chair, received messages from the others and from the Garvond. Its visor glowed with blood-lust.

The target is almost in range.

Bernice and Cheynor heard the voice clearly in their minds.

Cheynor shut his eyes for a second. Bernice did not know it, but there, momentarily, he had glimpsed the hand of his brother sinking into the mud once more.

Beside them, Strakk, in as casual a manner as possible, was repeatedly tapping the call button on his communicator. If any of the Time Soldiers had detected him, they would probably not have known what to make of the pattern of short and long strokes that he was sending out on the standard frequency.

The oaken door of the TARDIS library shook to the impact of a blow, then shattered into a million shards of light.

The creature that lumbered into the snowy alcoves was neither fully human nor fully alien. Its body was a larger version of Tom Cheynor, but the eyes burned with the deathly light of the Garvond, and the skin glowed as if putrid. Also, its hair was a brilliant white to match the snow on the bookshelves.

Within Tom, the Garvond could sense its source of power growing closer. Its link with the *Icarus* throbbed within it, sensing ripples in the software, meters crashing over into the red as the ship of Time swooped down closer to its target.

Something was tapping at the back of the Garvond's

sinuous mind. A pattern of long and short clicks, in repeated sequence. It thought it should recognize the system, from long ago. But the Garvond had more pressing matters to attend to.

At one junction, it found the book of poems lying face-down in the snow, and a toothy leer spread across its face.

The hybrid began to advance through the snow, following the tracks left by Ace and the Doctor.

It knew it was only a matter of Time.

Chapter 24

Undiscovered Country

'West of these out to seas colder than the Hebrides I
  must go,
Where the fleet of stars is anchored and the young
  star-captains glow.'
  James Elroy Flecker, *Golden Journey to Samarkand*

'Picking up a message from *Icarus*, Supervisor.'

Ballantyne was at the young operator's side in a second.
'Coded?'

'Yes, sir.' The young man's face was incredulous. 'Sir,
it's Morse.'

'Well, decipher it, man!'

The operator was shamefaced. 'I'm afraid it's not one
of my codes, Supervisor.'

Terrin cleared his throat. 'I did once do a course on
archaic ciphers,' he said. 'Only a day, though.' He turned,
looked up in hope at Rafferty. 'James?'

The Oxford Professor of Extra-Terrestrial Studies
rubbed his hands together with a slight squeaking sound
which set Terrin's teeth on edge.

'I can see,' said Rafferty, 'that you chaps still have a
few uses for the skills of pre-technological Man.' He held
out his hand for the TechnOp's headphones. 'Let's have
a bash, then, young fellow. Can't do any harm.'

On the screen, the *Icarus* continued to advance.

The Doctor stopped.

Ace skidded and almost fell on the snow.

'Now what?' she snapped.

Behind them, the heavy footfall and roars of anger were growing louder.

'Here,' said the Doctor. 'Look.'

She peered over his shoulder. The floor fell away, becoming stone-covered steps. Warmth gushed upwards, hitting her full in the face, and she heard the sound of trickling water. She saw it now. Light was fragmented in the ornamental fountain at the foot of the steps, and reflected in the pinkish marble of the flagstones. Ivy and other indistinguishable plants hung from the stonework.

'The reconfigured cloisters,' said the Doctor grimly. 'Come on. Let's get this over with.'

He ran to the edge of the water, followed by Ace. The marble echoed as if with the first footsteps in Time.

The Doctor stared impassively into the fountain. 'All right,' he said. 'We've found the source.'

Ace became aware of several things happening almost at once.

First, a noise behind her. She whirled round, ready to face the Time Focus with her blaster, but she found herself looking up the steps into the exhausted face of Tom Cheynor. The real Tom, with unlined skin, his hair its normal brown, his eyes devoid of the alien glare. He was leaning against the marble pillar – confused and nearly unable to support himself, but human once again.

She then felt herself grabbed with both hands, and found the Doctor's eyes looking urgently into hers. After a second his grip relaxed and his face lost its panic. Adrenalin turned to cramp in Ace's legs. She had just realized what the Doctor had instantly been looking for.

'Not in you,' he whispered, and his relief was genuine. 'So where . . .?'

And they heard the fountain change its note.

The water, glistening blood-red and emerald green, the colours of death on the battlefield, was being sucked into the centre of the fountain, as if Time were running in reverse. Around them, the cloisters darkened. Ace felt the marble throbbing beneath her feet. And then the water exploded from the nozzle, in a new shape.

'Oh no,' she murmured.

'...inversion.'

James Rafferty relayed the last word of the message, removed the headphones and let them dangle incongruously around his neck. He raised his eyebrows at Ballantyne, Vaiq and Terrin.

'Strakk,' Terrin muttered. 'Clever boy. It might work...'

Ballantyne was horrified. 'A force-field? Against a molecular accelerator? We'd need – '

'You'd need,' Terrin told him, looking him dead in the eye, 'all the energy this station can muster. Where are the deflector-fields usually regulated from?'

'Auxiliary control. But you – '

'Tell me how to get there, Ballantyne. Now!'

The supervisor hesitated. Somehow, Terrin sensed that he was still reluctant to try anything unorthodox.

Vaiq seemed to uncurl into action, snatching an instrument-box from a nearby rack. 'I'll take you there, Terrin.'

'You were just a carrier,' said the Doctor, in answer to Tom's unspoken question.

The boy stood by Ace, watching as water and space twisted into a towering figure. Sparkling like a mirror, its surface reflecting crackles of Time-energy, the Garvond grew as it drew its final strength from the power of the TARDIS.

The Doctor spread his arms out behind him. It was a simple gesture, but one which Ace knew. He was ushering her and Tom back, to protect them.

'I think,' the Doctor murmured, 'that I may have made another slight miscalculation...'

'What do you mean?' Ace hissed.

'The Garvond is integrated with the TARDIS.'

Ace looked up, up as if at a sheer cliff. The sparkling

Garvond stabbed at her eyes and she suddenly found she was meeting its hollow gaze.

It swooped.

Station Q4 was on red alert. The alarm echoed through its near-deserted walkways as Terrin and Vaiq ran, keeping pace with each other.

They leapt into the elevator, which took five seconds to convey them to the tiny auxiliary control centre of the station. Terrin saw an almost featureless room lined with slender consoles.

'You know where to look?' he asked, breathless.

She nodded curtly, tapping out a coded sequence on her wristband. A section of console pivoted, and the relevant hardware slid from its compartment into the room. Terrin saw a thick tube, bristling with circuit inlays and connectors.

'Field generator,' she said. 'We just have to persuade it to be a little ambitious.'

Terrin and Vaiq crouched opposite each other, one either side of the generator.

'If we don't get this rigged in time . . .' Helina Vaiq murmured, her dark eyes troubled, 'we could all be skinned and boned before we know it.'

Terrin shook his head, and grinned. 'I'm all right. I've been here next week, remember?'

Vaiq was making adjustments with a laseron probe, her face set with concentration. 'I reckon the Doctor would say that Time doesn't work like that.' She threw him another tool, which he caught instinctively. 'Patch in reinforcers to *all* the ectopic condensors on that side. And do it *fast*.'

Terrin gave her a a mock salute, and set to work with grim resignation.

The Garvond, looming in fire etched upon the water, directed its mental force. But Ace, steeling herself for the impact of blackness she had felt earlier in the engine rooms of the *Icarus*, sensed nothing.

Beside her, the Doctor cried out and fell to the cloister floor, clutching his temples.

He was in an open space, framed by concrete. Echoes bounced around him in the darkness. There was a noise, he made it out now, of dozens of revving engines, and a smell of fossil fuels. He stepped out, cautiously, feeling concrete beneath his toes, and the CityLink bus hurtled past him, thick-wheeled, dark-windowed. Heading out into oblivion.

The Doctor's hearts were pounding. He could see the Garvond, cowled and waiting like Death in Bay C of the bus station. So it was playing with him now. Playing off his deepest fears . . . Gritting his teeth, he strode out across the bus station concourse. He tried to ignore the lost luggage that swarmed like yapping dogs around his feet.

A table stood before the grinning skull of the Garvond. The Doctor, his face ashen, looked down.

The chessboard was of the highest quality pine and mahogany, beautifully varnished. Just a few pieces remained on the board, enough for the Doctor to recognize the paradigm, filched from his memory.

'Byrne and Fischer,' he whispered. 'Black playing the Gruenfeld defence.'

Just one game, Doctor. Always, it comes down to one set of moves, among so many. When you would explore, and play again and again..? Yes, I sense it now!

The Doctor gathered all of his weakening telepathic resources. But nothing, it seemed, could block out the Garvond.

Yes . . . not losing, no, that is not it. Rather the game left abandoned, of the enigma unsolved. The unexplored knowledge of the universe! There was a lilt of fascination in the Garvond's voice, an intrigued purr creeping into its inhumanity. *Yes, Doctor. THAT IS YOUR GREATEST FEAR!*

The Doctor was silent.

Around him, the bus station had shimmered into a dark

220

void once more. And towards him came another, familiar figure.

Ace had fought the tugging of her memories as long as she could. But now, the insistence of it overwhelmed her. She was no longer in the TARDIS cloisters with Tom Cheynor, shivering below a creature none of them seemed to know how to fight.

She was facing the Doctor.

He stood, pale, in a cone of blue light, his hands gripping the rail of the courtroom dock. And her own hands were tight around the butt of her gun.

Alight with unearthly power, the *Icarus* solidified fully, thundering on into the void.

On the bridge, the leading Time Soldier's fist clenched in triumph.

Our Lord Garvond has made contact!

The Time Soldier at the weaponry console seemed to shimmer with power, his hands uniting with the surface of the control panels.

Strakk exchanged a desperate glance with Bernice. She raised her eyebrows, as if coolly inviting him to do something.

You know he is guilty. You know he will betray you again.

The voice was lulling Ace, echoing in her mind like seagulls off a shore. She saw the faces of those she had known and loved, those who had died, and behind them, the agonized eyes of the scarred survivors. She saw death tearing through a world she had known as true and real, not too long ago.

She sensed the tears welling in her eyes. Meeting the Doctor's impassive gaze, she drew the pistol up.

The Garvond's voice became like a lead hammer, thudding into her brain. Riveting one single thought.

She fired, point-blank.

Around her, the water of the cloisters sprayed furiously onto marble, as the gun shattered into a million pieces.

* * *

Strakk's foot was curling, taking the strain. Bernice saw him. Her eyes said No. Alarmed, she looked at Cheynor for support. He was staring into space, distant, defeated.

Benny felt tragedy hurtling towards her in tangible waves.

When Strakk launched himself forward, she called his name, once, sharply, in anger.

He smashed into the weaponry operator's shoulder, and was hurled off in a blaze of sparks. He hit the deck at Benny's feet, just as the whole ship tilted, throwing the group of humans off-balance.

The engines were screaming now, blotting out all other sounds. All but one. The voice they had come to fear echoed round the bridge.

Target in range. Prepare for Time acceleration.

Vaiq's communicator hissed into life.

'*Vaiq! Are you ready? They're right on top of us! Now, Vaiq, d'you hear me?*'

'I hear you, Supervisor.' She snapped her panel shut. 'Just the final link.'

Terrin looked up. 'Right. So get out.'

Vaiq's face was hard with anger. 'We haven't locked into the main generator!'

'I know,' said Terrin. It looked, and sounded, as if this was something he had been planning for longer than Helina Vaiq could have known. 'When we lock in, there's bound to be massive molecular feedback. It's going to kick through every circuit in this room, and there's going to be one hell of a burn-up. The equipment wasn't designed for this kind of strain!'

She clicked her tool-kit shut. 'So we'd better not be in here.'

'Someone has to make that connection!'

'It would take two minutes at most to set up a simple remote – '

'We haven't got two minutes.'

'Terrin – '

'*Get out of here!*' he yelled.

222

For one brief, fragile moment, she saw the intensity in his eyes, and knew there was no use fighting it.

'Promise me you'll get out,' she said softly. 'If the relays give you time.'

He didn't look up.

Vaiq took a deep breath and slammed the elevator-control.

The hydraulic seal echoed with a snap of air, and she ducked out, her heartbeats shaking through her.

As the lift sped back to the upper levels, she swallowed hard. The fire was raging in her mind again, the intense, napalm-burn image, bringing burning tears to her eyes.

Somebody might have learnt how to fish today, Doctor, she said to herself.

'Come on, Ace!'

It was Tom Cheynor, pulling her roughly from behind, the water cascading all around them. Above, the Garvond was like a storm-cloud, etched in its own incandescent lightning, drawing its final surge of power.

'No!' she yelled. 'The Doctor!'

He was crouched on the soaking cloister stone, dwarfed by the time-creature.

The illusion had vanished around Ace when the gun shattered, and now she had realized what she had to do. It had come to her, in that split second when she'd realized she really was capable of pulling the trigger. She truly thought she'd done it.

So now, she just had to get him out of here.

Terrin could see the two zirconium connectors. All he had to do was slide one along the tube with each hand till they hit. Kissing with power in the centre. And there was no way of damping the feedback surge. Not now.

The communicator voice was yelling angrily at him, its sharpness driving into his mind.

He remembered Josh Kenley, his old friend, reduced to such a voice. His screams, filtered through the vacuum from that ghost settlement on Rho Magnus where he'd died. Coming out of the com-link grille, in the shuttle where Terrin had just hit escape velocity.

Screaming at him not to leave.

Only Kenley didn't know – had never known – that if he'd been taken back, then the berax spores that had infected his body would have killed the whole crew.

And Terrin would forever have been responsible for the deaths of two hundred. Instead of one.

He drew breath.

'Goodbye, Doctor,' he murmured. 'I wish I could come back to tell you what I find there.'

He slammed the connectors home.

Time can always be measured. There is a gap between a cause and an effect, no matter how small, even if no instrument in existence can measure it. But for Romulus Terrin, the effect could just as well have been truly instantaneous.

The white-hot burst tore the flesh from him, erupting outwards like an exploding sun. Black bones fountained up and cascaded in the glare, like nuclear ash. The walls of the auxiliary control room burned brilliant white.

And at the heart of the field generator, immense power coursed for one vital, inescapable second through the circuits.

The Time Soldier channelled *everything* that came pouring through its link with the Garvond.

Unstoppable, ripping Time apart in a beam of mutated molecules, the power flowed straight through into the weaponry subsystems.

Bernice, picking herself up from where she had fallen, saw the station in space on the *Icarus* monitor screen. And then, in the blink of an eye, she saw the beam.

It hit Station Q4's hub with an impact that should have ripped Time from its bonded steel, torn its infrastructure with the power of accelerated years.

Instead, the angry snake of Time-energy surrounded the station, picking it out for a millisecond in sharp relief like a great castle in a flash of lightning.

And then the power – the Garvond's energy of hatred, the blood of the Vortex, sent hurtling into space from its parasitic lair deep in the TARDIS – *came screaming back*.

Its point of impact was exactly the same as its point of origin.

The laser turret of the *Icarus*.

Benny, Strakk, Cheynor and the others grabbed onto whatever they could find when the shock slammed in.

Waves, torrents of green and red energy thundered through the bridge, moving at a tangent to real time, phasing by only a fragment of eternity.

Just like the Time Soldiers.

Benny was to remember afterwards that the discord of thrashing and screaming seemed to last forever.

Caught in the wash of their own inverted energy, the creatures were dismembered by jets of bright fire, by knives of light. The soldier at the weaponry console was first. Bernice saw it lifted high, almost to the ceiling of the bridge, screeching like a sacrificial animal. And then the time-winds whipped around it, slashing it to shreds, swallowing it.

The soldier nearest to Strakk opened its snout in a silent scream as Time-energy poured in. The creature's visored head exploded in what looked to Benny like a mixture of flesh and steel. And then the shower of shreds flipped into a two-dimensional plane, burning in a circle of red fire, and twisted away into infinity, falling like a stone cast into a bottomless pit.

The shrieks were pounding into Bernice's mind, battering her eardrums as they ascended towards the ultrasonic. In the haze of red and green, she saw Strakk trying to crawl towards her. He was holding one hand with the other. His mouth and eyes were open wide, she saw now, and he was screaming something about his hand.

All around the bridge, Time Soldiers were swept up in their inverted vortex, and consumed in spirals of phase-shifting fire.

* * *

'Well?' Ballantyne snapped.

Every system seemed to have gone down. The holograms were scrambled, like small storms of light in the control centre. Rafferty stood alone amidst the chaos, chewing on his index finger.

'We had power, sir,' called one of the TechnOps. 'It couldn't be sustained.'

'Was it long enough?'

The answer came from another operator. 'Energy source just relocated, Supervisor. Back to the survey ship.'

'Relocated,' muttered Professor Rafferty to himself. He wondered if that had other overtones, in the jargon of this alien century.

Another message came through. 'Major burn-out in auxiliary control. Dispatching fire drones to contain, sir.'

Ballantyne, from across the vastness of the Centre, dared to meet Rafferty's eye.

'They did it,' the supervisor said.

The Garvond bellowed in pain.

Ace gripped the Doctor's shoulders, trying to pull him back from the towering creature. He was pale, she saw. Maybe he really thought she'd done for him back there in the Garvond's virtual reality.

It dwindled now like a guttering flame. Its shrieks of anger were incoherent, a cacophony of tongues in many keys and at all levels of sound.

Energy seemed to rush in from all around Ace and Tom, passing them, uninterested, drawn instead to the vast magnet in the centre of the cloisters. A target. Bombarded with unremitting waves of its own energy, every burst of hate, the death of every Time Soldier crashing into it now with the power of ancient Time. And in the flickering tongues of light, it happened. The Garvond, its dragon-jaws forced apart in inaudible agony, whirled and shrank in its own typhoon.

The Doctor was struggling to stand. Ace saw that he was holding something out.

'What's he doing now?' Tom shouted. 'He'll get himself killed!'

Ace had no more idea than Tom. But she held him back, stopped him from pulling the Doctor aside.

She knew why. The Doctor knew what he was doing now. And what made Ace confident was one small thing that she thought she had lost.

Trust.

The Garvond, no more than a spinning globule of light, came to rest in the centre of the book that the Doctor held outstretched. Like a genie sucked back inside its own bottle, the Garvond vanished.

The Doctor snapped the book shut.

There was silence in the cloisters, except for the gentle splashing of the fountain and the drip, drip of water from the marble walls and the plants.

Ace and Tom climbed slowly to their feet. The young man pushed his soaking-wet hair back. He was wondering to himself if he would be able to get a decent hot bath in the very near future.

'Up the stairs,' said the Doctor with a smile, as he turned to face them. 'Second left, third right. Door marked with a small yellow duck.'

'Oh,' said Tom faintly. 'Right.'

'Doctor.' Ace's voice was low and urgent. She had taken her sunglasses off and was rubbing the splashes of water from them, but with her spare hand she pointed at the small red book he was holding.

'Oh, don't worry,' said the Doctor, as if suddenly realizing what she meant. 'He's back where he came from.'

Her mouth opened. She was wondering which question was the best one to put first.

'That's all you need to know!' the Doctor growled, and with a sudden burst of anger he turned and hurled the book into the fountain.

It was swallowed with an audible plop. But Ace knew it had not hit the water.

'Dimensional traps,' the Doctor muttered. He fished his hat out of his pocket and jammed it back on to his head.

'Nasty things. Lucky I never did take that book back to Gallifrey, though.'

Ace stepped forward, peered into the fountain. 'You mean the Garvond's –'

'These,' said the Doctor, 'are not the cloisters.' He sighed. 'Only I couldn't let you know that, or the Garvond would have read it in your mind.' He shook his head. 'It'll stay there now. Unless someone does something *very* stupid with the reconfiguration circuits.' He turned, and splashed back up the steps. Halfway up, he turned back to Ace and Tom.

'Well, come on,' he said. 'Unless you want to be stuck here for eternity too.' He took out his pocket watch, and his eyebrows shot up. 'Especially as it's almost time for a cup of strong tea and some almond slices.'

The bridge was like a granite shore after a storm, washed by the calamity, but unbroken.

There was a spontaneous burst of cheering as the Doctor and Ace emerged from the TARDIS: he had told Tom to stay in the console room. Benny, standing in front of the crew with her arms folded, just raised an eyebrow. The Doctor took it all in his stride, as usual. Out of the corner of his eye, he saw Ace's hand meet Strakk's high in the air, in a thump of victorious unity.

Cheynor stepped forward. He looked exhausted. Keeping a respectful distance from the Doctor, he folded his hands behind his back.

'What exactly happened, Doctor?'

'It would take far too long to explain the details,' said the Doctor quietly, leaning on his umbrella. 'I suggest you give Q4 a call. Captain,' he added, apologetically.

'Before that,' Ace put in, striding up to Cheynor, 'there's something I've been meaning to get you to do.' She held up her arm, showing him the limiter bracelet. 'Code-word?'

Cheynor reached out, rather awkwardly, and took her hand. 'Excuse me,' he said, and cleared his throat. '*Benedictus*,' he intoned.

The bracelet snapped open and clattered to the floor.

Bernice had strolled over to the Doctor. 'Feedback,' she suggested to him.

'More or less.' The Doctor's expression didn't change.

'Why didn't it affect us?'

'You're temporally stable. Most of the time. The Time Soldiers' waves were oscillating on their dimensional frequency. Hoisted by their own petard.'

Ace dropped into the Captain's chair, and put her feet up on his console. 'Zapped into infinity. Like our friend in the rec-room. Yeah?'

The Doctor nodded. His face half in shadow, he seemed to smile. 'Good,' he said.

Bernice's fringe was over her eyes, so the Doctor could not see them.

No, she was thinking. Not good.

Chapter 25

Reflections

They stood on a high platform above a cavern. Far below them, perched on a launch turntablc, squatted the grey shape, battered but intact, of the Survey Ship *Icarus*.

'Hides all sorts of things away, doesn't he?' said Benny. 'Fancy having one of these things in your cupboard-under-the-stairs.'

Ace was resting her chin on one hand, and with the other she was bouncing the yo-yo over the edge of the observation platform. She'd found the toy in one of the TARDIS's rooms of junk, and the Doctor didn't seem especially interested in it, so she had adopted it.

'Yeah,' she said. 'Pretty useful for the Survey Corps, having the Doctor help out. Being stuck a week behind yourself can't be much fun.'

When Cheynor and Ballantyne had exchanged official messages, it had not taken long before the embarrassing conclusion was reached – that the *Icarus*, thanks to its temporary occupants, was now in entirely the wrong time-zone. The Doctor, with only a minimum of fuss, had offered to arrange it. He'd said the TARDIS ought to be used to these short hops by now. The difficult part, he'd confided to Ace, had been materializing the TARDIS around the *Icarus* so that the Survey Ship ended up in somewhere that could accommodate it, rather than the swimming pool or the library, or skewered between walls.

'I suppose there must have been hundreds of casualties,' Benny ventured after a while.

'Everyone except the bridge crew,' said Ace quietly.

'And they lost three there as well. The Garvond wasn't joking.'

'And . . .' Bernice realised she was going to have to ask. 'Your friend?'

'No go.'

'No go? Come on, Ace, remember what the Doctor said. He's still got some time. A lot of time. And he's been promoted.'

'No, Benny. I mean I've spoken to him, and I'm not staying.'

Ace remembered.

He had sauntered over to her as they cleared up the mess on the bridge. There were more streaks of grey in his blond hair, while his bad arm was crooked and studded with med-implants.

With the other, he was holding a portable, suitcase-sized incubator. Under the perspex hood, baby Mostrell slept peacefully.

She acknowledged him with a grin.

'So,' he said, 'I'm condemned.'

Ace shrugged. 'You're one of the lucky ones.'

Strakk smiled. The same grey, bleak smile that she'd grown used to. 'Your friend seems to be a Doctor of everything. He gave me a look-over. Seems to think my body's ageing at twice normal rate at the moment, but that'll get faster. I might have . . .' He shrugged. 'Ten years in real time. At most.'

Ace was rubbing at an irritating itch under the sleeve of her combat suit. 'Yeah,' she muttered.

'Ironic that it's just my body. I can't get the experience at the same time.'

She shrugged. 'Lots of girls like older men,' she said with a feeble grin, but still didn't look directly at him.

He carried on, as if he hadn't heard. 'But, well, Cheynor's bound to get his own ship when we get back to Lightbase now, and he's pretty sure he can get me for his first officer, so long as I can manage it.' He sounded ridiculously cheerful. 'As for this old heap . . .' He thumped the nearest console. It was a tracking post. McCarran's. 'I'll miss her.'

Ace looked up. She couldn't see him clearly and she knew she was going to have to get out of the bridge, before she went and said or did anything stupid. It was crazy, but she knew she couldn't look at the blue eyes behind his grey quiff or she might end up staying after all.

'I have to go,' she said. 'You know that.'

Strakk rubbed his ear with his good hand. 'Yeah,' he said. 'Yeah, I know. I was just . . . passing time.'

'The Doctor hates goodbyes. Take one from me for him.'

'Will do.'

'You see – ' It was no good. She had to look him in the eye. 'I left him once before, a while ago, when something between us was half-finished. And even if I might end up topping him in a fit of rage, I can't walk out again.'

'I know.'

'I have to find out what he's about. I have to know what's really happening.'

'I know,' he said again.

She realized what he'd said. 'What?'

'I know you're going with the Doctor. He told me.'

Ace could have got angry. But she stored it. Maybe that would make sense later. Once it was really all at an end.

She nodded towards the baby. 'You got charge of him?'

He shrugged. 'I think I'm what they call *in loco parentis*. Until we trace his family.'

Ace smiled. 'Look after him. Not many people get a second go at life.' She sighed. 'That's why I have to leave in the TARDIS. I could be able to come back and see you. But with him – I only get one chance.'

Strakk seemed to understand.

Professor Rafferty's telephone was designed, he said, not to go off between twelve midday and two o'clock in the afternoon. It was what he called a lunchtime guarantee.

The Professor was serving the Doctor a plate of his

finest Parma ham and bean salad. Tom, in the other arm-chair in the study, was already well into his.

The Doctor was trying to explain something to Tom, with the aid of drawings on table napkins. 'You see, the force-field on its own wouldn't have been enough.'

'Why not?' Tom asked.

'The Garvond would simply have re-absorbed the energy and fired it back out with redoubled force. No, I had to rely on Q4's defences having been patched in by the time I had the Garvond trapped, where I wanted it. Where it couldn't use its power.' He heaved a deep sigh and leaned back. 'Poor Romulus. If I'd been there, of course, I could have shown him and Vaiq how to set it up on remote.'

'Helina was quite upset,' ventured Rafferty, passing the Doctor a knife and fork.

'Yes,' said the Doctor quietly. 'She'll get over it.'

There was a long, uncomfortable silence.

'Pleased to see you've got your appetite back, young Mr Cheynor,' said Rafferty dourly as he poured the Darjeeling.

The Doctor looked up from his first forkful. 'Voracious eating is perfectly normal in humans who've recently been possessed by alien entities, James. Replaces lost salt and protein. Take it from me.'

Tom nodded happily, and made indistinct noises of agreement.

'What, ah,' Rafferty ventured, handing the Doctor his cup of tea, 'what exactly *did* happen to him?'

'Ask him,' said the Doctor. 'He talks. Volubly,' he added with feeling, remembering Tom's incessant admiration of the TARDIS on their way back to twentieth-century Oxford.

Tom waved his fork in the air. 'It's fascinating, Professor.' He embarked on the same explanation which the Doctor had given him earlier. 'I was a channel between two unstable points in the space-time Vortex where the Time Soldiers were breaking through. And my link with the future was my great-to-the-power-of-something grandson, the acting captain chappie on the *Icarus* – who I was *forbidden* to talk to, I might add.' Tom glowered at the Doctor, who smiled inscrutably.

Rafferty sat down in his favourite chair. 'As usual, with the Doctor,' he said, 'nothing really makes sense when you look at it. I mean, you took those Survey Corps chaps home to base, in the right time?'

'Of course,' said the Doctor.

'And they were only sent out in the first place,' Rafferty said helplessly, 'to investigate a crisis on Q4.'

'Yes.'

'Which we averted.'

'Yes.'

'So they wouldn't have been sent out!'

'James,' said the Doctor, sipping his tea, 'you'll never progress until you forget all the *sensible* things you've learnt. Analyzing time-paradoxes from your armchair is like trying to read a book by staring at the dust-cover. Trust me. It works out.'

Rafferty shrugged. His hangdog expression seemed to have grown a little longer. 'I'd imagine all this has to be kept under wraps? People *notice* eccentrics who claim to have travelled in Time.'

'Even in Oxford?' asked the Doctor innocently.

'And another thing, Doctor – I've got to try and tell the Vice-Chancellor exactly why the President appears to have taken extended leave without notice.'

The Doctor leaned back in Rafferty's chair. He might have been smiling. 'Ah, yes,' he said. 'Epsilon Delta. You know, I think it's sad when a Time Lord doesn't realize he's as susceptible to Time as anyone. The Garvond offered him some sort of deal ... energy to revitalize his TARDIS, and then power over Earth and Gallifrey. He was convinced, by his own ego, that he was the Garvond's equal in the plan, when actually he was a pawn all along. One of his aliases, one he'd set up almost casually, was the Home Office Minister. It struck me when I had a good look at the photograph in the paper. And so all that time, the time-disruption that the President was plotting was his own assassination.'

'So he's dead?' Rafferty asked.

The Doctor spread his hands. 'He and Amanda fulfilled their purpose for the Garvond. They were disposed of, like everything else in the Garvond's way.'

'Am I meant to tell the Vice-Chancellor that?'

'I'm sure you'll think of something.'

'Hmm,' said Rafferty, and lapsed into a moody silence over his tea.

Tom leaned over to the Doctor. 'What's up with him?' he whispered.

The Doctor smiled. 'He's already said goodbye to Benny. I think that might have something to do with it.'

Bernice was sitting in the reading room of the Taylorian, deep in a copy of *Sur Racine* by Barthes. Even allowing for her fairly recent acquisition of pre-expansionist French, she wasn't all that impressed so far.

She sighed, put the book down on the pile beside her, which consisted of a copy of *Don Quixote* and a paperback, *500 Exciting Recipes with Root Vegetables*, that she'd found there on the table.

She took out a coin from her pocket, studied it. The head of the Queen, the year, 1993, and the words *Decus Et Tutamen* on the side. Tom had told her earlier that one of those could buy you two-thirds to three-quarters of a pint of bitter, or two packets of biscuits, or one-thirteenth of a compact disc. It was about to buy her something else.

Benny flicked the coin into the air, watching it spin through the dusty sunbeams. It reached optimum height, and began to fall.

This time, it was Ace who was standing by the pond in the Botanical Gardens. She was polishing an apple on her leather jacket. The shadow of a question-mark fell over her, and then the umbrella itself was planted in the gritty path at her feet.

235

'Reflections,' said the Doctor. 'They make you think backwards.'

She shrugged. 'They overestimated themselves. Didn't know their own strength could be turned against them.'

'Teamwork defeated them. Ours. Not that I'd get you to admit that just now . . . Anyway, that's not all I meant. The Time Soldiers were humanoids, once, you know. Or you'd guessed.' He held up a hand. 'No, don't say anything. Earth people, Gallifreyans, Tharils. Voyagers salvaged from the flotsam of Time, turned into ghosts. Shadows of themselves.' He tried to peer at her expression, frustrated as ever. 'That bothers me. It certainly ought to bother you.'

'They were evil,' she said, her voice flat. 'I saw what they did to Quallem and the others. They deserved to die.'

The rooks cawed high in the trees, and buses chugged in the High Street.

The Doctor took a deep breath of the November air again. 'Well, now I'm here . . . Out of all great evil must come something good, as someone said once. No, the Time Soldiers were pawns. The Garvond, that was an artificial creation. A creature feeding in all that was hated, feared. Nourished on minds from the Panotropic net and born through . . . a mistake.'

'You mean you thought you'd destroyed it.'

'Did I say that?' The Doctor pondered his reflection for a moment. 'Rather that I'd prevented it from coming into being. By removing something rather vital from the Net when I – ' He stopped. There were things which not even Ace was yet ready to be told. 'Well, never mind when,' he muttered a little grumpily.

The Librarian looked up sharply at the clattering sound.

Bernice made a gesture of apology, before looking at the coin.

Heads it was, then.

She returned the books, descended the stone staircase to the busy street, and headed back to St Matthew's.

236

There, in the quad where it had been left, the TARDIS was waiting for her.

There was silence for a moment in the gardens.

'It shouldn't have happened, you know,' he said.

Ace seemed irritated by his continued presence. She chomped into her apple.

'I knew you'd ask me what,' he said. 'Shuffling the pages of history, that's what.'

'Which you never do, of course,' said Ace indistinctly.

'This is different,' snapped the Doctor. 'First that alternative Earth with the Silurians, and then this. Those breakthroughs from a time-shift in Oxford shouldn't have happened. Nor should the Garvond's reactivation. *Not if everything was as I left it.*'

'Everything where?'

'In my past.'

There was another silence, broken only by Ace's munching.

'A pattern's emerging, Ace. Someone's playing games. Only this time I haven't been explained the rules.' The Doctor drew air in through his teeth. 'I may have to invent my own. Something that can control the Garvond can't be a fair player.' He turned to go. 'What are you doing now?'

'I'm going to the Queen's Lane coffee-house. Tom's promised me breakfast.'

'Don't be too long. We leave within the hour.'

He strode away, his mind a whirl of thoughts.

This time, the Doctor had cleared parking permission with the Head Porter, provided that he didn't use the grass.

He stroked the paintwork of the police box affectionately. 'Things will go better,' he murmured. 'You'll see.'

He took the key out and inserted it into the lock. We are both old, he thought. An Earth saying had come into his mind – 'Something old, something new . . .' How did it go after that? Then he remembered, with the result that he was wearing a broad smile when he entered the console room.

Bernice was perched on a turned-around chair, reading *A Brief History of Time*. A piece of wrapping paper and a ribbon were discarded on the floor at her feet. She glanced up as the Doctor entered and placed his hat on the time rotor.

'Ace coming?'

'Soon. Talk amongst yourself.' He was inspecting an upraised panel in the console.

Benny placed the book aside. 'What's *your* excuse?' she asked suddenly.

'Hmm?'

'The Garvond creature was a distillation of evil. You said so yourself. Sounds like it didn't have much of a free will struggle about killing, you know, no conscience and all that. Bit like the Daleks. But what about humans, and you?'

'You're implying,' the Doctor said, 'that we know better, yet we still do it.' He answered wearily, as if he had been expecting something like this.

'That's rather astute. I saw them die, you didn't. Did we have the right to do that to them?'

'The answer will come to you.' The Doctor looked up for the first time, and smiled past her. 'When you've lived a few hundred years, come back and I'll tell you if you've got it.'

'Thanks,' she muttered.

'Oh, please, don't worry.' The Doctor removed two printed circuit-boards and started rummaging in his pockets for the right tool. 'Age, you know, is more than just a shrinking of the skin on the skull, more than your hair falling out and your teeth going brittle. It's a slow, painful process. And on the way you find out what people were talking about all along.' He produced the probe he had been looking for, and beamed at her. 'You can't do a crash course in Time.'

Benny stood up, smoothing down her jeans. 'I'll be in the games room.'

The Doctor waved in acknowledgement. He was intent on the circuit-boards.

She turned to go.

'Happy Birthday,' he added.

Benny smiled wearily. 'You shouldn't have,' she told him, and left the console room with the book tucked into her pocket.

When she had gone, his face changed its expression very slightly. It was like the rippling of a flag in the breeze. When you're around, he thought, I feel uncertain, I lose sight of the plans I've made.

He let the circuit-boards from the TARDIS console fall from his hand and they hit the floor with a crash. The Doctor waited a few seconds to make sure Benny didn't come running back. Then he looked sadly down at the discarded circuits.

'Reconfiguration,' he said to himself. 'Dynamic forces of change.' He looked up at the softly glowing roundels of the console room just for a moment, remembering the confusion of the past few days. He nodded. 'But for whom?'

He knew the TARDIS would not answer.

'You know what I'm doing,' he said. 'I hope.'

When his foot stamped down on the two circuit-boards, the dozens of pieces skidded outwards like smashed pieces of nutshell, hitting all four walls of the console room before coming to rest.

Epilogue: Output

In the darkened, timeless room, the pendulum was still swinging, dripping condensation from its icy surface. Inside, something fluttered, stirred in agitation.

The prisoner was confused. It was being given conflicting information now in the data-rods which prodded it from all sides.

Thinking that this was a moment of weakness for its captor's powers, it rocked the sphere, straining again to escape. Fleeting images appeared against the surface – one could perhaps have been a screaming mouth, another might have been a large hand, its print outlined in condensation. But they lasted about as long as pictures in flurries of snowflakes.

Data was rushing through the attachments, bombarding the prisoner. And once again it heard that hateful echo, the voice of the being who had led it into a trap and now used it for manipulation of Time.

'An interesting experiment, don't you think?'

The prisoner, blind to anything but its own desire for escape, screeched soundlessly. It wanted no more. The energy it was using up was squeezing the life from its tired form.

'Oh, come now. Where's your scientific curiosity? Your race is meant to be intelligent, after all. Didn't you enjoy watching the Gavond gaining power ... growing ... Yes, yes, I know the Doctor knocked everything back into shape again, but he was never meant to lose. Oh, no, that wasn't the point at all.' The captor chuckled again. 'The experiment showed exactly what it was meant to show.

That within parameters, time *can* be changed. You and I, my friend, we made incursions into the fabric of the real universe this time . . .'

Trepidation seized the prisoner. It was clear that the ordeal was not going to be over yet.

It strained, with its failing faculties, to make out the other being's words. As if the captor knew how exhausted it felt, there came new, painful, invigorating pulses which wrenched its body, forced it to listen to the next words, which it heard with astonished clarity.

'The second phase is finished. It's time for something completely different.'

CAT'S CRADLE: TIME'S CRUCIBLE
Marc Platt

The TARDIS is invaded by an alien presence and is then destroyed. The Doctor disappears. Ace, lost and alone, finds herself in a bizarre city where nothing is to be trusted – even time itself.

ISBN 0 426 20365 8

CAT'S CRADLE: WARHEAD
Andrew Cartmel

The place is Earth. The time is the near future – all too near. As environmental destruction reaches the point of no return, multinational corporations scheme to buy immortality in a poisoned world. If Earth is to survive, somebody has to stop them.

ISBN 0 426 20367 4

CAT'S CRADLE: WITCH MARK
Andrew Hunt

A small village in Wales is visited by creatures of myth. Nearby, a coach crashes on the M40, killing all its passengers. Police can find no record of their existence. The Doctor and Ace arrive, searching for a cure for the TARDIS, and uncover a gateway to another world.

ISBN 0 426 20368 2

NIGHTSHADE
Mark Gatiss

When the Doctor brings Ace to the village of Crook Marsham in 1968, he seems unwilling to recognize that something sinister is going on. But the villagers are being killed, one by one, and everyone's past is coming back to haunt them – including the Doctor's.

ISBN 0 426 20376 3

LOVE AND WAR
Paul Cornell

Heaven: a planet rich in history where the Doctor comes to meet a new friend, and betray an old one; a place where people come to die, but where the dead don't always rest in peace. On Heaven, the Doctor finally loses Ace, but finds archaeologist Bernice Summerfield, a new companion whose destiny is inextricably linked with his.

ISBN 0 426 20385 2

TRANSIT
Ben Aaronovitch

It's the ultimate mass transit system, binding the planets of the solar system together. But something is living in the network, chewing its way to the very heart of the system and leaving a trail of death and mutation behind. Once again, the Doctor is all that stands between humanity and its own mistakes.

ISBN 0 426 20384 4

THE HIGHEST SCIENCE
Gareth Roberts

The Highest Science – a technology so dangerous it destroyed its creators. Many people have searched for it, but now Sheldukher, the most wanted criminal in the galaxy, believes he has found it. The Doctor and Bernice must battle to stop him on a planet where chance and coincidence have become far too powerful.

ISBN 0 426 20377 1

THE PIT
Neil Penswick

One of the Seven Planets is a nameless giant, quarantined against all intruders. But when the TARDIS materializes, it becomes clear that the planet is far from empty – and the Doctor begins to realize that the planet hides a terrible secret from the Time Lords' past.

ISBN 0 426 20378 X

DECEIT
Peter Darvill-Evans

Ace – three years older, wiser and tougher – is back. She is part of a group of Irregular Auxiliaries on an expedition to the planet Aracadia. They think they are hunting Daleks, but the Doctor knows better. He knows that the paradise planet hides a being far more powerful than the Daleks – and much more dangerous.

ISBN 0 426 20362 3

LUCIFER RISING
Jim Mortimore & Andy Lane
Reunited, the Doctor, Ace and Bernice travel to Lucifer, the site of a scientific expedition that they know will shortly cease to exist. Discovering why involves them in sabotage, murder and the resurrection of eons-old alien powers. Are there Angels on Lucifer? And what does it all have to do with Ace?

ISBN 0 426 20338 7

WHITE DARKNESS
David McIntee
The TARDIS crew, hoping for a rest, come to Haiti in 1915. But they find that the island is far from peaceful: revolution is brewing in the city; the dead are walking from the cemeteries; and, far underground, the ancient rulers of the galaxy are stirring in their sleep.

ISBN 0 426 20395 X

SHADOWMIND
Christopher Bulis
On the colony world of Arden, something dangerous is growing stronger. Something that steals minds and memories. Something that can reach out to another planet, Tairgire, where the newest exhibit in the sculpture park is a blue box surmounted by a flashing light.

ISBN 0 426 20394 1

BIRTHRIGHT
Nigel Robinson

Stranded in Edwardian London with a dying TARDIS, Bernice investigates a series of grisly murders. In the far future, Ace leads a group of guerrillas against their insect-like, alien oppressors. Why has the Doctor left them, just when they need him most?

ISBN 0 426 20393 3

ICEBERG
David Banks

In 2006, and ecological disaster threatens the Earth; only the FLIPback team, working in an Antarctic base, can aver the catastrophe. But hidden beneath the ice, sinister forces have gathered to sabotage humanity's last hope. The cybermen have returned and the Doctor must face them alone

ISBN 0 426 20392 5

BLOOD HEAT
Jim Mortimore

The TARDIS is attached by an alien force; Bernice is flung into the Vortex; and the Doctor and Ace crash-land on Earth. There they find dinosaurs roaming the derelict London Streets, and Brigadier Lethbridge-Stewart leading the remnants of UNIT in a desperate fight against the Silurians who have taken over and changed this world.

ISBN 0 426 20399 2